Finding Her Way

Riley Jefferson

Affinity
eBook Press
NZ
2014

Acknowledgments

As a writer, I have a supportive team working behind the scenes. Without these people, I would never have put words on the paper. I would like to thank some of them now…

I would like to thank the woman who stole my heart nine years ago. Michele my love, thank you for helping me fulfill my dream of being a publish author. I couldn't have made this journey without you. You have been my light in the darkness.

I would also like to recognize Mary, Richard, Kathleen, and Roger for their unwavering support of my talents. Without the support of loving, encouraging parents I wouldn't have made it this far. I would also like to express gratitude to the small group of cheerleaders that sit in the back, applauding my success.

Thank you Syd, you know what for…

Last but not least, I would like to show my appreciation to the wonderful people of Affinity E-book Press, Julie, Mel, Nat, and Nancy. You guys are awesome!

Dedication

For Darlene—
The lost love of a sister

Table of Contents

Prologue

"Thanks for escorting me up here. You really didn't have to," Jerrica Kerrison commented as she inserted her key into the lock on her office door.

"Oh, it's my pleasure," her companion answered.

The door opened with ease and they entered the darkened office. Using the starlight as a guide, Jerrica strolled to her desk, clicking on the small lamp. Walking around the corner of the desk, she slid out the top drawer. Snatching up the reason she had returned to the office, she turned to her escort.

"I told you I had left it here." She smiled broadly, holding up her wallet with satisfaction.

Jerrica suddenly stood still, inhaling deeply at the sight of the gorgeous blonde who had accompanied her. Standing in front of the windows, her companion's soft features were bathed in moonlight. Jerrica let the wallet drop onto the desktop in a load thump.

God, she's so beautiful, she thought.

"You have a nice view of the city. I never noticed it before."

Jerrica walked up behind her lover. "The view doesn't compare to your penthouse," she stated, sliding her arms around the woman's waist. "Tell me what you're thinking, Devin."

Devin turned to face Jerrica. "I'm thinking how much I enjoy our time together."

Jerrica pulled the taller woman closer, kissing her on the neck. Her smile widened as Devin tilted her head back, revealing more skin to caress. She growled into the soft skin, nipping it gently with her teeth. The tip of her tongue made a path to the delicate spot just below the left ear. Devin moaned as she sucked that sensitive spot. Jerrica knew she was driving Devin crazy.

Devin placed her hands on Jerrica's shoulders. With a tender push Devin made Jerrica step back, breaking the contact. A smirking Devin looked into confused eyes. "Who said you could do that to me?"

Jerrica grinned. "You didn't tell me I couldn't, nor did you tell me to stop."

"You think you know me so well."

"I wouldn't say I know you well, but I have learned what you like."

Sidestepping past Jerrica, Devin strolled to the office door, closing it. Gliding behind Jerrica's desk, Devin pointed a finger at her victim then curled it in, directing Jerrica to come to her.

Jerrica gulped hard watching the seductive woman beckon her. She tried to resist, but her feet had other plans. Not remembering taking the steps but suddenly finding herself standing right in front of Devin, she felt Devin's arm reach around her, the sensation making her eyes flutter closed. Jerrica gasped when the unexpected push landed her in a sitting position in her office chair.

"You think you know what I want." Devin leaned over a surprised Jerrica. "You have a lot to learn, Ms. Kerrison."

Devin took Jerrica's lips savagely, taking total control. Her captive groaned and freely opened her mouth. Jerrica arched toward her as their tongues engaged in sensual battle. Placing a stabilizing hand on Jerrica's arm, Devin pulled away, quickly returning to a standing position.

With eyes completely focused on her every move, Devin took full advantage of her audience. "Oh, honey, you think you know me," she purred, reaching down to the button on her pants and releasing the clasp.

Jerrica licked her dry lips as she watched her lover's pants cascade to the floor. She watched the sexy woman kick her pants aside. Her eyes slowly swept across the black heels, to shapely legs, to the lacy garter belt holding up her thigh-high nylons, and she gasped when she noticed Devin wasn't wearing panties. Staring as Devin slowly removed her top, she unconsciously tugged at her lower lip with her teeth.

Devin smiled at the frustration developing in the younger women's eyes. Almost totally exposed, she took the few steps forward to stand directly in front of Jerrica. With eyes locked on her lover's eyes, Devin straddled Jerrica's lap.

Beautiful naked breasts were inches from Jerrica's face. She reached up to touch the inviting nipples, but Devin slapped her hands away.

"Oh no, no, no…you don't get to touch until I tell you."

"You're a tease."

"Honey, I'm far from a tease. A tease works you up then sends you home unsatisfied. I, on the other hand, will make sure we are both satisfied…just on my terms." She grinned into desire filled eyes. "Now, let's continue your education…."

Chapter One

Jerrica nestled into a seat far away from most of the passengers that had already gathered in the train car, knowing the train would get more crowded the closer they were to Boston. She liked the quiet moments when she wasn't amid the chaos of the corporate world just yet. It made her sad to look at all the defeated expressions on the preoccupied passengers around her. At each train stop, Jerrica realized with exasperation that they were getting closer to where she worked. After six years at the same job, every day seemed an effort just to go in to work. Taking a deep breath, Jerrica mentally prepared herself for the day.

As the train reached North Station, its final destination, the passengers became restless with anticipation for the doors to open so they could exit the train. Jerrica knew that if she tried to enter the stampede of people, she would be in the midst of the madness that was the morning commute, the pushing and shoving that every passenger goes through, so she waited until the crowd thinned.

The walk from the station to the office wasn't too long and a couple of blocks seemed easy, though in the winter the freezing temperatures could chill you to the bone. Fortunately, today was a sunny, mild spring day and it was enjoyable to saunter a few blocks. Jerrica walked at a steady pace, often looking up toward the sky, enjoying the sunshine warming her face.

Consumed in thoughts about the impending day, she almost walked past the entrance to work. Stopping abruptly, she glanced at the building.

"Damn! I didn't expect to get here so quickly," she mumbled.

Walking across the decorative steel and glass lobby, she looked for an available elevator, but they all seemed filled. When impatience started getting the best of her, she squeezed herself into the next available one. Stuffed into an elevator like a sardine, she suddenly couldn't wait to get to her office. Not only did she not enjoy being in elevators, she disliked being in a crowded one even more. She could feel the warm breath from the tall man standing behind her. If her office weren't on the seventeenth floor, she would have taken the stairs. Jerrica practically jumped out of the confined space when the doors opened, startling the people still on the elevator. She politely smiled back at them as the door closed. Straightening her blazer, she exhaled in relief.

Three departments of Morrill, Hartford, and Donahue shared the seventeenth floor— accounting, public relations, and the overseas division. All the managers' offices hugged the outer wall, while the rest of the staff occupied cubicles in the middle.

Jerrica's loyal, bright, and intuitive personal assistant and friend, Lauren, rushed up to her. "Mr. Bisset has been waiting for you," she said.

"Good morning to you, too," replied Jerrica, walking toward her office, relinquishing her briefcase to her assistant.

"He's been here for ten minutes. He's in your office," Lauren stated nervously.

"I get the impression you don't like Mr. Bisset?"

Lauren placed the briefcase next to her desk. "He makes me uncomfortable. I feel he's looking down his nose at me."

Jerrica stopped briefly at her door, with her hand on the doorknob. She glanced back at her assistant with a wink. "He's not looking down at you, Lauren, he's probably undressing you with his eyes."

Jerrica quickly stepped into her office. When she latched the door closed, she heard a thump from the other side, which she assumed was a magazine tossed at her. A smile crossed her face.

She noticed Mr. Bisset standing near the windows looking at the street below. "Good morning, Mr. Bisset. What can I do for you this morning," she said, walking around her desk.

"Jak, why do you persist on being so formal when we greet one another?" Mr. Bisset commented, walking to the front of her desk.

Jak was a nickname from her youth that had followed her through school and now most of her male colleagues called her that as well. "It's a show of respect, Mr. Bisset, but if you prefer me to call you John, I will."

"I would prefer you call me John."

"So John, what can I do for you?"

"Well…I need to hire another PR person. I need you to look at yearly revenues for the past two years and compare them to this year's revenues up until today. I have to justify spending a huge chunk of money to bring in a well-established public relations representative," he said, not looking at her directly.

"That shouldn't be a problem. I can have Lauren pull—"

"I would prefer you to do all the numbers for me. If the brass or anyone else gets an idea of who I'm trying to bring in, they will say no and our competition will scoop her up."

"I trust Lauren to be discreet, but if you prefer, I will handle the project. I'll pull account reports today and I will have figures for you by lunchtime tomorrow. I hope the person you're trying to grab is worth all this trouble," she commented while jotting information on her notepad.

John stood and walked to the door. Turning to look at Jerrica, he grinned. "Thanks, Jak, and she is well worth it, trust me."

A puzzled look crossed her face as he left her office. *What is he up to?* she wondered as she paged Lauren.

Lauren entered with the briefcase in one hand and a cup of coffee in the other. She handed Jerrica the coffee, dropping the case on the desk. "So, what did that…I mean, Mr. Bisset, want?"

Jerrica looked up from her notepad. "He needs comparative figures."

"I can get those for you. What dates is he looking for?"

"Thanks, Lauren, but he has asked me to find the numbers for him. He wants to keep his request on the down low," Jerrica explained.

Lauren started to object, but it seemed as if she decided she didn't have anything nice to say about the situation. Faking a smile, Lauren turned and headed for the door. "If you need anything else, I'll be at my desk," she said, shutting the door loudly behind her.

Jerrica knew by Lauren's tone and quick exit that she wasn't happy about not being included in this big, secret project. Jerrica didn't even know why she hadn't told her more about it because she trusted Lauren not to gossip. Maybe the cryptic way John had asked had piqued her curiosity and she needed to see this through. She would work on his request later. She needed to go to the filing department, a couple of floors down, to get physical copies of the past couple of years' financial reports. She was already working on this month's figures, so almost one-third of the project would be easy.

There was a faint knock on her door. "Come in," she said loudly.

The door opened slowly and a tiny young woman stepped in. "Good morning, Ms. Kerrison. I have your messages from this morning and some new documents sent from Daniel & Daniel, Inc. for you," Jaime, her secretary, whispered.

Jerrica held her hand out to take the stack of paper. "Jaime, how long have you been working here?" she asked in a low voice.

"I've been here a little more than a year, Ms. Kerrison," Jaime replied quietly.

"How many times have I told you, that when you are in my office, to please call me Jerrica," she scolded while smiling at Jaime.

"Every time I'm in your office, Ms. Kerrison. I mean Jerrica," Jaime answered with a twinkle in her eye.

Changing the subject and being a little mischievous, Jerrica questioned her further. "Did Justin, our favorite delivery boy, drop these off this morning?"

Jaime's face flushed a bright pink as she looked down at her feet, shuffling them in embarrassment.

"I'll take that as a yes," Jerrica said and smiled at the innocence of Jaime's reactions.

As if not knowing what to say or do, Jaime tried to make a respectable exit before she totally embarrassed herself.

Jerrica opened the new files from Daniel & Daniel, Inc. Daniel Antiquities had started out as a small shop in Nantucket and they had been in business for twenty years and had made lucrative progress during those years. Then their daughter, their only child, had graduated from college and decided to take the little shop global. Devin Daniel, at twenty-five, had a talent for buying just what their patrons desired. She would travel the world, buying items and having them shipped back to the U.S. As the one shop grew, so did their reputation, which in turn started to attract wealthier clientele. After three years at the helm of her parents' company, Devin had opened another nine stores worldwide. When the company opened their ninth store, they started looking into an accounting firm to handle most of their enormous financial requirements. That is how the young and inexperienced Jerrica Kerrison met the beautiful, sophisticated, worldly Devin Daniel.

To Jerrica's surprise, on top of the papers was a note addressed to her.

Darling,
Have dinner with me tonight.
D.

Jerrica stared at the note. From Devin. This was a situation she was not ready to deal with at this moment. Crumpling the note, Jerrica tried shooting a basketball two pointer at her wastebasket. The small paper hit the rim and tumbled into the trash. She smiled with satisfaction. Inhaling deeply, she tried to get back to the other folders on her desk. Considering her next move she paged Lauren.

Sauntering in, Lauren took forever to cross the room.

With an elbow on her desk, chin on her hand, Jerrica waiting patiently for Lauren to reach her. "Are you taking your time on purpose or have you hurt yourself? Do I need to get you a walker or something," Jerrica asked.

"Funny," Lauren retorted.

"Ok, out with it Lauren. I know something is bothering you."

"I have a feeling we are going to be discussing the note from the wretched she-bitch that was just delivered to you," she said, plopping into the chair across from her boss.

"How did you know about the note," Jerrica asked, examining Lauren's expression. "Never mind," she said, rethinking the question.

Trying to stretch time so she could think, Jerrica picked up her pencil and doodled on her note pad.

"You're going to say no, right?"

Jerrica tilted her head up. "Yes," she tried to sound confident. "That is why I called you in here. I need you to call her office to decline the invitation."

"How's this sound for a message? Please tell Ms. Daniel to take her request and stuff it—" Lauren stopped mid-sentence, as if startled to see the obvious hurt in Jerrica's eyes.

Lauren's heart suddenly ached for her friend. Neither of them spoke as Lauren made her way to the door. Before she reached the door she turned. "Can I ask one question?" she asked, then not waiting for a reply. "How long did it take you to make that decision?"

She couldn't lie to Lauren. "I would like to tell you it was an instant decision, but I did ponder saying yes. Nevertheless, you have my answer. Please make the call."

Lauren didn't respond as she left the room.

Jerrica heard the door click but didn't really see Lauren leave. She was now staring at the tapping pencil in her hand. *I need to get back to work*, thought Jerrica. She would look at messages first, then e-mails and then spend the rest of the day working on reports.

Jerrica's morning became a blur of people coming in and out of her office and phone calls she effortlessly fielded to her staff. Just another day crunching numbers for clients, preparing accounts for auditing, or setting up new clients with accounts. It was the same routine every day. Jerrica focused on her numbers. Most times balance sheets and account records matched and the outcome was predictable, fitting into her no surprises lifestyle. On occasion, when Jerrica interacted with clients, she had a calming way that made them trust her from the start. She always adjusted who she was to whatever the client needed. The drawback was that no one got close enough to see the real Jerrica.

As she was clicking on the computer keyboard, there was another soft knock on the door. Jerrica wasn't sure she had heard it until it sounded again. Without looking up from her computer screen, Jerrica said, "Come in, Jaime."

The door cracked open and Jaime poked her head in. "How did you know it was me?"

"Well, let's see…Lauren usually pages before she comes in or she just comes in, and everyone else here knows to see Lauren to be announced. You are the only one I can think of who knocks."

Jaime smiled as Jerrica noticed the large stack of papers she was holding.

"Please tell me all those papers aren't for me?"

Jaime stopped in front of her desk "Just the top file is for you, and the rest of them I'm taking down to the archive department."

"Phew…I thought for a minute you were trying to load up my desk," she said letting out a breath.

Sometimes her workload would be a comfortable steady stream of paperwork going across her desk, but on more occasions then she liked to remember, the work was like a tidal wave. Ever since the business world started to downsize, her job had become busier. Clients wanted to know their financial bottom line and ways to cut their expenses. She tried not to think of all the people who might have lost their jobs because of the numbers she presented. She had to remind herself often that she was just an accountant analyst. Reaching up, she removed the folder from the stack.

Without a word, Jaime turned and, resembling a small child, skipped out of her office.

Jerrica sat back and thought about the first day she'd met Jaime.

†

It had been one of coldest days in Boston and Jerrica had made a non-scheduled visit to the human resources department. She knew it was time to split up Lauren's duties and get a secretary for the more day-to-day aspect of the business. As she walked into the waiting room of the HR department, she noticed what looked like a bundle of coats sitting in the corner with legs and holding a clipboard. She couldn't figure out if it was a male, female, or a yeti. She'd thought it was odd that, though it was cold outside, the person under all those layers hadn't removed any of them since they were now inside. She continued her journey into the human resources office shaking her head from side to side in amusement. Mrs. Maxwell, the HR manager, looked up from her computer and smiled.

"Ms. Kerrison, how may I help you today," she said.

"Good morning, Mrs. Maxwell. Please call me Jerrica. I need to add another employee to my staff, a secretary and was wondering if you had any eligible candidates."

"And you can call me Stephanie. I'm actually interviewing someone today who might fit what you need. I think she's in the waiting room now. Why don't you sit in on the interview and then give me your opinion afterward?"

Jerrica nodded her agreement and positioned herself in a chair near the corner of the room to observe the interview. She really didn't have time for this, but felt suddenly obligated to stay. Jerrica stared down at her hands in her lap while Stephanie went out to fetch the bundle of coats waiting in the other room.

This should be fun…not! she thought.

She heard the sounds of footsteps coming toward the room. Stephanie entered first stepping aside and gesturing to the woman to sit down and taking her coats from her. Jerrica was finally able to get a good look at the job applicant. To her surprise, under all those coats was a very petite, young woman in her early twenties, with long, dirty blonde hair. The young woman sat in the chair just vacated by Jerrica.

"Ms. Paisley, this is my colleague, Jerrica Kerrison. She will be joining us during this interview. She is only observing," Stephanie said as she looked at the woman's resume.

The young woman looked at Jerrica and gave her a brief, unsteady smile, then focused her attention back on Stephanie. They sat in silence until Stephanie cleared her throat and started the interview.

Jerrica cleaned her nails as she half-heartedly listened to Stephanie briefly discuss the resume verbally. She caught her name, Jaime. Jerrica still wasn't really paying attention to the interview until Jaime finally started to answer questions about her future goals. Looking up, she leaned forward in fascination, listening intently to this timid young girl. Jaime's rigid frame and unwavering eye contact showed hidden confidence. She could tell that under the meek and shy exterior there was an intelligent, willful, trustworthy young woman who might be a great asset to her department. If she did hire Jaime, it would give Lauren a new protégé. Jerrica smiled, thinking of how Lauren would handle training the newbie.

When the interview was finished, Stephanie pushed her chair away from the desk, and rose. She thanked Jaime for the interview and walked her toward the door.

Jerrica stood as well. "Stephanie, could you let me have a few minutes alone to talk with Ms. Paisley?"

Stephanie turned to Jaime. "Are you okay with this?"

Jaime nodded in answer.

Once Stephanie left, Jerrica motioned for Jaime to sit again. Jerrica walked to the front of the desk, seating herself on the top of it. Staring directly at Jaime, she spoke. "Can I be blunt?"

"Of course," Jaime replied.

"Good." Jerrica smiled. "I am a manager of a very busy department. Are you willing to work from forty to sixty hours a week and give me one hundred and ten percent toward your job performance every day? Plus my assistant will probably dog you for all those hours,"

"Your job offer is so tempting," Jaime responded, with a giggle.

"A quick thinker with a sense of humor, I like that. I can't promise you an easy job, but what I can promise you is that I am a fair employer. I will give you credit for any contributions you give. I will never hold you back if you seek a promotion in another department, and as a bonus I've been told that I am fun to work for. The most important thing that I can offer is the invaluable work experience you will receive being part of my team."

"Why are you giving me this chance? You really don't know me. You haven't even read any part of my resume."

Jerrica saw the doubt in the young eyes. "I know enough. At your age I would have loved to have a mentor to teach me this business. I didn't have that luxury. I'm giving you the opportunity I didn't have because I feel that if given the right environment to learn, you can be exceptional."

"Are you officially offering me a job?"

"If you are interested, yes, I am. It's for an entry-level position and the pay will reflect this arrangement. The job starts on Monday at nine am."

Jerrica slid off the desk, offering her hand.

Jaime stood, grasping the open hand. "I will be in on Monday."

"Great! I'll have Stephanie give you the details of the job. I look forward to seeing you on Monday."

Jerrica opened the door and motioned for Stephanie to come back in the room. Jerrica smiled. "Start the paperwork, Stephanie, I've hired her."

†

Jerrica's smile broadened as the pleasant memories flashed in her head. She had never regretted hiring Jaime, who always gave the one hundred and ten percent to every project. She was never late and had more energy than most of the people in the company. The only thing she wanted to change about her secretary was to break her shyness. She knew Jaime had talent, but her shyness stood in her way of moving up the corporate ladder.

I won't give up on her, she vowed to herself. The beep of the intercom almost startled her out of her chair.

"Jerrica," Lauren spoke. "Are you ordering lunch today?"

"I brought lunch."

Jerrica heard a quick reply just before the line went dead. Jerrica wasn't hungry and needed to get a lot of work finished before the end of the day. Usually Jerrica just worked through lunch anyway and that always bothered Lauren.

Jerrica cursed under her breath, remembering she had to go to the file department this afternoon to get the copies for Mr. Bisset's project. The file department is where all the paper account records were stored. They had everything on computers these days, but it still seemed important to have the original paperwork just in case of audits or mistakes.

Stepping into the main department, Jerrica took a quick look around the room. She noticed it was mostly empty, as people seemed to be at lunch. Lauren was gone but Jaime had stayed around to cover the phones. She would go to lunch once Lauren returned but usually on Fridays, they both ordered in and chitchatted at their desks. Lauren always said she barely tolerated Jamie's company, but deep down Jerrica knew she liked having her around.

Jerrica could see the top of Jaime's head over the top of the cubical wall. The cubical walls where just high enough to give each desk a little privacy. "Jaime, I'm going for a walk, I need to stretch my legs. If Lauren gets back before I do, please tell her where I've gone. Thank you."

"Yes, Ms. Kerrison I will," she said, obviously startled by Jerrica's sudden appearance.

Jerrica turned and walked toward the elevator. Once in the elevator she selected the floor the records department was located on. This mid-afternoon elevator ride was much more enjoyable then the morning's. The small box was nearly empty and she had plenty of room to move around. She was hoping that it wouldn't become too crowded before she reached her destination. Jerrica was only going a few flights down but it seemed like it was taking an eternity to get there. She heard the ding of the elevator, looking up just before the doors opened. The electronic numbers read that this was her stop so she adjusted her outfit and proceeded toward the records department.

The fourteenth floor, for some reason, always seemed much darker than any other department in the company. The layout was different as well. On the seventeenth floor, the floor plan was open. You can look around at all the offices and see just about everyone in their cubical. On the fourteenth floor it was like walking into an old-fashioned town office. After you walked through the glass doors, which still had hand painted File Room on them, you stood in front of a long wooden counter. The old florescent lights made the room and all its contents turn a pale shade of green. She disliked visiting this windowless department. Jerrica found the bell to ring for assistance and tapped it twice. With some amusement, she almost expected to see Barney Fife from Mayberry walk out to greet her. Looking around the dreary room, she detected a head poking out from between the racks.

With a wide smile, Leo walked toward her. "Good afternoon, Ms. Kerrison. How may I help you today?"

Pulling the request form from her pocket, she slid the paper in his direction.

Leo read her request. "I can have those copies for you in about ten minutes. Shall I send them to your office?" Leo asked, not looking up from the form.

"No, thank you, I'll wait. It's no trouble."

Once she had seated herself, she glanced up to find he had already disappeared. Hesitantly she removed her cell phone from her pocket. She should call her mom, but she wasn't ready for the speeches about her not visiting or that she's not dating…etc. Staring down at her phone directory, she had an overwhelming urge to call Devin instead. She knew she wouldn't, but just having the thought was upsetting enough. Slipping the cell phone back in her pocket, she heard the familiar sound of the copy machine. It wouldn't be long before Leo would be back with the papers she had requested. Brushing some lint off her lapel as she rose, Jerrica walked toward the counter. As she leaned on the counter, Leo appeared with a large manila envelope.

He dropped it lightly on the counter in front of her. "That will be five dollars," he said, with a sheepish grin.

"Put it on my tab," she replied, winking at the young man as she snatched it from the counter.

A quick look over her shoulder showed her a broad smile on his face as he watched her backside. *Ah, young men and their hormones*, Jerrica thought, laughing to herself.

Back on her floor, Jerrica felt more comfortable, more in her element. Strolling toward her office, Lauren suddenly appeared beside her. Jerrica watched Lauren glance at the envelope tucked under her arm. She made a scoffing noise under her breath, making Jerrica aware of her irritation. Jerrica and Lauren split ways returning to their respective desks.

Jerrica enjoyed the safety that her office seemed to offer today. She placed the unopened envelope on the side of her desk as she reclined in her chair. She decided she would have to take the project work home. The remainder of her day would be spent on other assignments that were more pressing. With a big sigh, she reluctantly started her other tasks.

After hours of burying herself in paperwork, she finally glanced at the clock. It read four forty-five. "Time to get out of here," she said aloud while piling all her paperwork together as she got to her feet.

Retrieving her briefcase, she slid the envelope inside. Inspecting the case a little closer, she noticed that her can of soup was still present. *Lauren would kill me if she knew I skipped lunch again.* Shrugging her shoulders in indifference, she proceeded to disconnect her computer. With ease she placed it into the case next to the can of soup. Rustling outside her door made her realize the stampede to leave the building had begun. Grabbing her jacket in one hand and her briefcase in the other, she headed out of her office. Instead of entering the crowd of people headed for the elevator, she took the stairs. Going down seventeen flights of stairs was much easier than climbing those same seventeen flights. Gravity would work in her favor as she stepped off the first step. Taking two steps at a time, she bounded down the stairs swiftly. When her shoe reached the last landing, she hit the exit door with her elbow, entering the lobby almost at a jog. She had sprinted from the building and down the street to the corner before most people exited the elevators. She hadn't seen her assistant before she left, but knew Lauren would check everything before she left for the day. Lauren lived closer to Boston so she always left a little later than everyone else. Entering the train station she glanced at the clock, five ten. Boarding the 181 train that would take her out of the city, she found a seat near the back and began to unwind for the trip home.

✝

A state of peace washed across her as she entered her large town house. Kicking the door closed with her foot, something caught her eye toward the living room. She smiled as she saw two balls of fluff spring in her direction. Before she could blink, Baby Kitty, the new kitten in the family, with unlimited energy and unlimited love, was at her feet stretching up on the front of her dress slacks.

"Let me put this stuff down first," she said, lowering her briefcase to the floor.

In one fluid motion, she set the bag down, and scooped up the kitten with the same hand. Baby Kitty was a small Ragdoll breed. Ragdoll kittens look like Siamese kittens but their temperaments are totally opposite. A friend back home had found the kitten abandoned on the side of the road. Jerrica, being a softhearted animal lover, adopted her. The older cat, Sassy, was not impressed with the new addition, but was at least tolerating her.

Placing the kitten on her shoulder, she headed for the kitchen, Sassy following close behind. She placed food-filled dishes down on the floor for her little monsters. While they were happily eating, she retrieved a bottle of Syrah from the rack and pulled a clean glass from the cabinet.

Jerrica suddenly felt her stomach growl, reminding her she hadn't eaten lunch. Leaving the now uncorked wine bottle on the counter to breathe a little, she went to the refrigerator and found a quick and easy supper—a plate of homemade beef and broccoli sitting in the front. After re-heating the food and pouring the wine, she made herself comfortable at the dining room table.

From her position, she could look at the water through a wall of windows. The back of the house on the first level had floor to ceiling windows that faced the bay. On the second floor, the master bedroom also faced the bay. Instead of large windows in the bedroom, she had a balcony. Jerrica loved having her coffee out there during the summer.

Picking at her food, Jerrica stared out the window at the evening's sparkles dancing on the gentle movement of the water. Pondering the events of the day, she just couldn't get the note from Devin out of her mind. Jerrica's eyes began to blur as her mind started paging through the memories of her first encounter with Devin Daniel.

"Oh Devin, why reach out now?" she said with a sigh.

†

Jerrica was having an extremely bad day trying to rectify statements and receipts that just weren't matching up. The buzz on the intercom brought her out of her private storm. "Your one o'clock is here," Lauren announced.

"Please tell them I'll be right with them."

Looking at the clock, she smiled. *Well, they're early, that's a good sign,* she thought

She was not in the mood to spend part of her day with some middle aged, disgruntled accountant who didn't want or need another agency looking at his books and Jerrica let out a sigh as she anticipated a long afternoon. Reaching for the phone, she buzzed Lauren. Jerrica pushed her seat back rising to greet this new prospective client.

Lauren stepped back and extended her arm out for the person behind her to enter the office.

Jerrica watched as an extremely attractive young woman flowed into the room.

Nodding her gratitude in Lauren's direction, the young woman confidently sashayed toward Jerrica.

Lauren made the introductions. "Ms. Daniel, this is Ms. Kerrison."

Jerrica extended her hand, but her eyes were fixated on the beautiful woman's face. Jerrica noticed Ms. Daniel was taller than she, with beautiful, flowing, sun-kissed blonde hair.

"Please, call me Devin," she said with a smile.

Jerrica's felt the silky smooth hand gently enfold her own. Jerrica's heart began to beat rapidly as their eyes locked onto one another.

This woman was stunning, Jerrica mused.

From her deep, ocean blue eyes, to her long silky blonde hair, to the magnificent tanned legs, Devin was an exquisite work of art. She was wearing a pin-striped, charcoal straight-line skirt that accentuated her curved hips and those long legs. The form-fitting white blouse opened just enough to show a little cleavage but still be respectable.

Jerrica held onto Devin's hand a little longer then she should have. Realizing her error, she quickly released it. Jerrica felt her throat start to restrict and her face blush as she averted her eyes. In a shaky, but professional as possible, voice Jerrica spoke. "Call me Jerrica. Please have a seat."

Jerrica motioned to the chair in front of her desk. "Would you like coffee? Tea? Something cold?" she asked, walking around to her chair.

Jerrica kept her vision glued to the top of her desk and not the exposed skin of the beautiful client. Opening the folder she had prepared for this meeting, she began her presentation.

"Morrill, Hartford, and Donahue have been in the business management and accounting field for more than fifty-four years. I have been employed here for five years, I mean six years and...."

Jerrica glanced up to see Devin watching her, listening intently. Jerrica lost her place as she stared into the inviting blue eyes. Jerrica skimmed her paperwork, trying to find her place. With great effort she tried to continue.

"I have worked with...many large corperations who...like your own company, were started...." Jerrica was tripping over her own words.

She felt nauseous and began to worry she might pass out. Nervously looking through her notes again, she felt a small bead of perspiration develop on her brow.

Lauren re-entered the office with a tray. Walking swiftly across the room she placed the tray with two glasses and a carafe of coffee on the table near the window. "If you need anything else I'll be at my desk," she said, as she pivoted and left the room.

Jerrica had watched every move Lauren made in some attempt to get her attention. She was secretly pleading for help but Lauren just went about her business, leaving Jerrica to handle her distress on her own. Jerrica cleared her throat nervously.

Devin broke the awkward silence. "Would you like me to get you some water?"

"Oh, I can get that," Jerrica choked.

"Don't worry about it. I'm not incapable."

Jerrica silently chastised herself. It's not professional to stare at the shapely backside of this beautiful woman who was graciously pouring her water.

Devin returned with the glass. "Can I be blunt…Jerrica?"

"Please."

Jerrica was scared of what she might say. Slowly lowering into her chair, Jerrica held her breath.

"I know you've probably spent a couple of days rehearsing your speech for me," she paused to sit. "And I appreciate the effort, but there is no need to continue…."

A hard knot developed in Jerrica's stomach. She had only spent ten minutes with this woman and already she had lost one of the biggest accounts MHD would handle. "I—"

Devin raised her hand, stopping Jerrica from interrupting. "I've already made my decision about Morrill, Hartford, and Donahue. My secretary started drawing up the contracts this morning. She will be faxing them to us before end of business today. I will be passing the domestic accounting department of my family's business to your company." Devin poured herself a cup of coffee and took a sip.

Jerrica was a little skeptical. "Why would you give MHD your account so easily? I mean, this is our first interaction. You know nothing about me or my work."

Devin leaned onto the desk. "Ms. Kerrison, I never enter an arrangement or contract without fully knowing who I'm dealing with. I did my own research on this company and on you before I even agreed to this meeting. If I hadn't approved of this collaboration, I wouldn't have bothered meeting with you today."

Devin's confident stare captivated Jerrica. Her gaze followed along Devin's jaw line down to her long neck, continuing to the open V shape of her shirt. She paused as she caught a glimpse of the frilly lace bra that had slipped out from under her blouse.

"Do you like what you see?"

"What?" Blushing she diverted her eyes to her computer screen. "What did you say?"

"Oh, nothing," Devin remarked with a sexy smirk, leaning back in the chair.

"So, why set up this the meeting if you had already made up your mind?"

"Well, I wanted to meet the person who would be taking on our books. I was also curious to encounter the woman that helped take a small hundred million dollar accounting management firm and turn it into a billion dollar company known worldwide in less than five years."

Placing her now half-empty cup on the desk, Devin rose and extended her hand.

Reluctantly Jerrica stood, taking the offered hand. Heat radiated through them as their hands touched. Jerrica's face flushed as she released the soft hand. "It was nice meeting you, Ms. Daniel. May I walk you out?"

"Thank you but I can make my way back to the elevator on my own," she said, reaching for the door.

Jerrica saw Devin look over her shoulder one last time with a twinkle in her eye and flashing a striking grin. Once the door closed, Jerrica felt the full emptiness of her office.

"What the hell just happened?" she muttered, dropping in her chair, exasperated.

✝

Jerrica wasn't hungry anymore as she swirled the food on her plate with her fork. She needed to stop doing this to herself, this remembering. Holding her glass in one hand and her plate in the other, she returned to the kitchen and refilled the wine glass.

Fetching her briefcase from the entryway, she headed up to her bedroom; the two little fluff balls right on her heels. She passed the guest room and bathroom on her way to the master bedroom. This townhouse was excessively big for just one person, but Jerrica knew she had to have it the moment she'd toured the property. It felt like home.

Dropping the briefcase on the small table near her dresser she rifled through the dresser drawers to look for her favorite pajama set. Once changed, she retrieved the computer from the briefcase. She cracked the French doors open to the balcony, knowing the sound of the waves on the rocks would be relaxing. She reclaimed her glass off the table before she positioned herself on the floor. A familiar purr from Sassy on the bed gave Jerrica comfort that she was not alone. Taking a quick look around, Jerrica saw that Baby Kitty was occupying herself.

Let's get to work, she told herself.

Jerrica hammered away on her keyboard. Papers were spread out on the floor beside her, graphs and charts were displayed on her computer screen. She immersed herself into the project, losing track of the passage of time. Hearing a noise she glanced around her computer screen. Baby Kitty had taken hold of one of her data sheets.

Sighing, Jerrica extended her arms toward the ceiling, stretching her back muscles. It was almost two in the morning she realized, looking at her watch. She had been at this a long time. Clicking the save button on her last report, she closed the computer and scooped the kitten in one hand and the documents in the other as she stood. She placed a quick kiss on the kitten's head settling it on the bed. Capturing the computer and the rest of papers off the floor, she returned them all to the safety of her briefcase on the small table. When she stretched again, she realized she was suddenly exhausted. She desperately needed sleep.

Jerrica went into the master bath to enact her nightly routine. Returning, she smiled at the sprawled out cats already asleep on top of the comforter. It was going to be a short night. Clicking off the light, she prayed she would find rest quickly.

Chapter Two

Sitting at her desk, Jerrica could feel the drain from not enough sleep. She had almost fallen asleep on the train. Then she missed the seventeenth floor, almost dozing off in the back. She had to ride the elevator four more flights before she was able to hop an elevator that was descending. It was going to be a long day if that kind of shit kept happening. Lauren had better bring coffee soon. Jerrica needed caffeine. To distract her climbing temper, she concentrated on the task at hand, opening e-mails. Scrolling down the page, she commented aloud.

"Nope, I don't need that one."

(Click)

"These two I'll forward to Lauren."

(Click...click…click)

"Nope, not this one either."

Jerrica had already sent John the numbers and graphs for his project so she had some free time. She should have stayed home today. When Lauren finally entered her office she was carrying two mugs of steaming coffee.

"Aww, you're my favorite assistant," she said as she was handed a mug.

"I'm your only assistant," Lauren said, not looking at all impressed with the compliment.

"Thank you for clarifying that for me. How about you're the best assistant ever?"

Jerrica sipped her much needed coffee.

"Now, that sounds a little better. You couldn't run this office without me," Lauren said and smiled.

"You're right, almighty one," Jerrica said grinning. "But I would like to think I have something to do with running this department."

"Ok, I'll let you think that," Lauren shot back, with intended sarcasm.

Jerrica tossed a paperclip in Lauren's general direction, making Lauren look playfully shocked. Jerrica's relationship with Lauren went beyond just boss and assistant. They had become friends along the way. Lauren had helped her get through some major troubles in her life. Lauren was the lighthouse in the dark, always showing her the way to safety. Jerrica was happy their paths had crossed.

She knew Lauren didn't have to work. Her husband, Brandon, a big-shot lawyer, could certainly support her. A trust fund and a small house on Cape Cod that her grandparents had left her didn't hurt either. But Lauren liked to feel useful, so she'd kept her job after marrying. Lauren and Brandon never had any children of their own, so they had somewhat unofficially adopted her as one of their own though Lauren was only ten years older than Jerrica.

"So, what are you doing this weekend?" Lauren asked.

"I hadn't thought about it. Why do you ask?"

"Well, I'm visiting South Chatham to finish opening up the cottage for the season. I thought if you didn't have anything planned, you would want to take a drive down and spend some time near the beach."

Jerrica loved South Chatham. Cape Cod was beautiful once you veered off the main highway and driving through the small towns was so relaxing. She couldn't get enough of the long beaches and gorgeous sunsets. She had even spent a short time living at the cottage in South Chatham a few years ago.

"I'm guessing that if you're asking me, Brandon will not be joining you?"

"No, he has a big case he needs to work on," she said rolling her eyes. "As usual."

"Well, then count me in."

"I would like to enjoy the house and beach before the tourists arrive. I think we all need a break and I hear the weather is going to be warm inland, so it should be mild at the coast. Also, remember, the house does have heat if it gets cold," said Lauren. "We could use some time together."

Jerrica could hear the soft pleading in Lauren's statement. "When do we get started?"

After pondering the question, Lauren responded. "I would like to be on the road right after work on Friday. We can leave here and be at the cottage by seven or eight at the latest. I can pack food for us for the whole weekend."

"I'm fine with that if you let me pay for steaks or lobster for Saturday's supper. We'll make a big dinner to celebrate the start of another great season at the cottage," Jerrica returned, watching Lauren stand.

"You have a deal," Lauren said as she left the office.

Now she had plans for the weekend. It was funny how life worked out. Sometimes. She had come in today not wanting to be there and now she had a weekend adventure ahead. Just the thought of going to Lauren's cottage made Jerrica's day brighter.

The intercom beeped, catching her attention.

"Ms. Kerrison, Mr. Bisset is on line one for you," echoed Jaime's voice from the intercom.

"Thanks, Jaime, I'll take it from here," Jerrica replied as she picked up the receiver.

"Hello, John. What can I do for you now?" Jerrica said in her friendliest voice.

As he rambled on, she really wasn't listening to him and barely noticed he had stopped talking. "Oh, I'm sorry John. Could you please repeat that last part?"

She heard him sigh aloud, then slowly repeat his information. She paid attention to his plans for the big meeting. *This information matters to me how*, she pondered, until he mentioned her attendance at the meeting.

"You want me to what?" Jerrica asked in an elevated tone.

John continued explaining to her why he needed her there for the meeting and how persuasive it would be if the person working in accounting presented the financials instead of the head of public relations. When John stopped talking, Jerrica sat back in her chair feeling cornered about the whole situation.

"Please, Jak, I need you to do this for me," John pleaded.

Jerrica had never heard him ask anyone so politely for anything. Surprised by his sudden, though short-lived sincerity, she agreed to attend.

John informed her that the meeting was at two in the executive boardroom. It was up there so the company's president, vice president, and CEO could leave for their overseas trip right after the meeting. She politely told him she would be there, then hung up the phone. She knew where the executives of Morrill, Hartford, and Donahue were traveling. They were flying to Europe to meet with the many small companies that were interested in testing the waters in the U.S. The results of these meetings usually meant more work for her department. They would have to sort out contracts and account information. The big shots brought the clients in, but she would do all the work and receive little of the credit.

Her face flushed as her temper increased at the picture that was forming in her mind. Same shit, just a different day. Jerrica pushed out her chair, leaning forward until her head was almost resting between her knees.

"Relax, breath slowly," she repeated softly.

She was concentrating so hard on her relaxation exercise that she wasn't aware Lauren had entered.

Lauren could only see the arch of her boss's back from behind the desk. Stopping in her tracks, she started backing up slowly. She had reached the door when Jerrica's muffled voice sounded.

"I didn't hear you come in but I do hear you trying to leave. Lauren, what is it?"

"I just wanted to check on you after that call from Mr. Bisset. His voice had an urgent tone," Lauren inquired nervously.

"He asked me another favor," Jerrica responded.

Lauren rolled her eyes, knowing she would be out of the loop on this one too.

When Lauren didn't respond, Jerrica slowly sat upright in her chair. She could tell Lauren was still irritated.

"I've decided you will accompany me to the executive boardroom at two this afternoon. I want you to be ready with a notepad, something to write with and color highlighters. Also, bring two bottles of water. You never know if they have anything to drink in that boardroom," she said, gathering papers on her desk.

A few seconds of silence passed and she realized Lauren hadn't left. With a question in her eyes, she looked up to see her assistant's confused expression. "I know this is sudden, but you have wanted to know what was going on so badly…well, now is your chance."

Jerrica waited patiently, amused, until Lauren had processed this new information.

"I'll be ready," Lauren muttered as she withdrew from the office.

Jerrica knew she had just killed two birds with one stone. Not only would she not be alone in the meeting, but she would also satisfy Lauren's curiosity.

At exactly one forty-five p.m. Jerrica stepped out of her office with her folders in hand and her best serious expression on her face. Her paperwork in order and her speech prepared. She'd spent the past hour getting everything together. She was ready for anything. She still didn't have a clear closing formulated in her head for her presentation, but she figured it would come to her when she needed to wrap up. Besides it was John's responsibility to sell them his idea to add another person to his roster. Jerrica was just in this meeting to give the financial aspect of his request.

Lauren walked up wearing her best smile. They nodded at one another in a silent acknowledgement, and then started toward the elevators.

Once inside the elevator, Jerrica felt the tension building in her muscles.

"You need to relax, Jerrica. You're going to make yourself sick."

"How did you know I was tensing?"

"I've known you long enough to know when you get tense," Lauren commented.

Jerrica tried relaxing her shoulders a little, knowing she wasn't doing this alone. As the elevator reached the thirtieth floor, Jerrica straightened her back, squared her shoulders, and readied herself.

Lauren's eyes widened as the doors slid open. The soft recessed lighting gave this department a luxurious atmosphere with its wooden floors and beige colored walls. *It was a huge contrast to any other department in the company.* She had to hustle to keep up with Jerrica. They were the first ones to arrive in the boardroom.

Jerrica set her folders on the oval mahogany table. "I would like you to sit in one of the chairs against the wall closest to the door," she said, turning to Lauren. "Those seats have a better vantage point."

Lauren nodded in agreement.

"I'll take care of the presentation," Jerrica continued, "I want you to keep an eye on everyone to catch his or her reactions, ones that I might miss during the presentation. I want to be able to have some kind of interpretation on how they felt or if they liked the information I present."

Jerrica is always her worst critic. With notepad and water bottle in hand, she made herself comfortable. Lauren knew Jerrica was insecure about her public speaking abilities. Later they would discuss what Lauren had observed and Jerrica would formulate a plan to build on her weak points.

Jerrica was busying herself with her financial paperwork when people started to file into the room.

Mr. Bisset rushed to talk to Jerrica the moment he spotted her.

Lauren couldn't hear what they were talking about, figuring he didn't want her to. She observed him pull out the chair right next to Jerrica, never acknowledging that Lauren was even in the room.

"Such an ass," Lauren whispered under her breath.

Minutes later more people appeared, filling the space to standing room only. The expressions on their faces showed that everyone would rather be somewhere else. When the door finally closed, everyone turned to Mr. Bisset.

Bisset stood to speak.

"Good afternoon, ladies and gentleman. I want to thank you all for attending this meeting on such short notice. Everyone received an e-mail this morning outlining the intent of today's meeting. I would like to start with the topic that's on everyone's mind, the added expense of this new position."

John turned toward Jerrica.

"For those of you who don't know her, this is Jerrica Kerrison," he said, placing a hand on her shoulder. "She is our top business manager and accountant and she has prepared a presentation for us. She is going to show us the financials for the past couple years to support the undertaking that I will present later."

Lauren thought it was strange that he would start with how to pay for his plan instead of explaining the project first. She watched as Mr. Bisset plopped back into his seat.

Jerrica rose from her chair. Lightly clearing her throat, she started her presentation.

Lauren glanced around the table, intrigued by how captivated everyone became as Jerrica spoke. Jerrica addressed the room with confidence, directing everyone in the room through the pamphlets containing her graphs that she had passed out earlier, and explaining in detail the current cash flow. Lauren felt a moment of pride watching Jerrica control the room.

When the presentation was over, Jerrica fielded questions. She was very pleased that everyone seemed satisfied with the information she had supplied.

Mr. Bisset stood and put a hand on Jerrica's back, "That was a very informative presentation. Thank you so much for your help. Ms. Kerrison will now be exiting the meeting and we will go on with the rest of the details."

Did he just rudely dismiss me?

Jerrica started grabbing her papers together, trying to control the anger that was building just below the surface. Walking toward the door, she motioned to Lauren. Most of the executives shook her hand offering polite goodbyes as she walked past.

Lauren followed her out, closing the door behind them. They both dashed for the elevator.

Jerrica was anxious to get back to her office. She couldn't lose her temper in the elevator.

"Jerrica, I'm sure he didn't do that on purpose," Lauren said, trying to soften her boss's irritation.

"I'm pretty sure he did. I wanted to smack that smug look off his face."

The elevator doors finally parted as they reached the seventeenth floor. Jerrica didn't even wait for Lauren to exit the elevator. She was at a swift run before Lauren even stepped out.

Jerrica's childish response made Lauren giggle in relief as she strolled toward her desk.

Jerrica rushed by Jaime's desk and right into her office, slamming the door behind her.

Jaime stood just in time to see the door close as Lauren reached her desk. "Did everything go okay?"

"The presentation was great. Mr. Bisset was an asshole. Give her at least a half an hour before you call or let anyone see her. I'm going to the lounge to get something to drink. I'll be right back," Lauren said.

"These two women are so confusing," Jaime mumbled aloud, shrugging her shoulders in bewilderment.

Jerrica tossed her jacket on her desk and started pacing her office. She had so much adrenaline going through her veins that she couldn't calm down. She continued replaying the meeting in her head. Her speech had been flawless given such short notice, but that wasn't what was bothering her. She was infuriated with the way John had excused her from the meeting. He made her look like a subordinate, not his equal. Why couldn't they have stayed for the full meeting? If he gets that new person he wants so badly, it will only be because she did the work for him. She would never do anything directly for him again. The more she pondered about it, the more frustrated she became. Stopping in front of the windows, she stared out into the city. "Breathe Jerrica…breathe."

She pulled a chair close to the window, dropping heavily onto it. Trying not to focus on one physical object, she let her eyes blur and her mind venture into nothingness. A loud knock on her door broke her trance. "Come in," she said in a scratchy, dry voice.

Lauren stepped around the corner with a mug in her hand. "Warm tea to help calm your nerves and to help ease your voice."

"How do you always know what I need," Jerrica replied, accepting the mug.

"I knew you would need something after that meeting. Mr. Bisset is a jerk. You were great!"

"Thank you. I don't feel like discussing the notes right now. I've decided to make it an early day," she said, sipping her tea. "I need to get out of here before I lose my temper, which means, in turn, I lose my job."

Jerrica retreated behind her desk. Placing the mug on the desktop, she turned to grab the briefcase from the floor.

"There's only two hours left in the day and I just need to cut out of here," Jerrica commented as she retrieved her coat. "Call me if there's an emergency. I'll handle everything else tomorrow."

Before Lauren could even get out of her boss's office, Jerrica was already through the doors, heading for the stairs.

Jerrica was down the stairs and out into the street in what seemed like seconds. She paused the moment her feet hit the sidewalk. A chilly breeze reminded her that it was still spring even though the bright sun warmed her face.

What am I going to do until it's time to board the train? she thought. *I guess I didn't think this through.*

She couldn't board her train for another two hours. Jerrica chose to walk toward the station hoping that something would catch her interest. The streets seemed busy for the mid-afternoon. She strolled along, trying not to walk into people who didn't even seem to notice her. She observed crowds rushing by in a hurry to get somewhere, talking loudly on their cell phones or into their headsets. Not one person was looking around enjoying the beautiful city that surrounded them. Jerrica realized that she was one of these people at times. She never took the time to look around anymore.

Have I become that shallow?

Crossing the street, she made the impetuous decision to stop at Equal Exchange Coffee House. She would treat herself to a warm latte and a much needed break. The sudden sound of her name made her pause. She thought she was imagining it and not wanting to look silly by stopping in the middle of the crowd to look around, she continued toward her destination. A few steps closer to the coffee shop she heard her name once more. She paused and looked around. Jerrica immediately recognized the woman pushing through the crowd. This day seemed to be getting worse by the second. Before Jerrica could convey her salutations, she was in an unwanted embrace. The embrace was blessedly quick, respectable since they were in public.

Jerrica stepped back. "Hello, Devin. How are you?"

"Hello…Devin? You don't sound happy to see me."

Jerrica knew Devin's deep blue eyes were staring at her and she blushed. Pausing a moment to regain her composure, she managed to flatly respond. "What kind of response did you want? How long has it been since we've seen or talked to one another? Do you even remember the last time we talked?"

Jerrica looked into Devin's eyes for a brief second, seeing the pain of the memories.

"Can we talk about this somewhere else?" Devin said, glancing around.

"That's right," Jerrica said in an elevated tone for everyone around the couple to hear. "You don't like to talk about us out in the open."

She could clearly see the discomfort in Devin's face and the uneasiness in her posture as she fumbled with her hands. Jerrica almost felt sorry for her…almost.

"Listen, I just want to talk," Devin said in a soft voice.

Jerrica could hear the begging in Devin's tone. She hesitated a moment, wondering why she was even considering this. "Fine. I'm headed for the coffee house, if you would like to join me, you are welcome to."

Devin reached out a hand, touching Jerrica on the shoulder as she turned to leave. "Jerrica, please stop. I would like us to talk privately. My car is waiting," Devin implored.

She wasn't obligated to Devin but felt compelled to give her a chance to say her piece. Jerrica nodded her acceptance. They walked together in silence toward the luxurious vehicle awaiting them.

Peter, Devin's driver, rose from the car as they stepped closer. "Good afternoon, Ms. Kerrison. How have you been?"

Peter held the door open.

"I'm doing well. It's nice to see you again."

She stepped into the car, sliding to the other side to give Devin plenty of room to enter the vehicle.

Devin didn't even acknowledge her driver, her current company her only focus.

Once everyone was settled, Peter reached for the handle of the driver's door. He situated himself behind the steering wheel. "Where to?"

"The usual place," Devin replied.

When the car pulled onto Main Street, Devin cleared her throat. "So, how have you been? I've missed you." Receiving no response from Jerrica, she continued. "Thank you for coming."

"Honestly, I don't know why I'm going anywhere with you, but until we get there I don't want to do small talk if you don't mind. We can talk once we get to our destination."

Jerrica stared out the window lost in her own thoughts. After plenty of silence and several blocks, Jerrica recognized the route they were taking.

"You're a little too predictable, Devin," she said, turning her head away. "You're taking me to your apartment. We are just talking, nothing else!"

Devin didn't even glance at Jerrica as her monotone voice retorted. "I figured it was really the only place we could talk privately and yes, it's just to talk."

"Oh, you mean a place that no one would see us together," Jerrica snapped.

"Jerrica, let's talk about this when we get inside," Devin said, responding to the bitterness she heard in Jerrica's voice.

Devin voice was not just angry but full of unspoken emotions, making Jerrica shift back to looking out the window. Pulling up to Devin's building, Jerrica sighed with dread of what her afternoon was turning out to be.

Peter opened the door at the curb.

"Thank you, Peter." Jerrica smiled to him as he held out his hand.

Jerrica felt a strange deja vu standing on the sidewalk waiting for Devin to exit the vehicle.

"Peter, please park the car in the garage. I'll call you when Ms. Kerrison is ready to leave."

Jerrica felt sorry for Peter because of the way Devin treated him. She smiled at him in hopes that he could see how sorry she was. Peter just shrugged his shoulders at her.

Devin didn't even take a second look back in his direction. She was already walking toward the main entrance of the building. "Jerrica, are you coming up?"

The door attendant opened the door as she approached. Jerrica followed Devin across the lobby to the elevators. Jerrica found that the exquisite lobby with its chandeliers and brass lighting didn't impress her anymore. Things had changed between them and that had tarnished objects she'd once thought were so beautiful. There was no conversation until they were safely in Devin's apartment.

"May I take your coat and briefcase?"

"Fine," Jerrica said, relinquishing the briefcase, then her coat.

Devin smiled as she placed the items in the entryway closet.

Jerrica instinctively walked across the open living room to the large windows revealing views of the park below and the beautiful harbor in the distance. This was one of the best views in the Boston area. Taking in the sight, she had almost forgotten where she was. Jerrica was just about to step back when she felt the warm body standing behind her. Devin stood an inch taller than she did but in heels she towered over Jerrica. Devin's warm breath was lightly brushing the back of her neck. Devin had removed her shoes, Jerrica realized. She stiffened, feeling Devin's hands brush up her biceps.

As if feeling the sudden chill in her companion, Devin dropped her arms to her sides, stepping back. "Would you like some wine?"

Not waiting for a reply, Devin headed in the direction of the kitchen.

Jerrica's current position made her feel like a trapped mouse. She needed to move away from the windows. She looked around the room and noticed that the furniture hadn't moved since she had last visited. Jerrica walked to the brunch table, taking a well-positioned chair that faced the room. There were four large chairs to this table, making plenty of room for an abrupt escape around either side.

Devin returned to the living room with wine glasses in hand.

Jerrica studied the woman with whom she was once involved. She was a beautiful but a complex woman.

Devin was a shark in the business world and sometimes that spilled into her personal life. Being an only child, her parents, especially her father, had indulged her every whim. As she grew into an adult, the self-centered attitude grew stronger, rooting itself deep inside her soul. When she wanted something, she moved heaven and earth to obtain her goal or prize. She could be genuinely caring and loving but also cruel and mean. Devin's father gave her everything but he took everything from her as well. She allowed him not only to steer her career but he also controlled her life. His influence kept her from being honest about who she was and from living the life she wanted. His controlling nature had ruined every relationship, male or female that she had ever had. Devin had become accustomed to hiding the fact that she preferred woman above men.

"I'm here."

Devin smiled, seeing Jerrica at her brunch table. She recalled the many times she had entered this room to find

Jerrica wearing nothing but one of her dress shirts, sitting in that exact chair, drinking coffee and reading the newspaper.

Jerrica, witnessing the soft change in Devin's face, knew she was reminiscing. She needed to remember to keep her distance from Devin. They had a history and some unresolved emotions between them. "So, I'm here. What is it you want to talk about?"

"I can see you want to get down to business. You never change, darling," she said, placing both glasses on the table.

Devin situated herself in a chair across from Jerrica so she could see every expression.

Not replying, Jerrica sat with her arms folded on her chest and waited for Devin to continue.

Devin pulled her wine glass closer, nervously rotating it in her hand. Softly clearing her throat again, she whispered. "I've missed you."

Jerrica reached for her glass, again adding nothing to the conversation.

"Jerrica, did you hear me? I've missed you."

"Is that supposed to make me swoon," Jerrica questioned, lifting her glass.

Irritated, Devin watched Jerrica slowly sip her wine. Devin observed, with great interest, Jerrica's soft lips brushing the cool glass as she tasted the liquid.

Jerrica thinks her cool exterior puts her in control. She's playing games with me, she thought.

Devin sat back in her chair, grinning.

She wants to play her cold games with me; I can play games too and do it so much better.

Seductively, Devin crossed her legs, making sure her skirt rode up her legs a little higher. The slit in the skirt revealed the lace of her garter belt to her guest.

Jerrica's face reddened when Devin caught her glancing at the open seam.

Let's see how far I can take this before I get what I want, Devin conspired.

"Are you playing some kind of game with me, Jerrica? I brought you up here to talk and you've barely said anything to me. Furthermore, when you do bother to say anything it's on the edge of being rude. I don't need this from you and frankly don't feel I've done anything to deserve that treatment." Devin voice was cold, easily baiting her prey.

Devin knew Jerrica would never walk away from a direct challenge. Devin slowly picked up her glass and just waited for Jerrica to respond. She watched the anger develop quickly in Jerrica's eyes. She knew she had pushed enough to make Jerrica erupt.

Jerrica stood quickly knocking her chair to the floor. Slamming both hands on the table, she began to speak. Her voice started low then amplified to almost a shout.

"Damn you, Devin! I didn't ask to come here, you asked me. You said you wanted to talk, so talk! You think I'm being rude. Have you conveniently forgotten everything that has gone on between us? You walked away from me, not the other way around. You broke my heart! After months with no communication you suddenly come out of nowhere. I guess I'm supposed to fall over you with gratitude because you say you miss me? You selfish son of a—"

Devin was up on her feet before Jerrica could finish her sentence, stepping around the table in one fluid motion, encircling Jerrica in a full embrace.

Jerrica didn't have time to react or think clearly when Devin lowered her head, covering her lips with her own.

She felt Jerrica resist but only tightened her hold.

†

I can't do this. This woman has caused me so much hurt. Jerrica's thoughts bombarded her. Jerrica's body overrode her sensibility, giving in to the heat that was growing deep inside her, molding her body to Devin. Every nerve in her body was coming alive and she hated herself.

Devin nibbled on Jerrica's bottom lip requesting entry.

In another moment of weakness, Jerrica opened her mouth surrendering to the deeper kiss. Both tongues danced a familiar dance. Jerrica arms reached up to the back of Devin's neck, intertwining her fingers in her soft, long hair. She relaxed, letting Devin control the moment, her mind no longer her own.

Devin slid her hands underneath the back of Jerrica's shirt. *Damn she was so soft and so beautiful.* She heard a soft moan as her warm hands caressed the smooth skin of Jerrica's back. The soft sound of this woman was fueling her desire. Devin broke the kiss, hastily placing kisses down Jerrica's exposed neck.

Jerrica's eyes closed lazily. She was lost in euphoria from the heat that was raging through her veins. She hadn't felt another woman's touch in so long. She tipped her head back giving Devin more access to her exposed flesh. The passion, long denied, spread like a wildfire from deep inside, heating her skin instantly.

Jerrica's tough exterior had cracked as Devin continued a trail toward the sensitive spot near her ear.

Devin, as if letting her ego get the best of her, gloated about her conquest. In a low sexy, raspy voice Devin reveled in her triumph. "I knew you couldn't resist me. You never could."

As quickly as the heat had begun for Jerrica, it vanished by the certainty of Devin's words. Reality shook her to the core. Jerrica roughly pushed Devin away. Glaring into Devin's face with hurt in her eyes and resentment in her voice, she yelled, "You bitch!"

She shoved Devin out of the way, rushing for the front door. She felt Devin grab her arm before she was out of reach.

"Jerrica, wait! I'm sorry. I didn't mean for that to happen." Devin said. "I mean, yes, I want you, but that's not why I brought you here."

Jerrica wrenched her arm out of Devin's hold and stormed toward the door.

Devin did not follow her. She had already made a mess of things and following Jerrica would only make it worse.

Jerrica snatched her coat from the hanger with one hand and swung the front door open with the other.

She paused and shouted into the apartment. "You are a cruel person, Devin Daniel! You're a cruel, evil person!"

Slamming the door shut, she left.

Jerrica hurried to the elevator, pushing the down button furiously. She kept looking over her shoulder hoping that Devin would not come out after her. Her heart was pounding so hard it was difficult to breath. Once out of the building, she felt the cool air blanket her skin, reminding her that she was holding, not wearing her coat. Sliding the jacket on, Jerrica glanced around the street hoping to catch a cab back to the train station. Her watch informed her that she had missed her train. The next one was an hour away.

I should have stayed home after all, she silently told herself.

"Ms. Kerrison?" A soft voice spoke behind her.

Turning around abruptly, Jerrica sighed. "Peter…you startled me."

"I'm real sorry, Ms. Kerrison, that wasn't my intention. Ms. Daniel asked me to take you home. Are you ok? You look shaken."

"I'm fine, Peter. You don't have to take me home," she paused to collect her thoughts. "Relay to Ms. Daniel that I am more than capable of finding my own way home."

"Please, Ms. Kerrison. If I don't get you home safely, Ms. Daniel will be very unhappy with me and when she's not happy… you know how she can be," he said, looking at his shuffling feet.

Yes, she knew how Devin could be. "Fine, I'll let you drive me home." Her voice sounded defeated.

"Please, this way."

Peter put out an arm for Jerrica to take as they both walked toward the car.

Peter was a good person, very polite, probably in his early fifties. *How did he ever end up working for Devin?*

Peter got Jerrica seated in the back and then settled himself behind the wheel. "Would you like the scenic route or the highway?" he asked.

"I don't want to keep you out too late, Peter, so you can go the highway."

"Don't worry about me. The wife is working a party for the elder Mr. and Mrs. Daniel so she won't be home until much later. I have the evening to myself," he said with a smile.

Jerrica smiled back at him in the rearview mirror. "I'll tell you what. You take whatever route you want. I know you wouldn't steer me wrong because I know your wife."

"My Molly would kill me if I didn't take care of her favorite Nantucket guest," he answered with a hearty laugh.

Jerrica liked his wife Molly. Every time they had gone to the Nantucket house, Molly always made sure Devin and Jerrica had everything they needed but kept her distance giving them privacy. Every employee knew the secret happenings at that house, but no one ever talked about it.

Devin has plenty of skeletons in her closet. I was one of those skeletons. If that house could talk, it would be scandalous, she thought and couldn't help but smile at the idea.

"It looks like it's going to be a clear night. I feel like a long ride this evening," Peter glanced at her in the rearview mirror.

"I'm in the car, you lead the way," she answered, leaning back into the seat.

Peter clicked the radio on to an oldies station and turned the volume up. Glancing in the mirror, Jerrica just smiled and knew it was going to be a relaxing trip. They drove out of Boston toward Lynn.

She knew exactly the route he was taking. When she was hired at MHD, Jerrica had made multiple trips around the area to find different routes to get into and out of the city. She sometimes would take this same route when she drove into work. Moving to the passenger's side of the back seat, she opened the window. The moon was full and the breeze coming in the window was a little chilly but she did not mind it brushing her face. She could smell the ocean when the vehicle crossed the bridge from Salem to Beverly. Beverly Harbor was so beautiful at night. The moonbeams dazzled on the few breaks in the water.

The breeze started getting cold, so Jerrica closed the window. She knew they were about halfway through the trip. Sitting back against the seat, Jerrica tried to relax from the totally wasted day. Trying to clear her head, Jerrica briefly closed her eyes.

"Ms. Kerrison," she heard a voice say.

Opening her eyes, Jerrica saw Peter standing just outside the open door.

"Ms. Kerrison, you're home."

"Thank you. For everything," she said touching his arm lightly as he helped her out. "Please be careful going back home."

"Ms. Kerrison, will I be seeing you with Ms. Daniel anytime soon?"

Hearing the concern in his voice, she responded as honestly as she could. "I hope not, Peter. I really hope not."

Jerrica waved as he drove away. She was ready to go to bed and forget today ever happened. Her body had betrayed her today and still ached to be touched. Two sleeping pills and hopefully she would forget all about this evening.

Unlocking her front door, feeling lonely, she yelled jokingly. "Honey, I'm home!" She knew no one would answer.

Chapter Three

The next morning Jerrica was startled awake as the lamp on her nightstand crashed to the floor. Turning, she was just in time to see the youngest kitty jump off the nightstand to investigate her prize on the floor.

Jerrica swung her legs over the side of the bed, stretching out her arms. Reaching down to pick the light up, she glanced at the alarm clock. It was five forty five.

Shit! I'm late for the train!

Tossing the blankets off, she leapt toward the bathroom. Abruptly stopping, she remembered she was taking her car today and not the train. Through the morning mental fog, she started making a mental list of what she needed to do to get ready. Shower, dress, do hair, makeup, pack for the weekend, call Mary next door to babysit the cats, feed the cats, and pack the car. Yes, that seemed organized enough to get her morning on track. Once she was happy with the list, she went about completing each task in order. She mentally checked off each item on her list as it was completed.

Working on the last chore, Jerrica fetched her packed suitcase from where she had deposited it earlier near the front door. Keys in one hand, suitcase in the other, she entered the garage. Popping the trunk she carefully placed the suitcase inside. She paused suddenly, feeling the dread that something seemed missing. Thinking through the list, she strolled back into her house. She retrieved the long coat she had chosen for the cold Cape Cod weather from the closet.

"Well kids, have a lazy weekend without me. Be good to Mary or she won't feed you," she teased as she lightly kissed each cat on the head as they ate breakfast.

Hand on the doorknob, she reached for her briefcase that was usually kept next to the staircase. Then realization hit her. "I forgot my briefcase!" Jerrica's voice was elevated in panic. "Where the hell did I leave it," she cried, quickly looking around the room.

Damn it all, she'd left it at Devin's apartment! How in the hell was she going to get it back without causing problems for herself? She didn't have time for this. She was going to be late.

Sitting in the car, Jerrica pushed the garage door button, remembering that her cell phone was also in her briefcase.

"Well, when I screw things up, I really screw things up," Jerrica said while turning the ignition.

The brand new silver BMW coupe convertible purred smoothly as if it was welcoming her home again. She looked at her well-used Land Rover sitting in the other parking space. "Don't worry, my friend, I'll take you out soon," she told it.

She should be taking the Land Rover to work but it had been so mild the past couple of days, she wanted to spoil herself. Backing out of the garage, slowly onto the street, she slid on her sunglasses. Shifting the car into first gear she punched the gas. She loved the power in this car. It was a gift to herself after the divorce became final.

She decided she would take the highway this morning. She knew traffic might get heavier the closer she got to work but there were always a few empty stretches where she could feed her need for speed. The nickname her father had given her was lead foot. Once off the exit and onto the interstate, Jerrica quickly wove through traffic. She made the decision to take interstate 93, which would be a longer commute but would be much more fun with its flat roadways. She needed to feel the rush of adrenaline that driving fast would give her. She wove in and out of lanes to find an open section of road. Her patience paid off as she came upon a section of highway that was clear for at least a mile with no on merging exits. Her pulse quickened. "Let's do this," she said, pushing hard on the gas pedal.

The speed limit was sixty-five in this area but Jerrica knew she could hit at least seventy-five and the authorities might not pull her over. She was willing to take that chance today. The exhilaration grew as the speedometer increased. Switching gears again, Jerrica pushed the gas pedal to the floor. Two hands on the wheel, adrenaline rushing in her veins and concentrating on the road, for a few moments she felt free. All of her problems took a back seat to the powerful feeling of the BMW. Easing up on the pedal, she noticed that traffic was slowing down in front of her. The bumper-to-bumper traffic was beginning as she drew closer to the city.

Approximately forty minutes later, Jerrica pulled into her reserved parking spot in the North End Parking Garage. Even though she took the train most days, she kept her reserved parking space for days like this when she wanted her vehicle nearby. The monthly fee didn't cost that much and she knew she could safely leave it here for the weekend. She would bring her suitcase into work hoping that Lauren wouldn't notice that she didn't have the briefcase. She had left her laptop on her desk so she could at least contact Devin discreetly about getting the case back.

Jerrica looked at the sky. Another mild day, the walk to work shouldn't be bad. Jerrica popped the trunk and grabbed her suitcase, realizing immediately that it hadn't seemed so heavy at home when she'd loaded it into the car.

"Ok…so this walk might suck after all," she said, laughing.

Stepping off the elevator, Jerrica was a mess. Not only had she walked from the parking garage to work in high heels, rolling a heavy suitcase, but also to make matters worse, the moment she stepped out of the garage the wind was hitting her in the face. Jerrica scanned the department to see if Lauren had seen her yet. The first pair of eyes that caught her attention belonged to Jaime. Within seconds Jaime was in front of her grabbing the suitcase.

"Are you all right? You look terrible."

"Yes, Jaime, I am fine. Thank you for the compliment. Could you please put that into my office along with my coat? I'm going to the ladies room to freshen up," she said, running her fingers through her hair. "Where is Lauren?"

"She's in the lounge preparing coffee. Do you want me to get her?"

"No that's fine. Just put that in my office and I'll be out in a couple minutes," she assured her, turning toward the women's room.

She looked over her shoulder to see Jaime rushing to her office. She smiled at the thought that maybe she wouldn't have to hear Lauren's lecture about the missing briefcase. Once in the restroom, Jerrica took a good look at her reflection in the mirror. Her hair was tangled in the back and standing up in the front.

"Wow, I look like shit!" she said aloud pulling her fingers through the mess.

The sound of a toilet flushing behind her made Jerrica realized she wasn't alone. Still working on fixing her hair, Jerrica tried, unsuccessfully, not to glance at the reflection of the farthest stall door opening. An unfamiliar woman stepped out, strolling to the sink next to Jerrica. Jerrica felt embarrassed by her outburst and tried not to make eye contact. Stealing short glimpses at the reflection of the mysterious woman in the mirror, Jerrica could tell they were of the same height, but the other woman's build was more muscular. Her hair was naturally black and wavy, just above shoulder length. The more Jerrica tried not to watch, the more frustrated she became trying to fix her hair.

After washing and drying her hands, the woman started searching in her pocket for something.

Jerrica found it hard not to stare. Even though she wanted to be alone to clean up, Jerrica couldn't concentrate on her task while being captivated by every move this other person made.

The woman turned to leave, unexpectedly pausing behind Jerrica. Leaning around her, she brushed up against Jerrica's arm and set something on the sink.

Jerrica froze at the feeling of this woman's soft skin against her arm. Jerrica closed her eyes, breathing in the intoxicating perfume that now surrounded her. Her legs felt like jelly, so she leaned into the counter for support. When she opened her eyes, the woman was standing by the door gazing at her. With the door opened, she commented. "No. You definitely do not look like shit."

With a smile on her face, she vanished into the corridor.

That was the strangest encounter I have ever had, Jerrica mused. Standing with both hands in her hair Jerrica glanced down to see what was on the counter. Picking up the ponytail tie, Jerrica chuckled.

Walking across the department with her new hairdo for the day, Jerrica stopped at Lauren's desk.

Lauren lifted an eyebrow. "Is it summertime already?"

"My hair and the Boston wind had a fight this morning. The wind won. Do I have coffee in my office?"

Lauren squinted her eyes in a mock annoyance, "Yes, your majesty. It's sitting on your newly polished throne."

Jerrica turned abruptly just to make her ponytail swoosh back and forth.

"Smartass," Jerrica commented as the door shut.

Leaning her back against the door, she sighed in relief. She had made it to the safety of her office. She rushed to her desk. The laptop only took seconds to load, quickly clicking the mouse to get into e-mail. Scanning the inbox, she didn't see anything from Devin. Should she e-mail her or call? Jerrica decided that e-mail would be safer. Opening a blank form, she began composing a letter when her intercom buzzed.

"Ms. Kerrison, there's a courier here with a package for you," Jaime's voice whispered from the speaker.

"Could you please sign for it and bring it in?"

"I'm sorry, I can't. The package has to be signed for by you only."

"Send him in," Jerrica said with frustration, completely losing her train of thought.

A scrawny young man entered the office with a large box in his hands. He placed the box on the desk.

"That's fine right there."

"Please sign here."

She signed the clipboard and handed it back. "Who sent this package?"

The deliveryman stopped just as he put his hand on the doorknob, "I'm not sure, Miss. A door attendant gave it to me and gave me instructions to deliver it directly to you. I was paid a lot of money to make sure you received it early this morning."

She thanked him as he exited her office. She grabbed the letter opener off her desk, slicing open the tape on the top of the box. Inside, wrapped in pretty tissue paper, was her briefcase with a letter sitting on top. Jerrica grabbed the letter and slid it under her computer. Pulling the case from the box, she moved the carton to the floor beside her desk. Jerrica touched the soft leather on the top of the case. Clicking the latches on the side, she opened it. With considerable shock, Jerrica reached in and picked up the new smart phone that was sitting on top of her files. She flipped it around in her hand to get a detailed look at it. She carefully placed the phone on her desk, and then drew her attention to the contents of her briefcase. Satisfied that everything was still there, she placed the case on the floor. Bringing her attention back to the phone, she moved it to the middle of her desk.

"I have to send this back," she mumbled.

When in the hell did she have time, between last night and this morning to get this phone?

"Wait…where's my other cell phone," she questioned aloud.

Not finding her other cell phone under the files, she grew annoyed. *Damn you, Devin, what kind of game are you playing now.* Jerrica picked up the new phone, placing it in the top drawer of the desk. At that moment she was not curious enough to turn it on. Not wanting to deal with this current mess, she decided to focus her attention on work.

In her non-caring style, Lauren knocked while entering the office. Leaving the door open behind her, Lauren moved quickly to the front of Jerrica's desk. "So, what was in the box?" Lauren inquired leaning on the desk.

"I don't really want to talk about it right now."

Lauren obviously could see the frustration in her eyes, so she instantly called off the drill of multiple questions.

"Lauren, trust me. When I'm ready to talk about it, I'll come to you first."

Lauren sensed it was time to leave. Showing an understanding smile, she left.

Jerrica put her head in her hands in defeat.

"Ms. Kerrison." The quiet voice emanated from the speaker phone.

"Yes, Jaime," Jerrica sighed softly.

"Mr. Bisset is out here and he would like to see you."

"Well, send him in."

"Umm…he would like you to come out here. He has guests."

"I'll be right out, " she said, cursing under her breath.

This isn't going to be my day, she thought.

She lightly tapped her forehead on her desk in aggravation. Jerrica sighed heavily, then headed out of her office. Once out in the main floor she noticed John standing near Jaime's desk.

He turned to see Jerrica approaching, instinctively holding out a hand to her. "Well, the board accepted my proposal, Jak," he said, shaking her hand roughly.

Jerrica felt uncomfortable, as her hand became a hostage of his sweaty grip. "John, that's great. I'm glad I could help," she replied, yanking out of his grasp.

Jerrica figured she might as well give herself some credit for helping, since he obviously wasn't going to acknowledge her input.

"Jerrica," John said motioning to someone behind her. "This is Olivia Hutten. She will be joining my PR department. She's the big mystery!"

Boy, John moved fast when he wanted something. Jerrica shifted her position to find a tall, eye-catching middle-aged woman standing a few feet behind him. The woman moved forward in her direction, putting her hand out to introduce herself. Jerrica extended her hand out again, for another greeting.

"Hello. Please call me, Olivia," she said, purring in a heavy southern accent.

Mr. Bisset interrupted their introduction by stepping in between the two women. He looked at Olivia as if he wanted to devour her, "Olivia, this is Jak. She's the one who helped me get you here."

Jerrica almost fell over. Did John just compliment her publicly?

"Jack? I thought Jack was a man," Olivia responded in a callous nature.

"Sorry to disappoint you, but no, I'm not a man. My initials spell Jak. It's kind of a nickname for people who know me well. My name is actually Jerrica."

Olivia looked uncomfortable with the new revelation.

John, not noticing the sudden tension, continued his introductions, "Oh, I almost forgot to introduce you to Olivia's assistant."

Standing just out of view on her left was the woman Jerrica had seen in the bathroom.

"Ms. Kerrison, this is Ms. Jeffery."

Stepping forward, she shook Jerrica's hand. Her face lit up when they touched. "I'm Madison."

Jerrica couldn't stop herself from staring into Madison's eyes. The color was a deep shade of brown with gold flakes around the iris. She could get lost in those eyes. When she smiled, they sparkled. Lightly tanned skin accentuated her full and inviting lips. Madison's unfamiliar scent was pleasing. Jerrica let her eyes close briefly to inhale the enchanting aroma. When she opened them, she realized Madison was looking at her intently. Releasing the grip, Jerrica observed Madison's eyes taking the liberty to size her up. She didn't know if she should be flattered or embarrassed. She blushed self-consciously.

Madison was trying, without great success, to hold back a giggle at Jerrica's shyness.

Jerrica looked around the small group of people to see if anyone else was witnessing their interaction. She was very pleased to see that John and Olivia were in deep conversation and hadn't even noticed the exchange.

"Well, it was nice to meet everyone," Jerrica said, wanting to make a quick exit. "Welcome, both of you, to the company. When is your first official day?" She directed her question to Olivia.

"Oh, we want to start right away. I will be moving my office in on Monday," Olivia said, responding with schoolchild excitement.

"Great. Then I'll see you around. It was nice to meet you, Olivia, and you as well, Madison. We'll have to do lunch once you get settled in," said Jerrica, excusing herself from the group.

Walking into her office, she turned to take a peek at the new PR department standing near her office. To her surprise, Madison was gazing in her direction with a grin on her face. Jerrica involuntarily blushed again and closed the door. Leaning back on her door, she envisioned Madison's bodily features. She hadn't missed that Madison filled out her blouse very well and her pants had a nice curve to them in the back. Jerrica felt an unexpected rush of heat from deep inside.

"Jerrica, stop," she scolded herself aloud. "It's so unprofessional to ogle the new employee."

Pausing a second, she heard the group of voices outside her office start to fade into the distance. Clearing her mind with a shake of her head, she moved back to her chair. Once settled in, she started working on quarterly reports. She would be sending her projected financial reports to her clients in a little more than a month. These reports were never part of the contract when clients signed with this company. She felt that giving them a little extra information free of charge is what kept them loyal patrons.

Scribbling notes on her worksheet, she cursed when her pencil broke.

Wonderful, what else won't go my way today? she griped silently.

Opening up her top drawer to claim her pencil sharpener, she encountered the new phone again. Her memory flashed to images of the evening's events with Devin. Retrieving the phone, she placed it on the top of her desk. Jerrica's mind was numb on what to do next. Suddenly, like a flip of a switch, she remembered the letter. Relocating her laptop a little to the side, she pulled on the corner of the envelope until it was free from its hidden home. Jerrica tapped the corner of the envelope on her desk then spun it in her fingers to tap the other corner of the envelope in nervous anticipation. She was extremely worried about what Devin had to say. Finding her letter opener, she opened the top with one smooth motion of her wrist. Carefully taking the letter out, she placed the empty envelope and letter opener on her desk. Taking in a deep breath and letting it out slowly, she unfolded the letter and began reading.

My Dearest Jerrica,
You know me better than anyone I've ever known. You should understand how hard it is for me to open up and share my emotions with you. I wanted to say I'm sorry for last night. It wasn't my intention to invite you into my home and assume we could pick up where we left off. I had planned to talk to you. I wanted to tell you what I was feeling. Unfortunately, having you in my place, seeing you at my breakfast table, brought back so many great memories that my old habits took control and I made a fool out of myself coming on to you. I won't deny that I wanted you, but I promise you that is not why I asked you there. I've been thinking a lot about you, about us.

I know our relationship was never smooth and I blame myself for all the problems we had. You were only being open, honest, and loving when we were together. Moreover, all I gave you in return was secrets, lies, and pain. I know now what I did was very selfish, but I wouldn't have admitted that when we were together. I have tried in the past few months to understand where I went wrong for myself and for you. I found I was afraid to let love into my life. I was afraid to let you love me. I found that my world is a very lonely place without you. I want you to know that I've missed you so much. I am so sorry for hurting you. I can never take back the things I've said, or the hurtful things I've done or I didn't do when we were together. However, I want us to try again. I want to show you how much I've changed. Show you the real me. Please give me a chance.

Lovingly,

Devin

PS. The phone is a gift from me. Please don't ask me to return it. I want you to have it.

Jerrica sat at her desk staring blankly at the letter. Setting it down, Jerrica felt hurt, frustrated and confused. She had spent months trying to get past the tornado that was Devin Daniel and now she saw herself stepping backward into the pain, instead of moving forward into her future. She turned to her computer and opened up a blank e-mail. Addressing it to Devin, she wrote:

Devin,

I received your letter. Thank you for returning my briefcase. Thank you so much for the phone. You really shouldn't have.

I need time.

I need to know first...
Have you admitted to your parents that you're gay?
Jerrica

She sat back in the chair, gazing at her computer screen, debating if she should hit send. Letting out the breath she was holding, she leaned forward, placing her hand on the mouse. Hesitating briefly, she clicked the button to send the e-mail. Grabbing the screen on her laptop, she closed her computer. At one time in her life she had been in love with this woman. For the first time in a long time, she felt overwhelmed with life and wanted to cry. There were too many emotions coming at her all at once.

Pressing the intercom to her assistant, Jerrica conveyed that she was not to be disturbed the rest of the day. She was going to lock herself in and get some important work finished.

"We are still on for the Cape, right?" Lauren asked.

"Yes, we are," she answered before ending the call.

Lauren knew this was a pattern for Jerrica. She would bury herself in her work to avoid dealing with emotional issues. Even though she had seen this before, she had no idea what she was hiding from this time. They would have plenty of time to talk it out on the drive to the cottage, Lauren consoled herself.

Lunch came and went but Lauren's anxiety was increasing by each passing hour. As she repositioned herself in her office chair for the hundredth time, she tried to concentrate on her own computer work. Every so often she received an e-mail from Jerrica for a project or a folder that she might need later. At least Jerrica was keeping her mind busy. The day seemed to drag on, but as long as she heard from Jerrica periodically, she felt some kind of normalcy in her day. Mid-afternoon, Lauren glanced at Jaime who was focused on her work and oblivious of the events around her.

I wish I could shut out the world as she does, Lauren thought.

After closer observation she realized Jaime wasn't focusing, she was softly crying behind her computer screen. Jaime turned her head as Lauren touched her shoulder, "Jaime, what's wrong?"

The tears that were few before, now flowed in abundance. In between tears and catching her breath, Jaime managed to answer. "This guy…I've been seeing for a few months just…broke up with me via…text message."

Lauren had been out of the dating game for quite a few years and found it hard to understand this blubbering girly stuff. "What happened?"

"I don't know. I thought we were serious."

"And," Lauren pushed.

"Well, we were finally…intimate and now he's breaking up with me," she explained as she wiped tears from her cheeks.

Lauren wanted to tell her this was classic for young relationships but seeing the hurt in her eyes, see decided that wasn't a good idea. "I'm sorry, Jaime,"

She felt remorseful for the younger woman. "Listen…Jerrica and I are taking a trip down to my cottage on the Cape this weekend. Would you like to come? It's not a total relaxation weekend, we are opening up for the season, but it would at least be time away."

She waited patiently as Jaime considered the proposal in between sniffles. "Are you sure I won't be a third wheel?"

"I wouldn't have asked if I thought that would be the case. I asked you because it's an all-girls weekend and honestly, I think it would be good for all of us to get to know one another better," she added in her best stretching the truth voice.

Jaime's eyes seemed to search Lauren's face for pity or embarrassment, but could only find caring. "I would like that a lot. But I don't have anything packed. What am I going to do?"

Lauren hadn't fully pondered that. "Well, you live in the Newton area, correct?"

Jaime nodded and Lauren continued, "I'll let you borrow my car to go home. You have two hours to be back here by the time we need to leave. Do you think you can make it?"

"You're going to let me borrow your car? Shouldn't we ask Ms. Kerrison if I can leave?"

"First off if you're going to spend the weekend with her, you need to start calling her Jerrica. Second, since she's closed herself off from the world today, I am in charge and I say you can go. I can handle it here. I trust you driving my car."

She reached back on her desk and grabbed her keys. Tossing them to Jaime she said, "You better get going. You know where I parked, right? Be back on time. I hate leaving late."

"I know where your car is parked. I'll be right back. Thanks, Lauren!"

She watched as Jaime rushed for the stairwell, disappearing behind the door. Lauren looked at her boss's closed door. *Wait until she told her what she just did.*

At almost five, Lauren glanced at the clock. Jaime had not yet returned nor had Jerrica come out of her office. She decided that if Jerrica didn't appear soon, she was going to force her way in. Just then, the office door opened and

Jerrica stepped out. Lauren notice that her face looked a little paler then it had earlier and her eyes were puffy. *Could she have been crying?*

†

Jerrica strolled to the desk, then glanced around the room. "It's almost quitting time. Where's Jaime?" she asked, pointing to the empty desk.

"Well, I sent her home but she'll be back," Lauren answered, eyes still focused on her computer.

"She'll be back? What did I miss?" Jerrica casually sat on a corner of the desk.

Blushing, Lauren's head tilted toward the floor when she began to explain. "Well, while you were hiding from everyone today, Jaime had an emotional meltdown."

Jerrica bent her head down in an attempt to see Lauren's face more clearly.

"I didn't know how to handle it, so I asked her if she wanted to go with us for the weekend," Lauren closed her eyes and waited for the scolding.

Instead, Jerrica touched her shoulder, "That was nice of you. So where is she?"

It was unlike Jerrica not to have an opinion on an unexpected change in plans. "I sent her home to get clothes. She should be back any minute now."

"Once she is here, let me know. I'm going to close up my office and then I'll be ready."

Back in her office again, Jerrica felt less stressed, but exhausted. She didn't have the energy to fight with anyone about the sudden change in status-quo. She was tired and just wanted to get out of there. Adding one more person to this journey put a crimp in her plans to bare her soul but she understood why Lauren had invited Jaime. Maybe this would be a good trip for all of them. They could spend time getting to know Jaime.

While shutting everything off and packing her briefcase, she reluctantly picked up the new phone. She could feel the tears at the edge of her eyelashes, but quickly wiped them away. Jerrica shoved the phone in her coat pocket. Walking toward the door, she heard familiar voices talking on the other side. Jaime must have made it back on time. Now they could go and have a great weekend.

Chapter Four

They had stopped briefly at Lauren's house in Dorchester to pick up food plus a few more necessities and Brandon gave his wife a good luck kiss. In less than twenty minutes, they were back on the road again. Jerrica nestled down in her seat preparing for the almost two-hour drive. The sound of random '80s music from a local radio station played softly in the background. She turned her head to look out her window. Maybe if she were lucky, she would nap on the way. Even as a child, she would fall asleep on long drives with her parents. She watched as the landscape changed, cities turned into towns and towns into large countryside. Jerrica glanced in the back seat to see Jaime concentrating on something on her cell phone. Jerrica felt her shoulders beginning to relax as she snuggled down in her seat.

"So," Lauren's voice broke through the silence.

Jerrica realized quickly that her peaceful moment was now over. She turned to look at Lauren who looked like she wanted to talk. Reaching, she turned the radio down.

"Are you going to tell me what happened today?"

Jerrica motioned her head toward the back seat reminding Lauren they weren't alone.

Lauren glanced in the rearview mirror at Jaime who was engrossed in her phone. Shrugging her shoulders, she lowered her tone, "Well, how about an edited version? You know I can't wait till we get to the cottage."

Lauren would be relentless until she got the answer she wanted. "Fine, I ran into an old friend yesterday and we had an argument. I left my briefcase at their house and the case was returned to me today. End of story," Jerrica blurted out quickly.

Lauren's scowling expression told Jerrica she was not happy.

"Jerrica…you're kidding me! I thought….well, you know what I thought and…this infuriates me. What the hell were you doing at…with that…?"

Jerrica found it a little amusing that Lauren was censoring her own language so she didn't give anything away to Jaime. Jerrica had to stifle the giggle. A noise from the backseat drew their attention.

"Are you okay back there," Lauren asked.

"Yes, I am. May I add to your conversation?"

Jerrica glanced at Lauren in confusion, nodding yes to Jaime.

"I understand you two have a close relationship and have been friends outside of work for a very long time. I know I'm only the new guy and you're trying not to get me involved in your personal life, but skirting around the truth is a little degrading to my intelligence."

"I'm sorry, Jaime. It's just there is a lot of stuff going on in my life, and the less you know, the less trouble you can get into in the future."

Lauren glanced in the rearview mirror to examine Jaime's expression.

After some deliberation, Jaime cautiously responded, "If you're talking about your past relationship with Ms. Daniel, I already know you two were involved."

Lauren's mouth dropped open with this new revelation.

Jerrica turned so she could see Jaime as she spoke.

"I know you two started dating or at least you were intimate approximately eight months after I started working at the company."

"How did you know that?" Curiosity was getting the better of Lauren.

Jerrica watched as Jamie's face flushed as she answered. "I saw…and heard them together."

The innocence in Jaime's eyes told Jerrica she was telling the truth, and she instantly felt mortified. Her whole body was blushing as she turned in her seat, staring out into the darkness.

"Oh, I have to hear the story to this, please continue, Jaime," Lauren said with a little evilness in her tone.

"It…was sometime around the end of September beginning of October, if I remember correctly." She paused to count the months in her head. "That was the first time it happened."

"Wait, there's more than just this one time?" Lauren shot a glance at Jerrica.

Jerrica slid down in her seat trying, unsuccessfully to find a place to hide.

"Jerrica, I'm sorry. Do you not want me to continue?" Jaime asked, leaning forward.

"Oh, you're with friends now, Jaime. Please go on with your story," Lauren prodded.

Jerrica's face paled.

"Well…it was a Friday evening, a few hours after everyone had left for the weekend. I had gone back to the office…."

Jerrica could picture in excruciating detail the event Jaime was about to describe. She hung her head in embarrassment.

"I had forgotten a file I had promised Jerrica I would complete before Monday. When I reached my desk, I noticed an unfamiliar coat tossed on my desk. I was pretty sure everyone had left for the day."

Jerrica did not want to relive that night or any night with Devin, especially from a different storyteller.

"I reached across my desk to grab the file and I heard some sounds coming from Jerrica's office. I didn't think anything of the simple noise. I mean Jerrica works late all the time. I continued my task until I heard what sounded like a loud moan."

Jerrica closed her eyes tight.

Lauren was smiling from ear to ear with the knowledge that this was completely embarrassing Jerrica.

Jaime paused, her face turning a light pink from the pictures flashing in her head, "My first instinct was that Jerrica was hurt and needed help. So…I ran to the door and opened it."

The pure horror of what she must have witnessed hit Jerrica full force. She leaned forward in her seat, putting her face in her hands.

Oh, this was too good. "Don't leave me hanging, Jaime. What did you see?" Lauren egged her on.

Jerrica wanted to reach out and choke Lauren.

Jaime obviously felt caught in the middle of this tug of war between these two women. She surely understood how uncomfortable Jerrica was at this moment, but she also knew that Lauren was the one who had invited her on this trip. Jaime was obligated to finish the story.

"When I opened the door…I saw," she said, gulping hard. "…the backside of a very naked woman straddling Jerrica's lap. I didn't actually see the woman's face, but that golden mane of Ms. Daniel's is unforgettable. I stood there briefly captivated at how beautiful they looked together. Realizing that the noises I heard were Ms. Daniel's cries of…passion. I quietly closed the door and left. I do have to admit she is a very striking woman. At least from the angle I could see."

If Jerrica could have crawled under her seat at that very moment, she would have. The car fell silent for several minutes.

"I'm sorry Jerrica. I didn't mean to, I mean…I didn't mean to walk in on your private moment. I just thought you needed help."

Lauren started to laugh so hard she was sure she would have to pull over. She couldn't see the road through all the tears in her eyes.

"It wasn't your fault. It's ok," Jerrica said softly. Reaching out, Jerrica slapped Lauren's arm to make her stop laughing.

The car was full of Lauren's laughter as they traveled over the Sagamore Bridge.

Jerrica squinted at Lauren. "Are you done laughing at my expense?"

"Don't get angry at me. I'm not the one who had sex in her office, and got caught."

Jaime sat quietly in the back seat.

"Jaime, do you think our client was getting her money's worth?" Lauren asked, wanting to get one more dig in, at Jerrica's expense before the conversation changed,

Jerrica's mouth dropped open in shock at Lauren's boldness.

"Well from what I saw, and heard that evening, I would say she received every last penny's worth."

Jerrica rubbed her eyes in frustration while Lauren bellowed in laughter even louder next to her.

Once past the hysterical laughter, she glanced at Jerrica who was staring blankly out into the darkness. "You're not seriously upset are you?"

"Not upset, just appalled."

"Appalled at what? You got caught, deal with it."

"I've built my professional life on following the rules. The first time I bend the rules, even a little, I tarnish my reputation in front of my employees." Disappointment echoed in her voice.

"I don't think any less of you," said a soft voice from the back seat.

Jaime leaned between the seats, speaking a little louder. "I respect you more for bending the rules. Seeing you that evening made me realize you are human and that you can have fun just like anyone else. That was also the night I found out you liked women." Jaime leaned back.

Jerrica sat quietly contemplating what to say next. "I don't advertise who I am, but if you ask me, I won't lie about it either."

Lauren started to feel remorseful for coercing Jaime into telling the story. "Listen, Jerrica, I'm real sorry for this and I'm sorry to you as well, Jaime. This whole thing was my fault. I started this line of questioning. So I am really sorry," she said staring at the long road ahead.

They sat in silence for a while, before Jerrica spoke. "It's fine, let's just enjoy the rest of our drive and our weekend."

Jerrica wasn't angry. She didn't have the energy to be angry. Her emotions were raw from the last couple of days and now this new revelation. Resting her head back on the seat, she finally dozed off. Flashes of Devin ran through her mind as she slept.

"Wake up sleepy head," Lauren's voice said.

Opening her eyes slowly, she blinked a few times to see Lauren standing outside the car.

"We are here," Lauren whispered, turning toward the trunk of the car.

Jerrica stood to exit the vehicle. Quickly grabbing onto the car door, everything around her began to spin. Her body slid down the inside of the car door as the taste of stomach bile penetrated the back of her throat. Next thing she knew, Lauren and Jaime were on each side of her holding her up under her arms.

"Jerrica, are you ok?" Lauren said.

Jerrica looked up at her with blurry eyes. "I don't know what's wrong. I don't feel so good. I think I'm going to vomit."

"Let's get her inside. We'll put her in the guest room upstairs on the right next to the bathroom," Lauren exclaimed as the two of them helped Jerrica into the house.

Once in the bedroom, they carefully laid Jerrica down on the bed. Jaime was scared, not knowing what to do to help.

"I know you want to help me, but right now you're only going to get in my way. If you want to help, go unload the trunk. I'll take care of her," Lauren said, taking charge of the situation.

Jaime nodded, leaving the room.

Lauren took Jerrica's shoes off and pulled the hair tie from her hair. Retrieving a blanket from the closet, she placed it over her sick friend.

Opening her eyes at the feel of the blanket she whimpered at her friend. "I don't know what happened. I was fine and…."

"Shh. Don't worry about it. You're just tired and I'm sure everything will be better in the morning. Now get some rest."

Lauren touched her forehead, no fever, but her skin had taken on a pasty color. She watched Jerrica's eyes flutter closed. Lauren reached the door, looking back only once and switched off the light, softly praying that Jerrica would be ok.

†

The morning sun leisurely rose above the delicately weathered cottage. Sunbeams cascaded in through the windows, illuminating the guest room. Squinting as the radiance of the day filtered onto her face, Jerrica slowly opened her eyes. Confusion filled her. *Where am I?*

Gradually she pushed herself to a sitting position. Leaning back against the headboard she slowly looked around the room. She was at the cottage, front room facing the water, room on the same side as the master suite. Lauren and Jaime must have brought her up here. She tried to remember what had happened. The memories all seemed hazy.

Throwing the blanket back, she cautiously got out of bed. When the spinning and nausea didn't return, she figured she might actually be finished with whatever had made her sick. Looking down, she noticed she was still wearing yesterday's clothes. Jerrica inhaled deeply as the aroma of coffee filled the small bedroom. She started toward the hallway, when she heard a door close. Changing direction, she strolled to the window. She watched as Jaime got into the passenger's seat of Lauren's car. *Where are those two going?* she wondered.

She stood in the window long enough to see them drive away. Since rushing downstairs wasn't a priority anymore, Jerrica started undressing as she moved toward the bathroom to take a shower. She found her suitcase sitting next to the doorway that led from the bedroom to the bathroom. *Great, she didn't have to go searching for it.* Entering the bathroom she smiled, seeing fresh towels on the counter.

"Thanks, Lauren, you've thought of everything," she said aloud.

Fully undressed, she stepped into the shower. The welcoming hot water flowed across her overworked body, caressing her aching back, tumbling down her tired calves to the open drain, where she hoped the water would take away all of her troubles. Wrapping the fresh towel around her wet hair she clutched the second towel in her hand and entered the bedroom. Mid-stride she stopped to inspect her exposed body in the full-length mirror. "Why do you bother looking?" she said to her reflection.

Glancing from head to toe she began the mental scrutiny of her appearance. The dark circles under her eyes made her look older than her true age. Her eye color was strange. Not just green, they were an emerald green, almost black at first glance. Hair was too long, skin was too pale. She needed to get back to tanning. Which also meant getting back to the gym, she reminded herself while absent-mindedly rubbing her stomach.

Her breasts were of average size. Her ass was firm, legs were long, strong, but still feminine. Her legs were her only two attributes she was proud of and didn't mind showing. She shook her head in disgust, walking away from the mirror. Jerrica tossed the suitcase on the bed and retrieved the items she needed, underclothes, her jogging pants, and an old sweatshirt from her alma mater. The aroma of coffee coming from the kitchen assaulted her senses again, giving her incentive to move more quickly. Once she had dried off and fully dressed, she journeyed downstairs. Entering the kitchen she viewed a full pot of coffee waiting for her. Selecting a mug from the cabinet she filled it to the rim. Glancing around, she noticed a note on the counter near a plate of croissants. Jerrica placed the pot in its holder, strolling to the food.

Good Morning Sleepy Head,
We hope you are feeling better this morning. We waited for you, but it started to get late. We have gone into

town for supplies. I'll pick up the steaks at the butcher shop. I'll buy you some ginger ale while we are out. If you need anything else, please call. There is cell reception anywhere on the property. We won't be gone long. See you soon.

Love yah,
Lauren

She placed the note back on the counter. Grabbing her coffee and a croissant, she headed for the back porch. A cool wind chilled her as she opened the back door. Snatching the comforter from the chair next to the door, she stepped out. The porch stretched the entire length of the back of the house. The cottage was a classic New England style beach home and she had fallen in love with it the first moment she had seen it. She lounged in the largest Adirondack chair she could find, wrapping herself in the comforter. With her stomach temporarily content, Jerrica tilted her head back against the chair and listened to the sounds of the distant waves crashing on the shore. Her eyes fluttered closed, letting her mind wander.

✝

"I'm here," Jerrica said into her cell phone, "Don't worry about a thing. I'll make sure I lock up after the weekend. Thanks for letting me borrow the cottage. Yes, Lauren, I'm fine. I'll see you on Monday. Goodbye."

"You didn't tell her I was here," Devin whispered in her ear.

"I think she knows you're here," Jerrica said turning into Devin's embrace, nuzzling her neck.

Devin tightened her grip, resting her chin on Jerrica's head. Her hair smelled like lilacs on an early fall day and she breathed it in deeply. In this moment, life was perfect. Devin sighed in contentment.

Jerrica pulled back to look into her eyes. "Is everything okay?"

"Yes, I'm fine honey. It's just nice to be here with you, just the two of us. Come on, let's go inside."

With an arm over one another's shoulders, they walked into the house closing the door behind them.

Jerrica grabbed Devin's hand and watched as Devin looked down at their linked hands.

"Let me show you the upstairs," Jerrica said with a smile.

Entering the master bedroom, Jerrica untwined their hands. Strolling to the French doors that led out to the balcony, she pushed them open. The sounds of the waves hitting the empty beach and the smell of the ocean filled the room. Stepping out into the fresh air, she slid her hands across the top of the hand-carved oak railing, tipping her head toward the sun.

Jerrica turned around, leaning against the railing. "What are you thinking about?"

"I was thinking how lucky I am to have such a beautiful woman in my life," Devin responded.

Closing the distance between them, she tilted Jerrica's chin up with her fingertip. She gently guided Jerrica's lips and Jerrica could feel the heat as their lips softy touched.

A soft moan escaped Jerrica as she surrendered. Her head began to swim and she didn't want the feeling to end. She opened her mouth to Devin's tantalizing tongue and the kiss deepened. Her body arched, trying to feel more of Devin's body against hers.

Devin teasingly pulled away. Hungry blue eyes held lustful green eyes captive as she reached forward, seductively unbuttoning Jerrica's shirt at the neckline. Goosebumps developed across the exposed skin.

Unlatching the last button, Devin slowly slid her hands up the seams of the open shirt. Her fingers tracing lightly over Jerrica's tight abs. Devin's hands slid up to the beautiful black lace bra. One twist of the front snap unclipped the confining lingerie with ease. In slow motion, Devin hands glided across Jerrica's shoulders, gently slipping off the restrictive clothing. The apparel no longer needed, cascaded over the railing, floating carelessly in the fall air until it touched the soft earth below. Devin trailed kisses down Jerrica's neck.

Holding onto the railing, Jerrica tossed her head back, encouraging Devin's continued path. The pleasure the soft lips were offering assaulted Jerrica's senses. Her knees were shaking as she released the railing. Running her hands through the golden tresses, she gently encouraged Devin's face to look at her. She could see the raw desire reflected in her eyes. "Let's go back inside."

Devin's smile broadened as she took her hand and led them back into the bedroom.

Jerrica stopped at the side of the bed. "Let me help you with this," she smirked.

Jerrica's hands moved down to the tiny stylish buckle on Devin's pants, pulling it free with ease. Her hand intentionally touched Devin skin as she lowered the zipper. She smiled as Devin released a groan. Working her hands around the waistband, she slid the pants down and watched them puddle at their feet. Jerrica sensually guided her hands under the hem of the turtleneck, lifting the garment. She grinned when she received hurried assistance. Once the shirt was off, Jerrica captured Devin's lips, kissing them softly at first and then pressing harder as desire grew.

Devin could feel a yearning from deep inside as she lowered their bodies to the bed. The kiss was broken with the urgency to breathe. Devin stared down at the beautiful woman who was lovingly looking up at her.

Jerrica's hand caressed Devin's flushed cheek. "I love you," Jerrica's voice said softly.

Turning her lips into the hand, Devin gently licked the exposed palm. Jerrica knew she was offering not only her body, but her heart as well. Smiling, Devin lowered her head, stopping millimeters from Jerrica's lips.

"I know you do," Devin whispered, selfishly capturing Jerrica's mouth, as their bodies became one.

Soon they would find the rhythm that would bring them to ecstasy…together.

They spent the weekend in bed, each enjoying what the other was offering. They left the room only for food or the bathroom. When the last hours of their perfect weekend arrived, they sat cuddled in a chair on the balcony, wrapped only in a blanket. Jerrica sat comfortably in Devin's lap as they witnessed the breaking of dawn. They had created this world just for the two of them. The rest of the world didn't matter and nothing else existed as long as they were holding one another. Jerrica angled her head to see Devin. "I hate to say this, but we have to go back today."

"I know," Devin's tone was flat.

"Are you ok?"

"I don't want this to end."

"I don't want it to end, either."

"This has been the best weekend of my life."

"It's been great for me, too. Unfortunately, we do have to return to the world sometime."

"Why?"

"We can't live off of love, Devin. I do have to support myself. Don't worry, everything will be all right."

Jerrica kissed Devin softly, wiggling out of the warm embrace. "I'm going to shower," She held up a staying palm. "Without you. I really need to start packing and if you join me, we'll never get out of here at a decent hour."

Devin smiled with pleasure as she observed a very naked Jerrica saunter her way into the bathroom. Devin caught the devilish grin Jerrica was wearing before she disappeared.

She hoped Jerrica was right, that they would be fine once they left the cottage. Deep down, Devin had her doubts that this relationship would have a happy conclusion. Standing with the blanket tightly around her body, she returned to the room, sitting on the edge of the bed. She heard the water running from the shower as she dug into her overnight bag to find her cell phone. They had promised one another, no contact to or from the outside world during their weekend alone.

Devin was about to break that promise. Finding the phone with ease, she flipped it to see the screen. Thirty-five missed calls, twenty-eight voicemails. She touched the screen to see who had called. More than half were from her father, a few from her mom, and the rest from her assistant. She groaned with the thought of having to explain why she had totally disappeared for the weekend. Turning to return the phone to her bag, it rang. His number flashed on the screen. The same number she had seen since her youth, her father's number. If she didn't answer it, he would keep calling and she would have hell to pay when she would see him. Touching the screen, she answered his call.

Jerrica could hear raised voices outside the bathroom door. She quickly finished rinsing and turned the water off. To her surprise, Jerrica could hear Devin's father. She knew Devin must be on her phone. His voice was so loud it was as if he was standing in the next room. The raised tones told her they were having an argument. Upset that

Devin had broken their agreement, she wrapped herself in the first available towel and opened the door. At first, she thought Devin had heard her, but after a few seconds she realized that wasn't true. Devin was standing out on the balcony, still wrapped in their blanket with her back to the room. Jerrica was about to announce herself, when a spout of venom came from the speakerphone.

"Then tell me where the hell you have been the past two days!"

"I told you, I needed some time away."

"Yes, I heard you say that. I didn't buy that expensive phone for you not to use, young lady."

"You didn't buy me this phone, Dad. Mom gave it to me for my birthday."

"Where do you think your mother gets her money?"

"Hypocrite," she whispered under her breath.

"What was that?" His tone elevated a little more.

"It was nothing, Dad. So what is so important that you called fifty million times?"

"Show me some respect young lady, I am still your father! You go off to God knows where, with God knows who, for two days without any contact. That's disrespectful to me and to your mother."

"I'm twenty-eight years old, Dad. I don't need to check in every day."

"Yes, you do!"

Jerrica could see the frustration in Devin's tense posture. She started toward Devin to comfort her but froze when the harsh voice came back from the phone.

"When are you going to stop fooling around with all these young men and settle down? You know your mom and I love you and worry about you. We want to make sure you have someone who will take care of you and give us grandchildren."

Jerrica almost choked as she felt the bile rise in the back of her throat.

Devin sighed. "Dad I'm not that old. I can still have fun from time to time. I'll find a man when I'm ready for a permanent relationship. You can't rush me into marriage or children."

"Well, we would like to see our grandchildren before we are too old to enjoy them."

"We keep discussing the same thing lately. I'm not ready. I've just started enjoying the life that I've built."

"Well, if you stopped spending so much time with your friends, you would have more time to look for the right husband."

"I don't want to discuss this with you right now. I'm on the Cape visiting friends and will be leaving for the city soon."

"Your mother and I are in Nantucket. I want you to come here. We have business to discuss and we can talk about your future as well."

"Dad, I carpooled down here, I don't have my own car."

"Fine, give me the address and I'll send my driver on the mainland to retrieve you."

"I would rather you didn't."

"Devin Lynn Daniel, you will come to the house! That's not a request!"

Devin lowered her head in defeat. Tears filled her eyes as she blurted out the address.

"That's a good girl. The driver will be there in less than an hour. He'll call you when he gets into town, so you can be ready. Now, be a good girl and say your respectful good-byes to your companions," he instructed. "Do you hear me, Devin?"

"Yes, sir."

"Good! I'll see you soon. Love you, baby."

"Love you too, Daddy," Devin returned her response lifeless.

Devin tapped the phone off and stared out into the water. Suddenly, Devin must have realized it was quiet in the house and there was no sound of running water. Turning around she saw a stunned Jerrica standing in the middle of the room. Devin rushed inside.

"Stop," yelled Jerrica, putting up her hand.

"Jerrica, let me explain."

"What is there to explain? I heard most, if not all of your conversation. You've been lying all this time. You've lied to me. You've lied to your parents. The saddest thing is you're lying to yourself. You're too scared to say no to Daddy. You let him control your life. To top this all off, I'm just a plaything to you, to pass the time until you find mister right. Did I miss anything?"

"Jerrica, you're not my plaything, nor have I treated you that way. It's just my...."

"I know it's all about your father. He runs your life and you let him. So, who's to blame here? I've been open with you from the start. I was in the closet for too many years Devin, and I won't go back there! I hurt many people pretending to be someone I wasn't. I won't hide and I won't lie for you."

Jerrica stepped back, contemplating her next move. Frustrated, she sat on the edge of the bed with her hands resting in her lap.

"Jerrica, please listen to me," Devin pleaded but didn't move toward her.

"I think you need to take your shower now. Your father's driver will be here soon to fetch you," she said looking down at her hands.

Devin was at a loss for words. Her heart was breaking, but she knew in some sense, Jerrica was right, her Father did run her life. The silence in the room became deafening for the both of them.

Jerrica's shaky voice whispered. "Please, take your shower. I need time to think."

Devin tossed the blanket that they had shared onto the bed and entered the bathroom.

Jerrica felt numb. *What am I supposed to do now? Get up and stand on your feet, you don't want to be in this room when she gets out of the bathroom.* Jerrica grabbed everything she could find that belonged to her and quickly stuffed it in her bag. "I'll get dressed downstairs," she mumbled to herself. "Right now I need to get away from her."

With one last glance at the closed bathroom door, Jerrica was out of the room and down the stairs in a huff.

Twenty minutes later, Devin appeared, carrying her suitcase and shoulder bag. Jerrica noticed that Devin had decided to pull her hair back, off her face, into a clip. She was wearing a familiar outfit, a pair of khaki pants with a white tank top. She glanced up, watching as Devin placed her bags near the entranceway then walked toward the kitchen. Jerrica was standing on the farthest side of the kitchen, putting distance between them, cutting vegetables on the middle island. As if a light switch turned on in her head, she remembered where she had seen the outfit.

Jerrica spoke first. "Did you bring your blazer?"

Confusion crossed Devin's face. "Sorry, I don't understand."

Still chopping vegetables, Jerrica continued. "I've seen you wearing that in your office. I'm asking if you have your blazer to complete your ensemble."

Devin answered the question in a dull tone, "Actually, yes. It's in my suitcase."

"Need to look all business when you see mommy and daddy?" Bitterness was evident in her voice.

"Are you staying," Devin asked, noticing all the cut vegetables.

"Not that it is any of your business, but yes. I'm not ready to face anyone so soon after this weekend."

"Jerrica, please, I don't want to end our weekend like this," Devin's voice was trembling.

Tears started to form in Jerrica's eyes. One tear bravely escaped and tumbled down her cheek. Jerrica whispered. "Devin, this is not only the end of our weekend but it's the end of us. I can't do the lying and sneaking around thing. It took me a long time to get to where I am today. I am proud of the person I've become and I will not hide for you or for anyone ever again. I don't trust you and if I can't trust you, then there is no reason for us to be together."

Devin gazed down at her hands that now rested on the counter top. Her heart was broken. "Don't do this, please. Jerrica, you don't understand? My life is complicated …well my…."

For a brief second Jerrica wanted to console her because she recognized the inner torment of what she was going through. She had traveled part of this road herself in discovery of her truth. However, she also knew that if Devin wanted to change, she would have to do it on her own and for herself.

Jerrica set down the knife, staring at the cutting board. Taking a deep breath and holding onto the edge of the counter, she uttered the last words she would say to Devin that weekend.

"I have always been up front with you, Devin, of who I am and how I feel. It kills me to admit this now, but I do love you…if you're not willing to fight for us then at least fight for yourself. My love for you is not strong enough to fight this battle alone. I can't and I won't pretend I'm someone I'm not."

Devin stepped back as if wanting to say something or anything that would make this situation right between them but nothing materialized. Devin's phone rang, breaking the silence. Retrieving it from her pocket, she tapped it. "Hello. Yes, I'm ready, five minutes, that's fine. I'll be waiting," she said into the phone.

Finished, she slid it back into her pocket. They stood in silence for what seemed like eternity. Devin looked up at Jerrica "Jerrica, I'm sorry. I care for you more than I've cared for anyone else. I'm sorry that it has come to this. I wish things were different but...."

Devin broke off as she saw a fresh flow of tears streaming down Jerrica's face.

Devin rushed around the kitchen island toward Jerrica. As she reached out for her, a car horn pierced the stillness and she froze in mid-stride. She let her arms fall to her side. The driver had arrived. Jerrica wouldn't even look at her. She just stared at the counter while the tears continuously fell.

Devin shifted backward as the horn sounded again. Not knowing what to say, Devin retreated to the front door. Once opened, the driver stepped in, picked up her luggage, and then disappeared outside. Devin stood in the doorway ready to leave. She could hear the soft sobs coming from the kitchen. Turning her head, she saw Jerrica's tear stained face.

"I'm sorry," she said.

Through tear-filled eyes, Jerrica watched the car pull away. Even though the car windows were tinted, Jerrica could tell that Devin wasn't looking back. Jerrica turned her back to the window, sliding down the cupboard doors to the floor, releasing the pain in her heart as she cried.

†

Jerrica let the memories fade, focusing on her current surroundings. She felt cold even with the comforter wrapped tightly around her and holding a hot cup of coffee. In the distance, she heard a door close. *Ah, the minions have returned*, she thought. Not getting up, she waited for them to find her.

"The back door looks partially open. I bet she's on the back porch," Lauren said.

"Maybe we shouldn't go out there. Maybe she doesn't want company. Maybe she wants to be left alone," Jaime responded,

"You know I can hear you, right?" Jerrica responded from the porch.

Stepping around Jaime, Lauren said with a smile. "I think she won't mind company. Good morning, sunshine. How are you feeling?" Lauren placed herself in the chair across from Jerrica.

"I feel a lot better this morning," she said, pulling the comforter from around her head.

"Well, you still look tired," Jaime added as she perched herself on the railing.

"Thanks for the compliment so early in the morning."

Jaime looked like she was about to panic when Lauren reached out and touched her knee. "She's messing with you Jaime, calm down."

She let out a breath and hopped off the railing. "That coffee looks good. I'm going inside to get some, Lauren, you want any? Jerrica, do you need your coffee topped off?"

Both women looked at one another, a little surprised by the energy level displayed.

"I could use a cup, thanks," answered Lauren.

"I'm good."

"Ok, I'll be right back," she said as she bounced into the house.

"That girl has way too much energy," Jerrica said.

"Yeah, I don't know where she gets it," she said, turning her attention back to Jerrica. "Seriously though, are you ok?"

"I'm feeling better than I did last night. I don't know what happened."

"Exhaustion, Jerrica. You've been working too hard."

"I doubt that, Mom. Did you get me chicken noodle soup while you were at the store?"

"As a matter of fact I did, and ginger ale as well."

"You're my hero, Lauren."

"I know."

The screen door flew open and Jaime strolled back onto the porch. She was holding two coffee mugs and a plate of cheese and fruit. Placing the tray and Lauren's coffee on the table between them, "I figured it was close to lunch time and you could use something to eat," she said, directing her comment toward Jerrica.

"That was kind of you." Reaching a hand out, Jerrica plucked a few grapes off the plate.

Grabbing a slice of cheese in one hand, her coffee in the other, Jaime hopped back on the railing.

Jerrica enjoyed the grape while she observed Jaime's actions. "I wanted to talk to the both of you about something," Jerrica said, sitting up straighter in her chair.

Lauren and Jaime exchanged glances.

"Since everyone is now aware of my relationship with Devin," Jerrica flushed. "I guess it's time to explain something about myself that you don't know."

Lauren sat back in her chair.

Jerrica noticed Lauren's sudden change in body posture. "I know there are things, Lauren, that you know about my past relationships, but there are many other things you don't know."

"Well, I'm not going anywhere." Jaime leaned up against the column attached to the railing. "Talk away."

Lauren sat with her arms across her chest, waiting for Jerrica to continue.

Jerrica's voice began to quiver as she recalled the events of the day she left him.

†

"I'm leaving!"

She rushed down the stairs with her suitcase in hand. On her heels was the man she was trying to escape. The strong hand grasped her bicep before she was able to reach the floor. The sudden jerk on her arm caught her off balance, sending her falling down the last four stairs to the marble-tiled foyer floor. Her suitcase slid across the floor beyond her reach. On her knees, she tried to crawl away from him. "Gregory, please don't do this."

"Don't do what, Jerrica?"

He hoisted her up like a rag doll and spun her around to face him.

She could no longer see the loving man she had once known, this monster she now feared had replaced him.

"You think you can just up and leave me? I have given you everything, you ungrateful bitch!"

"This shouldn't be a surprise to you. We haven't been in love for a long time," whispered Jerrica.

She could not stop him when he shoved her body violently against the wall. Her head hit hard, filling her eyes with stars. She felt his hands clutch her upper arms, keeping her from crumbling. The strong fingers dug painfully into her skin. "You're hurting me, Gregory!"

"You don't know what hurt is, Jerrica. You've broken my heart," he bellowed as he shook her, "I gave you my love. I bought you this damn house. I've given you everything. What happened to the promise you made me, until death us do part?" Gregory released her arms, stepping away, rubbing the back of his neck in frustration.

Finally, standing on her own feet, Jerrica calmed. "We made a lot of promises to one another, Gregory. To be faithful was one of those promises and you broke that."

She felt the pain the moment his palm connected violently with the side of her face. The force jerked her head to the side, almost knocking her off her feet. She grabbed the doorframe for support. The familiar taste of blood filled her mouth.

"I am the man of this house and you will not talk to me in that manner! This is entirely your fault! See what you made me do!"

Jerrica could feel a trickle of blood run down her chin as her cheek started to burn. Summoning courage from deep inside, she straightened her back. "Does hitting me make you feel like a big man. Go ahead, do your best, Gregory. You will never have me ever again." Jerrica closed her eyes, expecting him to release his anger, ending this torture.

Gregory forcefully grabbed Jerrica by the back of the neck, heaving her in the direction of the front door. "I love you and I know you love me. You just need time to realize that. We will be together. No matter where you are, you will always belong to me!"

Jerrica grabbed the doorknob, opening it quickly to escape. Her legs couldn't move fast enough as she sprinted toward the car.

"Remember, Jerrica, you are mine," Gregory yelled after her.

That was the last thing she heard him say as her tires squealed out of the driveway, the car jolted forward toward town. A quick look in the mirror showed the damage he had caused. The blood from her lip was beginning to dry but her lip was swelling. She could faintly see the bruise developing on her cheek. Tears filled her eyes. Flipping her cell phone open, she called the only person she trusted.

"Lauren, its Jerrica. I need your help. Is your cottage free?"

†

"I didn't want you to see the bruising, Lauren, that's why I wouldn't let you come down here for the first few weeks," Jerrica sighed.

"I always wondered why you didn't want to see me."

"I didn't want to see the look of disappointment in your eyes if you saw me like that."

"I wouldn't have been disappointed in you," whispered Lauren.

Exhaling heavily, Jerrica continued her story. She explained that her ex-husband wanted all her money in the divorce and that they still co-owned the house they once inhabited. She paused, laying her hands in her lap, re-grouping, and started talking about Devin. Jerrica's tone saddened as she recounted their history, Devin being her first real relationship with a woman.

To Lauren's dismay, Jerrica went into intimate detail about her feelings for Devin, using the word love often.

She described the last weekend they were together, down to the end. Jerrica's voice was so full of pain, she had to pause again and slowly sip her coffee.

"Wow, I had no idea that your feelings were so strong for her. I didn't know you had fallen in love with her," Lauren said softly, staring into her cup.

"Your ex-husband is a bastard," Jaime added.

Jerrica tried to flash them both a smile. "There's more," Jerrica said, looking at Lauren.

Lauren raised an eyebrow.

Jerrica confessed about the evening in Devin's apartment, the briefcase, and the new phone.

Lauren slumped more in her seat.

Jerrica could tell Lauren's mind was trying to piece everything together. Jerrica reached inside the mound of comforter and pulled out the new phone, setting it on the table.

Jaime and Lauren stared at the shiny object.

Jerrica leaned back in her chair, sipping her coffee.

Frustrated, Lauren abruptly stood, snatched the phone off the table. She pulled her arm back to throw it toward the ocean.

"Lauren, stop!"

"Why! You don't need anything from her!"

"I need that phone! She didn't return my other one."

"How damned convenient!"

"I know, but she kind of put me between a rock and hard place. So I need to keep it for now."

"I hate that woman," Lauren said, dropping into her chair.

Extending her arm, she tossed the phone on the table.

"I need something stronger than this coffee," Lauren said as she rose.

"Don't you think having alcohol this early in the morning is inappropriate?" Jaime whispered.

Lauren swung the door open, catching it in her right hand. "I think we're good."

Jerrica tried to hide the giggle.

"Are you feeling well enough to have one?"

"Sure I'll take whatever you're having."

"How about you," she asked, squinting at Jaime.

 "I'll have whatever you make, I guess."

Lauren shook her head and vanished into the house.

Now that they were alone, Jaime didn't know what to say to her boss. Her images of Jerrica were changing rapidly and she wasn't sure how to handle it. When she first started this job, she thought Jerrica was a control freak. Jerrica was fair, intelligent, but she always had to have her eyes on everything and everyone. Nevertheless, as time went on, Jerrica loosened her possessive grip on the department.

When life outside of the office was clouding Jerrica's judgment, she started handing off projects to her and Lauren more frequently. Then the night she saw her in her office with a woman, the picture was becoming clear as to where her mind had wandered.

Jerrica became even more aloof at the office shortly after that. She started hiding behind her office door, shielding herself, Jaime thought. Well she wasn't sure what she thought as all this transpired. Moreover, now she had all this additional information to add. Here she was, sitting at a beachfront cottage with a person she realized she really didn't know. Who at this very moment was an emotional wreck wrapped in a large blanket right in front of her.

"Say it, Jaime. I know you have something to say. It's written on your face."

"I'm just trying to understand you."

"What is there to understand?"

"When I started working for you, I thought you were a tower of strength. I idolized you."

"I'm guessing that's all changed now?"

"I think I've realized you're not the untouchable woman I thought you were. That you are human just like the rest of us, and your heart can be broken just as easily."

Jerrica ran her thumb across the rim of her mug and then placed it on the table. Leaning back in her chair she glanced at Jaime. "I never said I was untouchable. I'm not perfect, Jaime. I'm sorry you're disappointed in my actions."

Hopping off the railing, she walked toward Jerrica. Kneeling in front to her, Jaime took Jerrica's hand in hers.

Jerrica look directly into Jaime's face.

"Jerrica, I'm not disappointed."

"I'm only human," Jerrica said as tears filled her eyes. She was tensing, wanting to pull away.

Placing her other hand over Jerrica's, Jaime sensed the physical tension. "Let me explain. I'm an only child, and I didn't have many friends growing up. You've been the only one who has taken a chance on me and given me help to grow, personally and professionally. I've had you up on a pedestal for such a long time now. "

Jerrica noticed the tears filling Jaime's eyes as she lowered her head. Jerrica slid a hand out of her grasp. Lightly placing her hand on the top of Jaime's head, feeling the softness of her hair under her fingertips, she whispered. "I would like to have the opportunity to try to redeem myself in your eyes."

Tears rolled down Jaime's face. She leaned forward as Jerrica opened her blanket to hold her in her arms.

Jerrica glimpsed Lauren standing in the doorway with drinks in her hand.

"I leave you alone for two minutes and already you're hitting on the young girl."

Jaime stood and took one of the glasses out of Lauren's grasp. With a devilish smile Jaime responded, "If I were gay, you would be my first choice to help me cross over, sexy." Quickly leaning forward she planted a big kiss on Lauren's lips.

Jerrica grabbed one of the drinks from Lauren's hand just before she stepped back and started faking spitting in disgust. Jerrica and Jaime broke into laughter.

Lauren swallowed a big gulp of her drink and joined in the laughter. In jest, Lauren slapped Jaime on the back of her head as she passed by.

Jaime just laughed and hoisted herself back up on the railing, being careful not to spill her drink.

Lauren plopped down in her chair and stared at Jerrica with a somber expression.

"What?"

"I'm sorry."

"About what, may I ask?"

"Not being able to help you more with your ex-husband."

"Lauren you were my savior when I needed one. You couldn't have done much more."

"I feel like I should have, if you had just told me everything you were going through."

"You let me hide out in your beach house for months when he was trying to find me. You fielded calls for me when he called the office a hundred times a day. You were my leaning post. What more could you have done?"

Lauren sipped her drink, mulling the question. Then a smile came across her face. "I could have killed the son of a bitch!"

All three of them broke into hysterical laughter.

†

Jerrica wasn't sure how many drinks she had consumed during the past couple hours, but she was feeling rather happy. She turned her head to see Jaime sitting on the floor leaning up against the column, staring blankly at her glass.

"She looks plastered," Lauren observed.

"She's only had…what, three or four drinks. Jaime, you're a light-weight."

Lauren got to her feet, walking to Jaime. "Come on you. Let's get you at least seated in a chair."

She bent down to help Jaime stand. Lauren balanced Jaime's weight against her. Taking the now empty glass from Jaime's hand, she placed an arm around her thin waist, guiding her into the chair.

Jerrica stood as Lauren eased Jaime into the chair across from her. Jerrica removed the comforter and carefully tucked it around Jaime. Turning toward Lauren, she nodded. "Let's take a walk on the beach."

"That sounds great. I need to shake off this buzz anyways. I'll go grab our jackets." Lauren stepped into the house.

Jerrica reached out, placing a hand on the column. *I've been sitting too long.*

Lauren returned to the porch wearing her jacket and tossed Jerrica hers.,

"Now you sit in that chair until we get back. You should be warm enough with that comforter," Lauren whispered in Jaime's ear.

Jaime just nodded her head and closed her eyes.

"She'll be fine. We won't be gone long," Lauren told Jerrica.

They both left the porch, heading for the path to the beach.

"Be careful on the path, the rocks have shifted a little during the winter," Lauren said as she held out a hand to help Jerrica safely cross them.

When they reached the sand on the beach, Jerrica paused, closing her eyes and breathing in deeply. She loved the peaceful feeling she had being this close to the ocean.

"What are you thinking?"

"I'm thinking how much I love this place, the house, the beach, just everything," Jerrica said.

"There is a certain kind of peace here, isn't there," Lauren said, lifting her face toward the sun.

"Come on, let's walk."

With hands still interlocked, they started their stroll. They did not speak as they wandered down the beach; they were just enjoying the moment. Every few steps Jerrica picked up a rock, throwing it into the ocean.

Lauren started to hum a familiar tune.

Jerrica couldn't quite recognize the song, but enjoyed listening to the soothing tones.

Lauren spun suddenly to face Jerrica, pulling her into a secure embrace.

Startled, Jerrica enclosed her arms around Lauren's waist. They stood on the beach holding one another for a very long time.

Lauren tilted her head in toward Jerrica's neck to speak softly in her ear, "I'm worrying about you all the time lately."

"I'm fine, honest."

"I'm not sure even you believe that."

"I do believe it because it's true."

"Are you going back to her," she whispered.

The question just floated in the air between them. "I don't want you to do it. I want you to leave her in the past. I've seen what she does to you when she tosses you away like an old newspaper." Lauren's concern was apparent in her tone.

Jerrica put her head down, leaning harder on her shoulder, not knowing what to say.

"You deserve better. I know you think Devin was your first real love. I think you're confusing love with your first physical experience being fully open to yourself and to another woman. I know she will always hold a special place in your heart. However, know this, Jerrica, people like Devin are never going to be the people you want them to be or the people they should be."

Jerrica could feel the tears stinging her eyes. She couldn't stop them, not this time.

Lauren felt Jerrica's body tremble and felt the tears on her skin as Jerrica turned into her neck. "That's it. Let it all out, baby girl. Let the pain go. I am here. I'll always be here for you."

Lauren held her tightly, rocking back and forth allowing everything to pour out, all the hurt and pain Jerrica had held in for so long. She held her tight until there were no more tears left to shed.

Jerrica felt weak but safe in Lauren's arms.

"How do you feel?"

Jerrica pulled away enough so she could look into her face. "You are a special person, Lauren. How do you know me so well?"

"I just do."

"Thank you. I've been holding that in for so long," she said, lowering her tear stained face, placing her head back on Lauren's shoulder.

Lauren ran her hand over Jerrica's hair, hoping that her warm touch would give her some comfort.

"I think we should head back to check on Jaime," Jerrica remarked as she stepped out of Lauren's arms.

✝

Lauren lowered her arms to her side. She knew this was just a little piece of what Jerrica still had to deal with but she knew it was a start to the healing process. Lauren looked at the water, letting herself enjoy the peacefulness of the day. She felt a warm sensation cover her left hand. Looking down, she saw that Jerrica had slipped her hand around hers.

"Let's go….home," she said, making Lauren smile.

Lauren realized as they walked back toward the house, that she loved Jerrica. Loved and worried about her like the daughter that she and Brandon had never had. Smiling, Lauren glanced at Jerrica, who was looking at her.

†

Without a word, they both suddenly understood what the other one was thinking. With love in their hearts, they headed for the house.

As they stepped up onto the porch, they noticed Jaime was now sitting up and sipping coffee.

Her eyes still looked a little bleary, Jerrica thought as she leaned against the railing.

Lauren sat down in the chair next to Jaime. "Did the little nap do you any good," Lauren asked, putting a hand on Jaime's leg.

"I think so. I'm still feeling a little funny, but better than when I first stopped drinking. This is helping," she said, holding up her mug.

"You're comical when you're drunk. You sit like a lump in one spot, staring off into space. I wonder what you'd look like on drugs," Jerrica said and giggled.

"Well, I wouldn't know, I've never done them and don't plan to," Jaime said, trying to stand, still wrapped in the comforter.

"Here," Lauren said, standing at the same time. "Give me that hot coffee before you spill it on yourself or me."

"I'm good. I won't spill it," she promised, staggering a little.

Jerrica stepped in front of Jaime to help steady her. "Why don't we go in and start preparing supper? There are plenty of vegetables to cut for the salad and you can sit and supervise," said Jerrica.

"Sounds good to me," slurred Jaime.

Lauren rushed around both of them to hold open the door. As they passed by her, Lauren laughed. "You two look like an old married couple."

Jerrica deposited Jamie in the first kitchen chair she came to. "Remember, you're older than both of us."

Lauren picked up the kitchen towel off the counter, tossing it at Jerrica. She caught it in her left hand, returning it with haste.

"You throw like a girl," Lauren said, grinning.

"I am a girl! I can prove it if you would like evidence." She winked at her.

Jaime straightened herself. "Oh, please no. I've seen enough nakedness where you're concerned."

Jerrica playfully swatted at Jaime.

Lauren just started laughing as she pulled the vegetables out of the grocery bags.

"Can we stop talking about what you saw in my office? I would like to try to get past the fact that you saw us."

Jaime sat back in her chair with a smile across her face. "Well, I don't have much of a sex life anymore. So, we might as well talk about yours," she said.

"Oh please, if you've had sex in the past two months, you're having more than I am," Jerrica added.

Jaime's cheeks got red, but her facial expression seemed sad.

Lauren picked that time to jump back into the conversation. "Leave her alone, Jerrica. Her boyfriend just broke up with her."

"I'm sorry. I didn't mean to tease you," replied Jerrica.

"Yes, you did."

"Yeah, I kind of did, but I didn't know about your recent break up. I just heard you had a meltdown, but nothing specific."

Jaime looked to Lauren who was avoiding eye contact by bending down looking for a clean knife on the lower shelves. "Thanks, Lauren! You told her I was having a meltdown."

"Well, I didn't know how else to describe it," Lauren shot back, still searching for the knife.

"Hey, no arguing, you two. We're all friends here," Jerrica said, acting like a referee.

Jaime slouched in her chair with her arms crossed, pouting.

"Hey, give Lauren some slack. She doesn't understand the younger generation these days," Jerrica teased.

"And you do?" Lauren said standing up with the clean cutting knife in her hand.

"I think so," she answered, pretending to be afraid of the knife.

"I guess we brought the comic relief this weekend. Why don't you stop running your mouth and help me with this salad," Lauren ordered.

Jerrica put on her best frown, walking around the counter to wash vegetables. Once she had thoroughly washed all the vegetables, she placed them in a bowl she had lined with paper towels. She took the bowl to the counter on the island, placing it directly in front of Lauren.

"Thank you, my dear," Lauren said with a smile.

"So, I want to hear about Jaime's relationship problems."

Jaime groaned loudly. The women just stared at her until she realized she had better talk or supper might be out of the question. Jaime let the blanket open around her shoulders, sliding it off to puddle on the arms of the chair. Softly clearing her throat, she began her embarrassing tale.

They had met at one of the many parties that Daniel & Daniel, Inc. had thrown. He was a dashing young executive from their company. He had the bluest eyes she had ever seen with chestnut color hair. Jaime sighed at the memories. They started sending e-mails and texting. After a week or so, he asked her out on their first date. He had made them a picnic in Boston Commons, took her to Fenway Park and the Boston Opera. Wined and dined her, but never pushed the subject about spending the night. Then about two weeks ago on what would be their last date, she took him home to spend the night.

"Spend the night? That's all we get. How about a little more detail?"

"Lauren, leave her be. You sound like a horny teenager."

"Maybe I am. It's been so long since Brandon and I have had sex."

"Umm...I don't need to hear this," Jerrica said, putting her hands over her ears.

Lauren laughed at how silly Jerrica looked. "Anyway, Jaime, please continue," Lauren, said.

"That was pretty much all I'm going to tell you. I've called him maybe three times during the past two weeks. Then today I received a text that he doesn't want to see me anymore."

A thought dawned on Jerrica, "Please tell me he wasn't your first?"

"Does it matter?"

"Yes, it does," Jerrica and Lauren, said in unison.

"No. He wasn't my first. I just can't believe I was so stupid to fall for his fake lines. I thought if I took my time, making him wait, it would be different this time."

"All men are scum," Jerrica proclaimed. "Except Brandon of course."

"Thank you for clarifying that, but at least tell us it was fun."

"You are incorrigible, Lauren," Jerrica rolled her eyes.

"I imagine if I don't give her something, she will just keep hounding me."

"You're getting to know Lauren, pretty well."

"Ok, fine. The sex was ordinary, I've definitely had better," Jaime said, raising her pinky in the air.

Lauren started to laugh as Jerrica squeezed her eyes shut in horror.

Jaime just smiled as she wobbled to the refrigerator.

"Whoa, take it easy, speedy," Jerrica reached for her.

"I'm ok. I'm coming out of it."

Retrieving a bottle of lemonade from the fridge, Jaime stated, "So, when are we going to eat?"

"Oh, sure, she's been drunk most of the afternoon and now that she sobering up, she's hungry," smirked Jerrica, "I'll go outside and start the grill, your highness."

✝

"That supper was wonderful," Jaime exclaimed plopping down on the couch and rubbing her very full tummy. "I might burst."

"I'll second that. Those steaks were cooked just right," Lauren complimented Jerrica, setting down a newly opened bottle of wine on the coffee table.

"I'm not the greatest cook, but I do know how to cook a great steak," Jerrica boasted, looking at her friends with a smile.

"It's getting chilly in here," Jerrica commented as she picked up a couple of small logs to place in the fireplace.

A small chuckle escaped Lauren. "I keep forgetting you stayed here for a while, so you know how to do that."

"I'm not powerless." Jerrica reached for a few more items to get the fire started.

Jaime watched as Jerrica lit the match, placing it under the little tee-pee of wood and paper she had made in the fireplace. To her amazement, the fire didn't start blazing as you see in the movies or on television. The bright colorful flames slowly crept their way up the paper. As it lightly licked the logs, she was sure it would go out when the colors dimmed only briefly and then the flame expanded, its brilliant colors covering the first log. Only then did the flame crawl across the other pieces of wood continuing its mesmerizing show.

"Earth to Jaime," Jerrica said, waving a hand in front of her.

"Sorry, Jerrica. I must have zoned out."

Jerrica just smiled, getting comfortable in the recliner. She knew what Jaime was feeling. She had felt the same thing the first time she stayed at the cottage. The cozy beach décor rooms, the soothing accents of Lauren's impeccable taste splashed in different places and now, seeing the exceptional fireplace roar to its full potential. The experience could be overwhelming, but heartwarming at the same time.

"Well ladies, let's toast." Jerrica raised her glass. "To a wonderful weekend, to great friends, old and new. And to the future, may it be everything we hope it will be."

They talked then. They shared growing up and family stories. They all learned something new about their associate, boss, and now new friend, bringing them all closer to one another. The evening hours passed by as quickly as a blink of an eye as they opened up to one another, drinking wine and laughing.

Jaime yawned and looked down at her watch. "Wow! Its eleven thirty already!"

"What, are you going to turn into a pumpkin at midnight?" Jerrica inquired.

"If I'm going to help with this house tomorrow, I need my sleep." Jaime stood, strolling toward the stairs.

Just before she was out of sight she turned, "I would advise you two to go to bed soon. We have a lot to do tomorrow."

Jerrica looked at Lauren. "You haven't told her what opening up the cottage entails, have you?"

She looked up and smiled. Lauren's idea of opening up the cottage for the season was making all the beds and placing any dirty sheets from the first weekend into a laundry bag then uncovering the rest of the furniture and leaving.

Lauren had a maintenance man, Willard who would come in and do the rest of the opening. He would take the dirty sheets home for his wife to clean and return them the next time he was at the house. Willard used to take care of the beach house when it belonged to Lauren's grandmother. Therefore, it was natural to keep him on when Lauren took the house. Jerrica had met him when he opened up the cottage the months she went into hiding. "You can be so evil sometimes, Lauren."

Lauren's grin broadened as she stared at the fireplace.

Jerrica slid her hand around the stem of the glass left by Jaime and stood. After depositing the glasses in the kitchen, she wandered back to the living room. Stopping behind Lauren's chair, she leaned forward so her chin was on the top of Lauren's head. "I'm headed up too. Don't stay up too long, okay?"

Lauren lifted her hand to Jerrica's cheek, "Don't worry, I won't. I'm going to spread the fire out and watch it go out some more. Then I'll be up."

Jerrica smiled at the comforting gesture. Softly kissing her on the head, Jerrica backed away.

✝

Within seconds, Lauren was alone in the living room. She loved being in this house. She loved having her friends here. When she was a child, she used to be scared of the noises the house made at night. Her grandmother used to tell her the house was like an old friend. In the silence of the night, it would share stories to those who listened. Lauren understood as she grew older what her grandmother had meant. The house had been a reliable friend for her and her family.

Leaning her head against the chair, she closed her eyes, listening. Sounds emanating from soft creaks on the ceiling, told her that someone was still awake upstairs. A light wind was blowing outside and she could hear the wind chimes on the back porch. She heard the soft sounds of the waves quietly rushing onto the beach, than retreating quickly, just to repeat the action again.

Lifting her head up, she stared at the fireplace, thinking of Brandon. She suddenly missed him. His job was very demanding and she didn't get to see him as often as she would like. They used to spend almost every weekend at the cottage together when they were first married. Now, she was lucky if he made it down for one week in the summer. Lauren started to feel sad about the time they'd wasted being apart. She decided she would call him first thing in the morning. After separating the logs in the fireplace,

Lauren decided it was time for her to retire for the evening. Standing before the staircase Lauren glanced around the first floor, speaking softly into the silence. "Goodnight, old friend."

†

As the sun awoke above the cottage, three very unique and special women lay sleeping, unaware of its arrival. Lauren was the first one to stir. The sun was patient in its pursuit to slowly raise the other two from their slumber. One by one, they all found themselves half-awake sitting at the breakfast table. Jaime pulled her sweatshirt hood over her head and gently lowered her head to the table.

"How did everyone sleep?" Lauren asked as she poured her second cup of coffee.

"Ok, fine," mumbled the two sleepy women.

"I would suggest getting some breakfast into you before we start working on the cottage."

Setting two plates of food and two cups of coffee on the table, she continued. "Once we are done, we can all take turns showering. I would like to leave around one. We can catch lunch on the drive back."

Jaime never picked up her head.

Jerrica's eyes looked in Lauren's direction, sleep still in them, "You're joking right? It's only seven thirty in the morning."

"Best time to get started," Lauren answered, heading up the stairs.

Jerrica slowly shook her head in disbelief. Cautiously she lowered her head onto her crossed arms, leaning on the table and within minutes, she was lightly snoring in tune with Jaime.

Chapter Five

"Don't drop that!" bellowed a heavy southern accented voice on the other side of Jerrica's office door. "That's irreplaceable!"

It was too early on a Monday morning to hear yelling already in the office. Making her way to her door, Jerrica saw what all the commotion was—Olivia had two movers carrying a large wooden desk across the department. By the strain on the workers' faces, the desk was as heavy as it looked. With her shoulder leaning against the door frame, she watched in amusement. Olivia was giving them so many different directions it wouldn't surprise Jerrica if they set it down in the middle of the walkway and left it there. She grinned at the thought of Olivia's horrified expression if they did just that.

"Good morning. What a devilish smile on such a beautiful face. What were you just thinking?"

Jerrica swiveled to see Madison standing next to her. "Hi. Ms. Jeffery, I mean…Madison. I didn't see you there," she said, her gaze falling to the floor as her face flushed with embarrassment.

"It's okay, Jerrica, you really don't have to answer my question. I'll use my imagination."

Looking up from the floor, she tried to redirect the subject, "Why does Olivia have such a large old desk? She has plenty of financial backing to get new stuff."

Madison smiled at Jerrica's awkwardness. "She's had that desk for as long as I've known her. She told me it has special meaning to her because it belonged to her father. He was a very successful southern lawyer."

"Oh, so you come from the south?" Jerrica avoided eye contact. "How long have you worked for Ms. Hutten?"

Madison stepped forward, entering Jerrica's personal space. Leaning in toward Jerrica's ear, she replied in a sultry tone. "If you want to get to know me, Jerrica, you're going to have to buy me dinner first."

Jerrica's eyes fluttered closed smelling the intoxicating musky perfume now surrounding them both. She could feel Madison's soft black hair graze the side of her cheek sending electrifying chills up her spine.

This woman is so sexy, Jerrica thought frantically.

Madison stepped back, staring at a very flushed Jerrica.

"Madison, can you help me with these guys? Nobody's listening to me," Olivia bellowed from across the room.

Madison sighed in frustration but waited a few extra seconds for Jerrica to say something. When it was apparent the friendly banter was over, she commented graciously as they parted. "I'll catch you around."

Jerrica watched as she strolled away, taking in the gentle sway of her hips. It was mesmerizing to observe how her pants hugged her hips, thighs and the pair of shapely legs. Jerrica suddenly realized she was staring. Looking around to see if anyone had seen her, she stepped back into the office and closed the door.

Madison heard the office door click closed. A nervous feeling started in the pit of her stomach.

Maybe I offended her, I shouldn't have said that to her, she thought, agonized.

Madison didn't have much time to ponder those kinds of questions for very long as Olivia's temper was skyrocketing. "Olivia, why don't you go to the lounge and get yourself something to drink. I'll handle this," she said, putting a hand on Olivia's shoulder.

Olivia nodded in agreement. Walking around the struggling workers, she disappeared around the corner.

The moment that Olivia was out of sight, Madison had the men set the desk down.

Lowering the desk to the floor, the workers bent in pure exhaustion. Their chests heaved to intake as much air as they could get, as they tried to stand erect again.

Madison waited patiently until breathing returned to normal before she would negotiate with them.

"Listen," she said, putting her hand on the desk, "I know this desk is heavy. I know that Olivia can be a handful."

Madison watched as both men glanced at one another. "But I'll make a deal with you. If you get this desk in her office, exactly where I tell you before she gets back, I will give you a bonus of one hundred dollars each."

The men smiled at one another. They picked up the desk again, bringing it carefully into the office. When Olivia returned, Madison was in the office wiping off the top of the desk. "The movers will be back shortly with more stuff. Olivia you need to remember to be patient, we are just moving in. You wanted this job and I'm making it happen for you. You need to relax. It will all come together sooner or later."

Olivia walked to Madison, placing her arms around her. "Thanks, my friend. You're always here for me."

Standing in the middle of the office, with the door open, in the arms of her boss was not what Madison wanted to be doing the first hour of a new job.

"Olivia," she joked, talking into her ear. "Please let me go. You don't want the movers to think there's something going on in here, do you?"

Olivia released her from the hug, smiled, then walked to the windows.

Madison knew her boss needed a few minutes to collect herself, so she left the office to look at her own workstation. Standing next to her cubicle, she glanced back at Olivia in her big office.

One day Madison, you'll have an office like that, she thought, straightening her posture in pride.

Sitting down at her desk, Madison looked around at her new home. The cubicle had three walls that were tall enough for privacy, but short enough that she could glance over them. She had two file cabinets on her left that extended one wall. It wasn't the greatest desk she had ever had, but she would make do. As she surveyed the department, she noticed she could see Jerrica's office door from her seat. She leaned back in her chair with a huge grin.

Well at least this job does offer some benefits, she mused. I wonder what her story is.

From the moment Madison had laid eyes on Jerrica, in the women's room, she had fascinated her. Her dark green eyes added to Jerrica's mysterious qualities. Madison didn't want to admit that she felt heat rising from inside whenever she was around her.

She's way out of your league, anyway, she told herself. Besides she's probably straight.

If Jerrica wasn't into women, then that would explain why she looked like a deer caught in headlights when Madison flirted with her. And, if she was straight, at least Madison would have the pleasure of looking at that beautiful body throughout the day. Shrugging her shoulders, she started pulling items from boxes.

"Good morning," she heard a soft voice say.

Madison looked up from her cubicle. Smiling, Madison stood, walking toward the welcoming smile. "Good morning. I'm Madison, Ms. Hutten's assistant," she said, extending a hand,

"Hi, I'm Jaime. I'm Ms. Kerrison's secretary," Jaime said, shaking hands.

A small silence fell between them. "So are you new to Boston?"

Why was everyone so nosy about her past living situation? Madison thought. "Ms. Hutten and I just transferred from the Carolinas. She enjoys the winter season in New England."

Jaime nodded her understanding, as if not sure who should talk next.

"Since I'm new here, would you like to have lunch with me," Madison blurted out before she realized the commitment she was making.

Jaime smiled from ear to ear with a twinkle in her eyes. "I would love to. I have lunch after Lauren comes back from hers. Lauren is Jerrica's, I mean, Ms. Kerrison's assistant. Lauren doesn't really have a set time she goes to lunch. I just go after she gets back."

"My schedule is pretty open. My boss is flexible with lunches and breaks," Madison replied.

"I'll stop by your desk before I take lunch and we can go together. Sound good?"

"Great. I'll see you then." Madison returned to her desk.

Jaime was elated. No one here had ever asked her to lunch, except for Lauren. Her other co-workers thought she was a snob because she was quiet and kept to herself. Glancing back at Madison, Jaime smiled at the thought that she might have found a new office friend.

Madison went back to organizing her desk as the movers made many trips with boxes into Olivia's office.

After five or six trips by the movers, she thought it might be time to check on the progress. Peeking in, she noticed that Olivia was still standing at the window looking out. *Not surprising*, walking up beside her, she leaned her shoulder on the window. "What's going on?"

Letting out a sigh she glanced at Madison, "I'm just adjusting to the change."

Madison felt a little frustrated with Olivia's reaction. "I know moving up here has taken you hundreds of miles away from your family. However, Olivia, this move was your idea, remember?"

"I know. It's just the physical moving, that's the hard part, first my office, then my apartment."

"Olivia, give it a week, next week will be better." Madison turned so she was leaning fully against the window, looking at the mess in the office.

"I can rectify this for you," she said, snapping her fingers. "Why don't you go to the spa, then take yourself out to dinner. Tomorrow, take the day off. The movers for your apartment will be done today. I can handle the movers here and the rest until you return. When you come back on Wednesday, everything will be in its place."

Olivia pondered her suggestion and sighed. "That's fine, Madison. It will give me time to relax."

"Good, you have a ten thirty appointment at ECI salon and day spa. So you'd better get going." A wide smile crossed Madison's face.

Without a word, Olivia went to her desk, picking up her bag. "You know me so well, Madison. What would I do without you?"

That was a rhetorical question, Madison knew. As Olivia left the office, she waved, disappearing around the corner. Madison loved when Olivia left her to her own devices. She could handle getting everything organized by herself without the stress of Olivia and her temper.

When the movers were done, Madison passed them their bonus, thanking them for a job well done. She started back on the task of setting up her boss's office the way Madison would want it to be, if it were hers. Everything would be within Olivia's reach and Madison would know where to find it if her boss couldn't. Four boxes into unpacking, sitting on the floor, she noticed the time. It was close to noon. She should be hearing from Jaime soon. A knock on the door startled her out of her unpacking trance.

"Come in," she said still sitting on the floor.

As the door slowly opened, she heard a familiar voice before the figure appeared around the door.

"Olivia, I was wondering if you…" Jerrica's entered the room seeing Madison sitting on the floor.

"Olivia is off for the next couple days. She will be back on Wednesday. Is there anything I can help you with?"

Jerrica was surprised by the undeniable sensual tone in Madison's voice. "I was going to…ask Olivia out for…lunch," Jerrica mumbled, "But…umm would you like to go instead?"

Jerrica was shifting her weight from one foot to another, but not looking directly at Madison.

She smirked at Jerrica's embarrassment. Standing, Madison brushed her pant legs off saying, "Thanks for the offer, but I already have a lunch date."

Jerrica's face was blushing when they made eye contact, "I wasn't asking you out on a date. It was just a friendly lunch."

Madison tried not to giggle. "Well," she said, stepping closer to her, "Maybe we can take a rain check, Olivia and I?"

Jerrica felt a little dizzy as the sweet aroma of Madison's perfume wafted around her. "That's fine, maybe next time," she said as she turned, leaving the office in a rush.

"I'll hold you to that," Madison answered as Jerrica disappeared. She stared at the empty doorway, grinning.

Jerrica quickly retreated to her office. Her hands were shaking as she closed the door. What is wrong with me, she chastised herself. I don't understand why she has this weird effect on me. She has been flirting with me since we met.

She had never felt so unnerved by anyone, this was new to her, and she was scared. She walked to her desk, trying to shake off the strange feeling she had in the pit of her stomach.

Lauren walked into her office just as Jerrica reached her desk. In each hand, she was carrying two vases with what looked like a dozen roses in each. Lauren's frown on her face pretty much said it all. "These are for you."

"They're from, Devin, aren't they?" Jerrica lowered her chin to her chest in distress.

"Do I really have to verify that for you?"

Jerrica's head snapped up in sudden anger, "Stop answering my questions with a question! Are you trying to piss me off?"

Her tone had flipped from being distressed in seeing the flowers to the anger that Lauren had unintentionally invoked in her.

Walking in silence to the table near the window, Lauren placed the vases there. Without glancing at her boss, Lauren left the office, closing the door behind her.

Jerrica knew there was no logical reason she should be this upset, but it was too late to stop it from taking over. The uncontrollable fury raged through her body. Her fists balled up as hatred for everything that had gone wrong in her life overtook her. She charged the table. When both hands hit the top of the table, she yelled in anger as she forced the vases off the table and into the air. "Stay out of my life! I fucking hate you!"

The vases soared across the room. The first vase crashed on the floor depositing its contents on the carpet. The other vase hurtled farther, shattering as it struck the door with force. The impact sent shards of glass, rose petals, and water flying about her office. Jerrica's legs weakened and she dropped to her knees in front of the window. Using the edge of the table to hold onto, she lowered her head and closed her eyes. Tears nudged at her eyelids wanting release, but she was determined not to be weak and cry. Breathing deeply she tried to contain the frenzy inside that had made her lose her temper. She hated when she allowed herself to become this angry. Still on her knees, leaning back on her heels, she dropped her hands from the table, letting them hang at her side. Her mind was numb as the storm drained out of every pore. Every muscle felt weak.

✝

Lauren had closed the door quietly behind her. The tone in Jerrica's voice and the glare in her eyes had said everything. Lauren had exited the room as quickly as possible. She had just arrived at her desk when she heard the scream, then the loud smash against the door. Lauren lowered her head and closed her eyes. Her heart ached for her friend. A soft touch on her shoulder startled her. Turning her head, she saw Jaime standing behind her.

"Is everything ok?"

Lauren tried to stay calm and not let Jaime hear the worry in her voice. She was about to answer when she saw someone out of the corner of her eye. She could see

Madison watching them with curiosity. Lauren deliberately lowered her voice as she leaned in toward Jaime. "She just received flowers from Devin."

"No!" Jaime gasped putting her hand over her mouth.

Lauren nodded her head in confirmation. "I'm guessing from the recent sounds, she threw them across the room. I bet it's a mess in there." Lauren glanced at the closed door, "Listen let's just get back to our routine. I'll look in on her later. She needs time to deal with things."

Jaime knew that Lauren was right. Jerrica would want normalcy when she reappeared again. Jaime found herself struggling with the invisible line between employee to employer and caring friends. She wanted to rush in there and tell her everything would be okay and that she was here if she needed anyone. She looked at Lauren. She could see the same anguish running across her face. She noticed Madison hadn't moved from her standing position next to her desk since they had gotten back from lunch. The look of confusion on her face compelled Jaime to go and talk to her.

"What happened?" Madison whispered.

"I can't really talk about it," she answered, looking down at her feet.

"Jaime, I'm not going to push you for information, but I heard the same noises you did and I'm concerned. Is your boss okay?"

Jaime looked up and saw the worried look in Madison's eyes. "If I tell you, you'll have to promise not to tell anyone."

"I promise!"

"Jerrica's ex has been bothering her a lot lately and today flowers arrived. I think she's just frustrated with the things going on in her life right now."

"Oh, so the noise was probably her response to getting the flowers," Madison said, understanding the situation a little more clearly.

Both women stood together, preoccupied with their own thoughts.

Lauren's sharp voice echoed from across the room. "Jaime, get back here. You have plenty of work that needs to be done."

Jaime's face reddened in embarrassment. Smiling shyly at Madison, she quietly walked back to her desk.

Lauren locked eyes with Madison. At that moment, Madison knew Lauren had summed her up and by the look on her face; she didn't get high marks in her book.

Lauren severed eye contact only when she felt she had gotten her silent message across to the new girl on the floor. Lauren shifted paperwork as she slyly observed Madison disappear into Olivia's office.

There's just something about that woman I do not like, she thought as she watched Jaime sit down. *She's going to be trouble; I'm going to keep my eye on that one.*

✝

Time passed slowly. Jerrica wasn't sure how long she had been kneeling on the floor, when the ache in her legs brought her back to reality. Reaching up, she grabbed the edge of the table with both hands, balancing her frame. With as much energy as she could muster, she pulled herself into a standing position, not releasing her grip on the table. Taking a deep breath, she wobbled to the side window to look out, placing a warm hand on the cold window to steady the shakiness. Her mind was running through a thousand thoughts at once. Thoughts of her empty life flashed through her mind, conjuring images of Devin. She quickly placed a hand on her chest as the pain of their past break-up and most recent interaction shot through her heart.

Behind her, a familiar noise captured her attention, but she did not turn away from the window. The office door opened cautiously. Jerrica saw Lauren's reflection in the window.

Lauren glanced around the room at all the broken glass and flowers flung everywhere. She obviously wanted to comfort Jerrica. Avoiding the problem in front of her she spoke quietly. "Jaime and I are leaving for the day. Do you need me to stay to lock up?"

An eerie silence befell the room until Jerrica whispered. "I'll lock up tonight." She was standing motionless.

Lauren paused a moment, as if wanting to say something, anything, but obviously decided to leave her in peace. She closed the door.

Jerrica heard a soft goodnight as she heard the latch on the door. Alone in her office once more, she took in a deep breath; releasing it gradually.

I'm almost thirty and I'm alone, she commiserated.

Lowering her head, leaning it against the window, she closed her eyes.

What have I done with my life? One failed marriage and one painfully failed relationship.

Both relationships had taken their toll on her heart. She had always had her career to fall back on. She could always depend on her drive, personality, and intelligence to succeed in her career. But her career didn't keep her warm at night. As she straightened up, pushing her head away from the window, she realized, in a moment of clarity, that her career was not enough to fulfill her life anymore. She wanted, no...deserved, more than this. Her eyes focused beyond the window, on the city, as the shadows of dusk blanketed the busy streets of Boston below.

†

Hearing the movement of people outside the door, Madison glanced at her watch. It was quitting time, confirmed by the timepiece. Brushing off her pants as she stood, she surveyed her progress. Two large boxes with Olivia's junk inside and a small one of desk stuff was all that needed to be unpacked. Not bad but now it was time to get out of there.

About to exit the office, hand still on the doorknob, she noticed Lauren standing in Jerrica's open doorway. She froze. Madison could see a side profile of Jerrica standing near her windows. She watched as they exchanged words, but Jerrica didn't move. Madison couldn't see the expression on Jerrica's face from where she was standing. When Lauren slowly closed the door, walking back to her desk, Madison recognized the expression on her face.

The concern and uneasiness she had seen on Lauren's face earlier had returned. Not wanting to attract Lauren's attention or her wrath, Madison took a couple steps back into Olivia's office, quietly pushing the door shut. In the silent office, Madison listened for noises on the other side of the door to diminish. She finally heard what she thought might be the last of the bell ringing on the elevator so she cracked the door open and peeked out just in time to see the elevator doors close.

After a quick scan around the department, she determined Lauren had finally left. Madison strolled to her desk, picking up her coat. She was going to have to find a way to get along with Lauren or working on the same floor was going to be hell. It was only the first day, maybe she would soften up as time went on.

Madison slid her jacket on, proceeding toward the elevator. Once there, impatiently she pressed the down button several times, as she waited.

†

Jerrica hadn't left her spot near the window. Her eyes were clouded with thought. She could tell by the stillness in the air that everyone had gone for the day. Everyone had gone home to a loved one or a loving family for the night. Not her, she would go home to an empty house. Where did she go wrong? The sky had darkened as night crept in, only a few speckles of starlight scattered scarcely amongst the darkness. Tears filled her eyes as she continued to analyze her life.

"Are you all right?"

Alarmed Jerrica spun around to see someone standing in the doorway.

"I knocked, but I guess you didn't hear me." Stepping closer, she inquired again. "Jerrica, are you okay?"

"Madison?" Jerrica replied, blinking back the tears.

Not being able to stop the tears cresting her cheeks, Jerrica turned back to the window, hoping Madison hadn't seen them. "I'm…sorry…I…didn't hear you come in."

Jerrica's voice was shaky, Madison realized. She had seen the puffiness around Jerrica's eyes before she turned. "Jerrica, is…can…I mean…can I help in anyway?"

Jerrica quivered as she used her fingertips to wipe the tears, but could not reply. She didn't want to turn around, she didn't want to talk to anyone at this moment, didn't want anyone to see her in this weakened state. The room went silent. Jerrica's spine stiffened as the smell of perfume surrounded her. Suddenly she felt the warmth of Madison's breasts pressed up against her back.

Madison delicately slid her hands up to Jerrica's shoulders, gently brushing the soft skin of her biceps on the way. She waited for some indication from Jerrica to stop, but it never came. Madison wasn't sure if Jerrica was trembling from her touch or from something else. Sliding her arms across Jerrica's upper chest, she held her in a caring embrace.

The warmth of Madison's arms made Jerrica feel unexpectedly safe, as she leaned back into the inviting tenderness.

Madison felt the overwhelming need to comfort Jerrica. She felt the body in her arms relaxing and heard the soft, sniffling slow. She could feel Jerrica's silky hair on her cheek, breathing in the light lilac scent. *I could hold this woman forever, she realized.*

Jerrica stepped forward, stopping the moment she no longer felt the comforting warmth. She turned to face Madison, not looking into her eyes. Without any verbal exchange, Jerrica stepped back into Madison's embrace.

Madison's heart jumped as Jerrica laid her head on her shoulder. Madison enfolded her arms completely around Jerrica, resting her check on the side of Jerrica's hair. She was amazed at how well their bodies fit together. Madison didn't want the contact between them to end, but secretly wished this moment was for better reasons. She felt Jerrica pull her head back, their gaze locking. Madison could see the tears that still clouded those beautiful green eyes. She closed her eyes as the soft touch of Jerrica's palm caressed her cheek. She became increasingly aware of Jerrica's thumb delicately skimming her bottom lip. Without warning, she felt the velvety touch of Jerrica's lips brushing against hers. Her knees became weak, holding on tighter to stay standing. *I should stop this…I need to….*

†

Jerrica lightly licked Madison's bottom lip, being rewarded when they parted. Their tongues stroked and played. A moan escaped Madison's throat. The emptiness that had engulfed Jerrica compelled her to want more and Jerrica reveled in the taste of this exquisite, sensual woman. She had never been so excited just kissing someone. She knew she should stop, but couldn't help wanting more.

Feeling the urgency intensify in Jerrica's kiss, Madison ran her fingers through the silky, auburn hair. Fingers entwined in Jerrica's hair, she wrenched their lips apart, gasping for a much-needed breath. She looked into Jerrica's flushed face, watching as her eyes slowly opened, baring all of Jerrica's raw desire. Trying to manage the fiery passion that was building inside her, Madison loosened her arms, taking a step back.

"I can't do this. Your emotions are everywhere, Jerrica. You're not thinking straight. I just can't do this, not here, not like—"

Jerrica lifted a finger to Madison's lips stopping her from continuing. With unwavering wanting in her eyes, Jerrica breathed, "Then take me home.

Chapter Six

As they entered the darkened apartment, Madison turned to Jerrica. "Please, wait here," she said, disappearing into the void of the room.

Blinking repeatedly as a light illuminated the space, Jerrica tried to focus in on the surroundings. Madison was standing in what looked like a living room. The room had two neutral tan colored couches running almost parallel to where Madison stood. There was a small green recliner to the right, and a small television on a stand across the room to her left. This apartment reminded Jerrica of an ordinary hotel room, nothing flashy, no personality, no personal effects.

"This place is temporary until I get my stuff shipped back and settled," she said, looking around the room. "Would you like something to drink?"

"Yes, please," she said, watching Madison hurry into the kitchen.

"You can place your jacket anywhere. Make yourself comfortable."

Wiggling out of her jacket, Jerrica placed it over the back of the recliner. Now that her head was clearer, she started struggling with doubts about her recent actions.

What am I doing here? Why am I doing this? This is so unlike me, to be a one-night stand. Going home with practically a stranger is not my style at all. Then again, what has my style done for me so far in life? she thought.

Determined to see this through, she was going to feel first, worry about the consequences later. Other people did it, why couldn't she?

"I hope you like diet soda, that's all I have right now," Madison commented as she entered the room.

Jerrica spun instantly in the direction Madison's voice was coming from. Pushing her thoughts aside, she rushed toward Madison. Placing both hands on either side of Madison's face, Jerrica passionately kissed her.

†

Madison released the glasses, letting the contents plummet to the carpet, pulling Jerrica tightly to her. Their tongues hungrily explored one another, tasting, caressing. She wanted this woman, she needed this woman in her bed. Madison slid her hands across the soft material covering Jerrica's back. With one meticulous tug, she released the tucked in shirt. Sliding her hands underneath, stroking the muscular back, she felt the skin tremble under her touch. The sensation made her dizzy.

Liberating her lips from the intensity of the kiss, Jerrica tipped her head back, releasing a low sensual sigh as Madison trailed kisses down her neck.

Slowly Madison kissed the base of the exposed neck, leisurely nipping and licking her way up to the soft earlobe. Running her tongue along the rim of her ear, a moan escaped Jerrica's lips. Steadying her breathing, she whispered, "Tell me this is what you want. I need you to tell me this is what you want."

Jerrica could hear the wanting in Madison's plea. Breathing in deeply, Jerrica shifted out of her arms, stepping just out of Madison's reach.

Madison paused as if afraid, holding her breath in apprehension. Was she afraid that Jerrica had changed her mind?

Jerrica watched the conflicting emotions play across Madison's face. Pausing for a moment, she slowly glided her hands down the fabric on her side, capturing the hem of the shirt with both hands. Drawing the shirt over her head, she casually tossed it on the couch. "I want this. I want you," Jerrica replied, extending her arm out and taking Madison's hand.

Madison released Jerrica's hand as she reached for the light on the nightstand. The light gave the bedroom a soft glow. She directed her attention to the woman standing in front of her. Tenderly she passed her fingers across the exposed forearm, trailing up to the soft skin of her bare shoulder. It felt as soft as fine silk.

Gazing longingly into one another's eyes, Jerrica's skillful hands ran up the front of Madison's dress shirt, expertly releasing each button. Once the skin was exposed, her hands drifted under the shirt, pushing the material off broad, quivering shoulders, letting the garment tumble to the floor.

✝

Madison could feel her temperature rise each time their skin brushed together. The ache of desire that had started in Jerrica's office was intensifying to a blaze that might consume her. "Take this off," Madison groaned as she delicately slid her index finger under a bra strap.

Submitting to the hungry stare that wanted to devour her, Jerrica reached behind her, unclipped the garment, removing it quickly. The private show for Madison continued when Jerrica reached down to her waist where she hastily opened her pants. With a little wiggle and a small side step, Jerrica was standing only in her panties, her pants now a puddle on the floor next to her.

Madison's heart almost jumped out of her chest as she watched Jerrica remove her clothes. Her eyes appreciated Jerrica's almost naked form standing like a goddess in front of her. Madison's gaze washed Jerrica's velvety auburn hair brushing against her perfect ivory skin, ending a little above her firm, full breasts, down to the flat stomach and muscular abdomen. The vision of tiny red panties made her body jolt with excitement. She resumed her admiration down to the chiseled thighs that complemented Jerrica's incredibly strong legs. *Was this really happening or was she dreaming?*

†

Jerrica was captivated watching the intense desire grow in Madison's eyes as her gaze raked the entire length of her body. Jerrica seductively brushed by her toward the bed. She turned with her back to the bed. The coolness of the bed frame lightly brushed her calf when she took a small step back. Gradually, she lowered herself onto the edge of the bed, making sure wanting eyes were locked on her every move. Leaning back on her hands, she slid herself back so she could stretch on her side in the middle of the big bed. With legs crossed, bending an elbow, her head leaning on her hand, she breathed out. "It's now your turn. I want to see all of you."

Unclipping her bra in the front, Madison let it tumble to the floor. Her shaking hands yanked the pants fastener and zipper open. The slacks descended to the floor. Kicking them off, she strolled to the bed.

Jerrica watched Madison with great admiration. Every line, every curve was perfect. The tanned skin was flawless from the broad shoulders to the perfectly round, petite breasts. As her stare followed the curve of Madison's hips and muscular legs, Jerrica noticed no visible tan lines. A bolt of electricity surged down to her core at the thought of Madison sun bathing nude.

Her attention shifted to refocus on the warm hand sliding up her thigh. Madison was kneeling on the bed in front of her. Staring into eyes filled with yearning, she reached for the back of Madison's neck, enticing her closer. Their lips met softly this time, savoring each caress. Entangling her fingers in Madison's thick hair, Jerrica pulled her harder against her lips, deepening the kiss. Hands gently explored the curves and hollows of unexplored terrain, taking precious time to remember every inch of exposed skin.

Pulling away, Madison nipped on Jerrica's bottom lip. She trailed kisses down the delicately defined neckline, nestling in the base of Jerrica's neck. Her low husky voice whispered. "You are so beautiful."

Madison began a slow, tantalizing descent, kissing and licking every delicious inch. Tilting her head, she took the soft nipple into her mouth, teasingly circling it with her tongue. A long moan escaped Madison's lips as she nibbled the taut bud.

Jerrica whimpered, arching her back, filling Madison's hungry mouth with her breast. She trembled with excitement as a skilled hand caressed her side, sliding down to her hips. Madison released a growl as she dragged her fingernails up her back.

Positioning herself to lavish the other breast with attention, Madison's hand continued to flick and pinch the already sensitive nipple her mouth had just awoken.

Jerrica's body was alive, every nerve was ablaze, arousing her to the edge of her sanity. She raised her hips, caressing herself against Madison's thigh, increasing the hunger that was building in her core.

The wetness from Jerrica's panties coated Madison's thigh. Madison positioned herself above Jerrica, releasing a small gasp as their bodies fully touched. Jerrica's dark green eyes were almost black with desire as Madison bent to devour her lips. Wiggling a hand between them, she captured the waistband of the red panties. She worked them low enough so Jerrica could kick them off. Sliding her hand between Jerrica's legs, she enticed a soft moan from her lover. Madison ground her teeth together when she felt the moisture coat her finger. She buried her face into the neck of her exquisite companion as her own arousal was building to a fever pitch.

Jerrica's head tilted back into the pillow, as a skilled finger encircled her, stroking the flames of ecstasy burning inside. Jerrica bit her lip, stopping the blissful cries from escaping. She had never been vocal during sex, so the urge to scream with pleasure was foreign to her.

Madison glanced at Jerrica's upturned face. Her eyes were clenched shut, teeth deeply indenting her lip. Brushing her cheek against Jerrica's, she whispered softly. "Don't keep it in, sweetheart," she begged. "I need to hear that I am pleasing you."

Jerrica lifted her back farther off the bed, groaning, "Oh, my…oh…Madison, you feel so…."

Grinning, Madison slid two fingers inside.

Jerrica words became inaudible, as she was lost in the haziness of the journey, the climb taking her to places she needed to reach. Jerrica wrapped her legs around Madison's waist giving her deeper access to the depths of her passion. The thrusts came faster and deeper.

"That's it…," she exhaled between ragged breaths.

Jerrica had never been so free, so uninhibited. Her need for release was frantic as she held onto Madison. A heavy sheen of moisture developed between them.

Using her thumb to massage Jerrica's already sensitive core, Jerrica knew Madison could feel the muscles tightening around her fingers. Madison had to feel Jerrica was close to orgasm, she was increasing the rhythm.

Jerrica closed her eyes, surrendering to the rapture, nails digging into delicate flesh. "Oh, God, yes …ooh…yes," she moaned as her body tensed, the climatic explosion erupting from deep inside her, sending her soaring between the clouds, into a limitless abyss between fantasy and reality.

Flinching with delicious pain on her back, Madison held her tight as multiple spasms ripped through Jerrica's body. Madison softly kissed Jerrica's neck as she floated back onto the bed. Madison could feel Jerrica's heaving chest under hers. When the waves of ecstasy gradually subsided, Madison regrettably withdrew her fingers from the warmth.

Jerrica released her embrace on Madison, letting her arms and legs fall to the bed. "That was…indescribable…" she was able to whisper.

"It was absolutely beautiful," Madison responded in a throaty voice.

Post orgasmic eyes fluttered open to glance into dark, lustful ones. Jerrica was surprised to feel a twinge of arousal rising again. Placing her palms on Madison's shoulder, Jerrica used her body weight to push Madison off balance and onto her back. Jerrica quickly took her lips furiously. She used her knee to nudge Madison's legs, parting them with ease. She slid her body between them.

Madison pulled her mouth away, releasing a strained groan when Jerrica teasingly rubbed her body against hers. Madison was on overload as Jerrica teased her breast with kisses and nipping.

Methodically, Jerrica circled an erect nipple with the tip of her tongue.

An experienced hand worked the other breast, until she couldn't take any more of the exquisite torment Jerrica was inflicting on her. Her need for release was beyond teasing foreplay as she grabbed Jerrica's hand, directing it in between the mist covered skin and the fabric.

"A little impatient, are we?" Jerrica said, smirking with satisfaction.

"Please…," Madison breathed.

Jerrica pushed her hand farther under the fabric, feeling Madison's arousal on her hand. With feather-light touches, she caressed her. Madison started trembling uncontrollably underneath her, as her head swayed from side to side. Jerrica felt her own sexual arousal rise again in fervor. Jerrica entered Madison with intensity. She heard a growl as Madison's back arched off the bed.

Madison slid her legs open farther to adjust to Jerrica's fullness.

Jerrica's talented fingers orchestrated a delicious symphony of pleasure deep inside the depths of Madison's soul.

Trying to hold onto every feeling, Madison lifted her hips in rhythm to receive everything Jerrica was offering. "Oh, you feel so good, oh…don't stop," Madison said through clenched teeth as she grabbed the tangled bed sheets.

She could feel the tension building quickly as her body craved for release and her eyes fluttered closed. Madison cried out as the rapture of her climax rumbled through her.

"Oh, yes! Oh…God, yes…I love you, Jerrica!" Tipping her head back, Madison fell into the abyss of complete orgasmic pleasure.

Jerrica's head snapped up to look into the upturned face that was concentrating deeply on the euphoria. *Had she heard that right?* Not wanting to stop the pleasure,

Jerrica continued stroking her lightly until she felt the spasms decreasing.

Madison's body began to relax, bringing her back from the clouds.

Jerrica slowly withdrew her hand, caressing the soft skin up to the heaving chest. Cuddling into the base of her neck, Jerrica lightly kissed the moist skin. When breaths traveled from light gasping to a steady even flow, Jerrica whispered. "How about that drink now?"

Madison grinned as her eyes opened lazily.

"Well, thanks to you, the first ones are on the living room floor," Madison said, turning her head to look into beautiful green eyes.

Sitting up, Jerrica straddling Madison's hips., "Are you really going to hold that against me? Besides..." Jerrica's words trailed off as she noticed Madison seemed pre-occupied.

Madison couldn't stop staring at Jerrica's shapely body towering above her. Gentle hands traced the strong thighs, slowly moving up together just beyond the tiny patch of hair above her parted legs. Sliding her hands up Jerrica's abdomen, slowly onto her breasts, Jerrica's nipple hardened in her palms. Jerrica quivered as she kneaded the full breast.

Jerrica's arousal started building the moment Madison caressed her skin. Jerrica lifted her arms behind her head, elevating her breasts, allowing Madison to hold them firmly in her hands. *How can this woman have such an effect on me?* she wondered.

Sitting up, Madison placed a hand on Jerrica's back so she could pull her forward, placing a nipple into her mouth. Wetness pooled between her own legs.

Jerrica moaned as Madison's fingers filled her. Using her strong legs, Jerrica started thrusting her hips against Madison's hand. She lowered her arms to hold onto

Madison's shoulders for support. It felt so good to have Madison inside her.

Pulling her closer, Madison met every downward thrust with a slight upward intensity, increasing the fever forming inside. The intense climax hit quicker than the first and Madison gasped in pleasant surprise.

Clutching Madison's shoulders, Jerrica threw her head back, releasing a deep primal moan as the surge of spasms tore through her. Each spasm followed another, taking her higher and higher until every oversensitive nerve was on overload, leaving her content and extremely exhausted. She floated forward into the safety of Madison's arms.

Madison held her closely, feeling Jerrica's heartbeat near her cheek. Time seemed to stop when Jerrica was in the security of her embrace. With great ease, she leaned back, laying them both on the bed.

"You are amazing."

"I think you're the one who is amazing," Madison replied while placing a kiss on Jerrica's forehead "Would you like that drink now?"

Not bothering to open her eyes, Jerrica just nodded.

†

Madison involuntarily shivered as Jerrica slid off her and onto the bed. Madison stood and hurried toward the kitchen hesitating only once at the doorway of the bedroom, to look back at the bed, admiring the statuesque beauty lying motionless in post rapture. On her way back she glanced down at the mess on the living room carpet, Madison smiled as she relived the night's events. "I made it back without—," she stopped just inside the bedroom.

With a contented grin, Madison walked to the nightstand, setting the glasses on top. Reaching out she lightly touched the tousled hair of the now sleeping beauty in her bed. *How precious*, Madison thought as she flipped the light off. Picking up the blankets, she cuddled up behind Jerrica, spooning her in a warm embrace.

A small sigh escaped Jerrica's lips as Madison's warm arm wrapped around her waist.

Kissing the back of her neck, Madison lowered her head onto the pillow, letting her own blissful exhaustion overtake her.

Chapter Seven

The peaceful sound of a city sleepily awaking for the day was abruptly interrupted with the sounds of a ringing cell phone. Rushing out of bed to find the disturbing noise, Madison fumbled through items on the floor looking for the culprit. Once she exhumed the phone from her pocket, she clicked it on to stop the annoying sound.

"Hello," Madison said in a hushed tone.

"Good morning, my partner in crime," bellowed the southern voice from the speaker.

"Olivia? It's kind of early," Madison turned scanning the bed for Jerrica. It was empty. "What do you need?"

"Ah, sugar, it's not that early, it's a little after nine. I thought I would find you at work by now, but when I called, they dropped to voicemail. Therefore, I thought I would check your cell. Honey, you ok?" Olivia voiced concern.

Madison glanced at the pile of clothes on the floor, only hers were there. An uneasy feeling began to creep up Madison's spine. The room was empty and the apartment seemed quiet. She could hear Olivia blubbering about something on the phone, but her attention was on finding Jerrica. As the panic started to spread, she rushed to the bathroom. The silence she heard from within only accelerated the tension she was feeling.

Quickly opening the door, Madison met a bright, empty room. She felt like someone had knocked the wind out of her as she leaned heavily against the doorframe for support.

"Hello? Hello? *Hello*?" Olivia's voice increased in elevation.

Placing the phone to her ear she replied. "Sorry, Olivia, I'm here. I didn't mean to be late. It's probably my body adjusting to New England time."

"Honey, have you called your parents yet? I bet they would love to see you," Olivia said sympathetically.

"I will, Olivia, sometime soon. I don't have time to think about that right now. Did you need me for something?" Madison was trying to keep her on track without losing her own mind in frustration.

"Well, since you're not at the office yet, I need you to stop by my place and pick up some files. I have notes and calls I need you to arrange for me."

"That's it? It couldn't wait till tomorrow when you return?'

"You know me."

"Yes…yes I do," she said, shaking her head, "I'll try to be there in about an hour."

She didn't wait for Olivia to respond but clicked off the phone, tossing it helplessly on the bed. Madison pushed herself off the frame and flipped the light off in the bathroom. Looking across the room, she felt her heart sink.

Jerrica didn't wake me when she left, she thought sadly.

Madison needed to talk to her right away about what happened between them last night. She needed to know why she left without saying goodbye. She had so many questions that only Jerrica would be able to answer. Snatching a towel from the rack, she returned to the bathroom and began her preparations to start the day.

†

Waking with a start, Jerrica looked around, confused. She froze when a peaceful moan of slumber emanated from behind her. In a flash, that evening's exploits filled her mind.

"Oh no…what have I done?" Jerrica whispered.

Madison shifted behind her, pulling her closer.

Please don't wake up, she prayed silently.

The feel of Madison's arms wasn't at all unpleasant, but Jerrica was becoming unnerved, needing to flee from the situation she knew she had created. With great caution, she rested her hand on Madison's wrist, carefully lifted her arm. Sliding out from under the warmth, Jerrica glanced briefly at the delicate hand that had given her pleasure only hours before and guilt quickly replaced thoughts of pleasure. Once free of the arm, Jerrica slipped a pillow where she had been laying for Madison's arm to rest on. Trying to be as quiet as a mouse, she gathered up her clothes in the bedroom, slipping into the bathroom to dress.

With most of her clothes on, she looked in the mirror. With her hands in her hair, she assessed her reflection. She was a coward, running out like this. They were both adults, they could handle the situation, but instead she was running. Looking away from the mirror, she hated herself.

Peering out, Jerrica confirmed Madison was still asleep as she made her way across the bedroom to leave. *She is beautiful,* Jerrica thought, taking one last look before closing the bedroom door. As the door clicked shut, remorse consumed her. Her shame wasn't because she didn't find Madison attractive, or hadn't had fun the past evening, it stemmed from the feeling that she had used someone for her own gratification.

Rushing toward the living room couch, she seized her shirt, slipping it on. Turning she scooped up her jacket, and headed for the door. Her hand on the doorknob, she stopped.

Can I really do this? Am I that kind of person who just leaves in the middle of the night? A person who can't face her own faults?

With slumped shoulders and head down, she turned the doorknob, leaving the apartment. *I guess I am that kind of person,* she answered herself as the elevator doors closed.

✝

Madison went through her morning preps at high speed, anxious to get out of the apartment, especially the bedroom. The memory of Jerrica was everywhere. The hot shower water hit the scratch marks on her back, making her wince for more than one reason. Once dressed, she headed toward the kitchen as quickly as possible, needing coffee. The empty glasses on the carpet reminded Madison why she was rushing to get out of her apartment.

"Shit," she mumbled. "Screw the coffee. I'll get it at work."

Madison grabbed her jacket and headed out the door, locking the memories in her apartment.

Any minute now, that phone will start ringing, Madison hoped as she stared at her cell phone.

Hailing a cab, she instructed the driver to drive directly to work. She didn't want to face Olivia and have to lie to her. She was in a hurry to get into work, anxious to talk with Jerrica privately. A messenger sent to Olivia's apartment was the best she could do right now. She was tempted when she arrived to ask to see Jerrica, but instead went to her own desk. Everyone was so busy working that no one noticed her arrival. Madison knew she had to go into Olivia's office to finish unpacking, but she didn't want to leave her desk just in case Jerrica exited her office. She tried not to stare at the closed door as she sat, willing it to open.

"Good morning."

Madison bolted to a standing position, knocking her chair into the person behind her.

As Jaime bent in agony, she whimpered at Madison. "Didn't mean to scare you."

"Oh, Jaime," Madison quickly moved the chair away, placing a comforting hand on her friend's back. "I am so sorry. You startled me."

Madison softly rubbed Jaime's back until she started to right herself. "Did I hurt you?"

"I'm fine. It's my own fault. I shouldn't have walked up on you like that." Jaime rubbed her tummy a couple of times. "Would you like some coffee? I'm headed for the lounge to get a cup."

"I'll come with you. It will be hard to carry four cups of coffee all by yourself," she said, subtly baiting Jaime for a revealing response.

"Oh, I was only getting two anyway," Jaime, replied in her innocent way.

Not exactly the clear answer I was looking for, Madison thought.

Walking into the lounge, Jaime was talking about winters in New England or winters near the water. Madison wasn't sure what Jaime was saying as her mind was preoccupied with getting information about Jerrica. Jaime pulled out three coffee cups when Madison spoke waving her hand at the third cup. "No thanks. I think I'll start my day off with a diet soda, my morning's already thrown off. I was told we were getting low on cream anyway."

Jaime filled the two cups with coffee, than grabbed two packets of sugar, depositing them into one cup before answering. "My whole day is all screwed up if I don't start it with coffee. I mean it has to be made just right, sweet, and light." As she stirred in the creamer, she continued, "Jerrica likes hers a little darker than mine, but Lauren likes it black. Yuk! Maybe that's why she's always in a bitter mood," Jaime giggled, than glanced around the room quickly to make sure no one else heard her.

Madison had retrieved her beverage from the vending machine. With her back against the counter, she waited to see what Jaime did next. She watched closely as Jaime grabbed the cups off the counter, spinning on her heels to leave. Madison felt her stomach flip as she glanced at the cups, one light in color, and one dark. "So no coffee for the boss lady today?" she asked, trying to hide her disappointment,

"Nope," Jaime said as they walked out of the lounge, "She's not here today. Working from home I'm told. It's just Lauren and me to hold down the fort today."

Madison thought she might heave, but since she hadn't eaten since yesterday, there wasn't anything left to bring up. Trying to get rid of the sudden cottonmouth feeling, Madison sipped her soda, giving herself time to think in the process. "I know what you're going through. Olivia is out until tomorrow and I still have to get her office ready. She's not capable to set it up herself. So I'm here doing my job and hers at the moment."

Jaime nodded her head in understanding as they reached Madison's desk. With a sweet smile, Jaime walked back to her department, depositing a mug on Lauren's desk before she crossed to her workstation. Jaime waved then turned to pull out her chair, returning to work.

Madison's head was whirling. Grabbing stuff off her desk, she entered the solitude of Olivia's office.

Chapter Eight

Jerrica arrived home just as the glimpse of daylight was appearing in the sky. She had stopped by the office to retrieve her briefcase before going home. She left a message for Lauren letting her know she would be working from home today. Dropping her briefcase near the staircase, she slid off her jacket, tossing it toward the kitchen countertop. Her first priority was to put out food for the animals. When that task was completed, she dragged herself upstairs for a shower.

In the bedroom, she started removing clothes as she crossed toward the bathroom. Jerrica switched on the shower, adjusting it to the right temperature. Removing the last piece of clothing, she paused, sighed heavily, and entered the cascading water. Placing her palms on the warm moist tiles, Jerrica leaned her head under the water spray. Each drop of water tumbling down her body made Jerrica wish her troubles would wash away as well. Several minutes passed before she mustered up enough energy to start the task of cleaning herself. Her mind was racing with images of Madison's face, images of them making love. Sliding her hands down her sides to rinse off the soap, she could still feel the electricity of Madison's touch.

Finally rinsed, Jerrica stepped out of the shower, encasing her tired body in a towel. Leaning on the counter, she again stared at her reflection. Jerrica's thoughts were cruel toward herself.

What were you thinking? You initiated this whole thing. She doesn't deserve this from you. She is a wonderful, giving person and you used her. Then you didn't have the balls to stick around and face her this morning. You are a terrible, thoughtless person Jerrica Abigail.

Jerrica lowered her head, letting the tears flow. "What have I done," she sobbed.

Jerrica left the bathroom emotionally and physically exhausted. She needed to get some rest, then maybe she could think a little more clearly. Drying off, she slipped into her sleepwear. She grabbed the sleeping pills that she always kept in her nightstand, popped a couple, and closed her eyes tight, hoping restful sleep would find her soon.

†

Madison busied herself with unpacking Olivia's office, but her mind kept wandering back to Jerrica. She has never given herself to someone so completely or enjoyed someone so much. Last night had been the best sexual encounter she had ever had, but it had been so much more… somehow. It had been heavenly until she woke up alone this morning. She needed to talk to her! She needed to know Jerrica's side. The wait was going to be agonizing.

†

Lauren spun her chair toward Jaime the moment Madison disappeared into Olivia's office.

"What were the two of you talking about?" Lauren asked as she crossed her arms.

Continuing to click her keyboard, Jaime answered absently. "Nothing really."

"You two seemed to be gossiping on your way back from the lounge," an irritated Lauren snapped back at Jaime.

Turning her head in Lauren's direction, Jaime responded coolly, "We talked about coffee, doing someone else's job, oh, and she asked me about Jerrica. That's it," Jaime swiveled, going back to her computer work.

"Why did she ask about Jerrica?" Lauren inquired harshly.

Jaime spun her chair to totally face Lauren, "Do you have something against Madison? You seem to bristle every time her name is mentioned and you don't even bother hiding your dislike from her or anyone else."

The expression on Lauren's face never wavered. It was stern, and her jaw was firmly clenched. She answered, between gritted teeth. "I do not have to like everyone we work with. They do not pay me enough to be nice. Besides, I don't need to explain to anyone why I don't like her."

"I think if you gave her the chance, you would find her a very likable person," Jaime offered, shaking her head in disbelief.

Scoffing, Lauren slid her chair around to face her computer, ending the conversation.

Chapter Nine

"Olivia, it's in the folder on the corner of your desk. I told you it was there this morning!"

This was the third time Olivia had called Madison looking for that same folder. "Hold on, I'll be right in," Madison slammed down the receiver.

Pausing to take a few calming breaths, she stood, feeling everyone's eyes on her, and moved into the office. Not wanting any confrontation, she strolled to the desk, picked up Olivia's bag with one hand, and retrieved the file from underneath it with the other hand.

Snatching the folder from her hand, Olivia made a huffing noise in disapproval.

Madison smiled weakly at her, turning to leave.

With the door partially open, Olivia's voice boomed out. "What the hell is your problem lately?"

Madison blushed, quickly closing the door, hoping no one had heard Olivia's loud voice. Rotating on her heels she looked directly at Olivia as she walked toward her, "If we weren't friends, Olivia, I would knock your block off for talking to me that way."

Olivia, now looking concerned, stood to respond. "Honestly Mads, what's wrong? You have been off your game for weeks now."

Madison plopped herself into the chair in front of the desk. She looked at the hands she had folded in her lap. "I have been a bitch, haven't I? Do not answer that. I'm sorry, Olivia."

Returning to her seat, Olivia leaned on her desk to look at her friend more closely. "Madison, what is it? How can I help?"

Madison could hear the genuine worry in her voice. She had known Olivia for six years now and knew she did care about her. She realized she had been like this for a while now, since she last saw Jerrica. Letting out a long sigh, Madison began her short version. "I hooked up with someone a couple of weeks ago, and I can't seem to get her out of my mind."

"Wait…we've only been in New England a little while. Wow, you're quick, girlfriend," Olivia said, obviously a little surprised.

Glaring at her friend, Madison continued. "It only happened once, but I know it was more than just a physical act between us. I felt a deep connection to her and I know she felt something for me. I know she did! I mean when we hooked up, it was like we had been together for years and knew exactly what one another needed."

"So, what happened?"

"Nothing happened, that's the problem. She left during the early morning hours. I woke up alone." Madison voice was cracking under the emotional stress.

"Oh, come on, Mads, it was just sex. She needed some, you're a good lay, get past it. Madison, she is not worth all this emotional baggage, especially if she leaves your ass in the middle of the night."

Madison looked up from her lap shocked at her friend's brash words. "You can be a bitch sometimes, Olivia. It's not like that. I know she felt something and I think—"

"And you think what, Mads? You enjoyed one another, nothing more. Boston has plenty of lesbians you can date.

Chalk it up to a night of great sex and move on to someone else."

Olivia gave her a wink and a knowing grin, obviously baiting Madison to say more.

Madison stood quickly, pounding her fists on Olivia's desk. "Screw you, Olivia," she shouted, "It's not like that! I can't move on, I'm in love with her!"

Olivia's evil grin transformed into a huge smile as Madison slowly returned to her chair, the realization of what she just admitted hitting her.

In a soft voice Olivia spoke to a bewildered Madison. "I know you are honey. I know you are…."

The perplexed look on Madison's face made Olivia's heart go out to her.

Confused, Madison replied, "How did you know when I didn't even know myself? I didn't know until I just heard myself say it. How can someone fall in love so fast? It is not possible! It's just not possible!"

"You knew. You were just hiding it from yourself because there's pain attached to thoughts of her. I do believe in love at first sight…so anything is possible."

"I knew there was something between us the moment I saw her. I just didn't recognize what it was," Madison admitted to herself as well as Olivia.

"Love at first sight. I never, in a million years, would have thought that would happen to you. You are always so calculating with everything you do. So, what are you waiting for, go to her," Olivia said with determination. "I need my assistant back!"

"It's more complicated than that. It's not just the fact that I don't know how she feels about that night or even me, there are just other things at play." Madison released a heavy sigh.

"What other things," Olivia's curiosity was piqued, "I can't help you if you're not telling me everything. What is standing in your way, besides yourself?"

Madison lowered her eyes again, debating if she should divulge the rest. They sat quietly waiting for Madison to decide. "I hooked up with Jerrica," Madison paused, "she's the one I brought home."

"Ok, so what's the problem?" Olivia asked innocently.

Madison raised her head looking at her absentminded friend. "Geez, Olivia don't you remember anything? You've met her, Mr. Bisset introduced you two."

Madison waited for Olivia's memory to kick in and when it didn't, she continued. "He introduced her as Jak and you offended her by saying you thought she was a man because of the name."

Olivia's face lit up with acknowledgement. Then she covered her mouth in shock. "Oh, wow…Madison, not exactly your league," Olivia muttered.

"Thanks for the words of encouragement," Madison retorted.

The wheels in Olivia's head began to turn as she started putting invisible puzzle pieces together in her head. "You slept with her the first week we got here." Trying to put the pieces together, she continued. "And she hasn't returned to work. Am I correct?"

Madison was not ready to do a timeline of her life, but answered anyway, "No and yes. We didn't hook up the first week we started here, it was the first Monday and yes, she hasn't appeared at work since?"

"Damn Madison you're good. On the first day? Wow! So what's the problem? Call her or go to her house. Make her talk to you."

Madison's heart sank lower in her chest. "Her personal numbers and home address aren't in the directory. I tried the HR department, but could not sweet-talk any information from her. Her assistant doesn't like me, so I stay clear of her. I just cannot come out and ask her secretary without raising red flags. I've tried, Olivia. I guess she just doesn't want to see me. I'm sure if she did, she would have called me by now."

Madison stood. "Well, now you know it all. I'm sorry I've been unbearable to work with lately. I will try to be better. I'll be at my desk if you need anything else."

Olivia watched a very dejected Madison leave her office.

†

After two days of working at home, Jerrica decided to write a letter to the board of Morrill, Hartford, and Donahue. The letter included that until further notice, she would be working off site. She would be working from her home office, but if given enough notice would travel to the office for projects that needed her personal attention. In her closing, she emphasized her many years of service to their company and if this wasn't acceptable, she would tender her resignation. She only had to wait two hours for their response along with clauses to her demands. The board granted her the right to work off site, under the stipulations she specified in her letter, but interjected that this was only a temporary situation. Jerrica was satisfied with the compromise.

On day three, she wrote a long e-mail to her staff, explaining the new arrangements and how it affected their specific jobs. Jerrica figured between e-mails, phone calls, the occasional messenger, things would run just fine for a while. The e-mail was vague on her sudden disappearance from MHD, but nobody was ready to ask her questions. That is until that second Saturday morning after receiving the e-mail, when Lauren showed up unannounced on her doorstep.

Jerrica was sitting in her pajamas at the breakfast table staring out at the water, her first cup of coffee in hand, trying to relax. The ringing doorbell caught her off guard. Before she could even get out of her chair, Lauren was using her key to enter the home.

"Maybe I shouldn't have given you that key after all," Jerrica commented flatly, looking back out the window.

Jerrica turned to see if she had actually come in. She bolted out of her chair as an angry Lauren rounded the table.

They were standing toe to toe and Lauren's face had reddened in frustration. "Who do you think you are?" she yelled. "Don't you ever talk to me it that manner again! Do you hear me? I'm not shit on your shoes, Jerrica and I'll be damned if you will treat me that way!"

The two women stood frozen, staring at one another, both full of rage. As time started to pass, Jerrica found she couldn't stand the infuriating look in Lauren's eyes and bent to pick up the chair that she had knocked askew in haste. Setting the chair upright, Jerrica sat, folding her hands on the table.

Lauren took a deep breath as Jerrica returned to her seat. Seating herself across from Jerrica, she could see the bay in the background. They both sat quietly, waiting for tempers to decompress.

Lauren had shaken Jerrica to her core. She had never witnessed Lauren so angry, never mind having that anger directed at her. More in control of her tone, Jerrica whispered. "I'm sorry."

Lauren reached her hands out, covering Jerrica's hands with her own. "I'm sorry, too."

Silence crept between them again for several minutes, each waiting, hoping the other would speak first. Trying to break the tension, Jerrica spoke. "There could have been an easier way to get my attention, you know?"

Lauren tried not to smile, holding onto the little anger she had left. "What has happened to you, my friend?"

Slowly dragging her hands out from under Lauren's, Jerrica tried to think of something to say.

"Jerrica, look at me."

She didn't want to answer the question, nor did she want to look at Lauren. She reluctantly lifted her face to look into her friend's eyes.

Lauren's eyes filled with tears as she took a long look at the pain and exhaustion in Jerrica's deep green eyes.

"Don't! Please, don't," Jerrica managed to say before hiding her face in her hands.

Lauren could hear the soft sounds of sobbing coming from Jerrica. "Jerrica, talk to me. You're scaring me. What is going on with you?"

Jerrica turned to the windows, wiping the tears away with the back of her hand. Lauren could tell Jerrica was struggling with her emotions. The house fell silent. The only sound that seemed to echo through the house was the soft ticking resonating from the antique clock on the bookcase.

Not changing her position, Jerrica's pain filled voice stated simply. "I'm a coward."

"That's not helpful, Jerrica. Explain to me what is going on," Lauren replied.

"If I'm going to talk to you about this, I need you to promise me some things. I need you to promise me you won't judge me. I'm doing that enough for both of us. And you will not retaliate in my name or interfere."

Lauren paused before answering. "Whatever you need me to do, that is what I'll do. Jerrica, please, talk to me."

Jerrica was trying to speak without breaking down as the memories flooded her mind. "The last Monday I was at work, after everyone went home, I went home with someone, and I really shouldn't have."

"You went home with someone? Wait, didn't you get the flowers from…on Monday?"

Jerrica took a deep breath. "Yes, that was the same day. I was experiencing many conflicting emotions that day. I was a basket case, you remember. After everyone left, she came to me. I needed to feel something, Lauren, even though I knew in the back of my mind it was just a temporary solution. I'm not saying it was right, but it happened and I can't take it back."

"You've got to be fucking kidding me, Jerrica! I thought you were done with Devin. After yelling at me in your office about letting those flowers into your office, you turn around and go home with her!"

Jerrica continued to stare out the window, delaying her response until Lauren finished her rant. "It wasn't, Devin," Jerrica said, somberly, turning to look directly at Lauren. "It was Madison Jeffery."

Jerrica saw Lauren trying to hide her surprise, but her eyes betrayed her feelings. "I know, Lauren. I messed up. I broke my own personal rule of not getting involved with a co-worker and my own rule about one night stands." Jerrica turned back toward the window.

"Well, that clarifies a few things," Lauren sat back in her chair thinking, "Ms. Jeffery has been a little nosy the last couple of weeks, indirectly asking questions about you. She is becoming real tight with Jaime."

"Nothing is her fault, let me clarify that for you. It's completely my fault. I'm the one who told her to take me home and the one that made the first move once we were in her apartment," Jerrica admitted.

"I kind of understand now why you haven't returned to work, but that doesn't explain why you think you are a coward."

Jerrica flinched at the word. She had said it first, but hearing that word repeated by someone else stung a little. "I'm a coward because I left in the early morning while she was sleeping. I let her wake up alone with no explanation or anything. Lauren, that's not me, I don't just hop into the sack with someone and then leave in the middle of the night like a prostitute."

"Stop that, you're not a prostitute," Lauren commented, trying to think. "I don't think either one of you are at fault, honestly. You two just met, you needed someone, and I'm guessing she did too. You're both consenting adults, things just happened. That doesn't mean you have to hide from her. You've changed your complete working career just so you won't see her, that's a little extreme. Don't you think?"

Jerrica took a couple of seconds to contemplate Lauren's words as she watched her stand. "The evening with Madison was just the straw that broke the camel's back per se where work is concerned. The past few months have been hell for me at MHD. It takes everything I have just to get out of bed to go to work. Then once I get there, all I want to do is come home. I'm beginning to re-evaluate my career choices. Then add Devin into the situation and now Madison, I needed an undetermined leave of absence from that place."

"Jerrica, re-evaluating your career is a good thing. Everyone does it in their lifetime at least once, maybe some even more. I know I have, plenty of times throughout my career. I do believe a break right now would be good for you. I've noticed your heart hasn't been in your work for a while now. Nevertheless, you left Jaime and me in the dark. I thought we were all friends and you left us just dangling in the wind. Then out of nowhere we get a formal e-mail announcing your plans and nothing, but work correspondences since then…and,"

"And what?" Jerrica's low tone interjected.

"I still stick with my first analysis, two consenting adults just enjoying one another. That's it, not complicated."

Lauren grabbed the cup off the table. "I need some coffee. I'll refresh yours while I'm at it."

"I'm sorry about not taking you and Jaime's feeling into consideration. It just happened so quickly I went into self-protection mode. Upper management suggested the formal e-mail. That was not my idea. I am so sorry."

Jerrica tried mustering a smile but felt a little relieved when Lauren was busy with the coffee. She wouldn't have to think or talk for a few minutes.

"So, do you feel any better?" Lauren's voice sounded from the kitchen.

"Not really. It's more complicated than that. Nothing is ever simple in my life."

"See, that's your problem," Lauren said entering the room and placing the cups on the table. "You make this situation more complicated in your head than it really needs to be."

In almost a whisper, Jerrica tried to explain the biggest complication. "She told me she loved me."

Lauren choked on her coffee and fetched a napkin to cover her mouth. Lauren was baffled by this new information.

Before Jerrica could turn her head, Lauren gently touched the bottom of Jerrica's chin. Slowly lifting her head, making her keep eye contact, "Jerrica, I'm only going to ask you this once and I want you to be honest with me. This is very important. Do you love her?"

Jerrica tried tilting her head, but Lauren prevented her from looking away. Jerrica closed her eyes in a desperate attempt to hide her emotions. She paused, taking her time to answer truthfully. "I don't know."

Lauren sat back in her chair, perplexed at what had just happened.

The tears started to slip out behind Jerrica's closed eyelids. "I don't really know what I feel. I don't think I've ever been in love with anyone before, so I can't honestly answer yes or no. I just don't know." Jerrica laid her head on her crossed arms on the table and started to sob openly.

Running her fingers through Jerrica's hair, Lauren spoke softly. "Honey, are you sure you're not confusing a great night of companionship and sex with something more?"

Raising her head, Jerrica brushed tears from her cheek. "It wasn't just sex, Lauren. I craved her touch and ached to touch her. When she stared at me with those deep brown eyes, it was as if she was looking right into my soul. It's really hard for me to explain all the feelings that were going on."

Oh my friend, you have it bad, Lauren concluded.

Chapter Ten

Days turned into weeks and weeks turned into a month and still Jerrica hadn't returned to work. Madison was getting discouraged of ever seeing Jerrica again. "Hi, Mom, it's me," she said into the receiver one day at work.

She had been dreading this call since she moved back. She would have to tell them she had been in New England for a little while and why she hadn't called until now. "Yes, Mom, I'm working in Boston now, with Olivia."

Her mother started complaining about something going wrong at the house, but Madison had tuned her out until she heard her name being repeated in a high pitch. "Sorry, I'm at work right now, trying to do two things at once." She tried to pay closer attention this time. "I know its last minute, being Thursday, but I was planning on coming this weekend. Maybe stop by early Saturday and leave on Sunday. How does that sound?"

The ecstatic voice on the phone made her feel warm inside. "That's great. I'll call when I'm on my way. Okay, I will, you too. Love you."

Hanging up the receiver Madison released the breath she had been holding in since she dialed.

"I'm glad you took my advice and called your parents."

Frightened, Madison spun around in her chair to see a grinning Olivia leaning on her cubical wall. "Are you trying to give me a heart attack," Madison said as she put her hand on her breast in surprise.

"Baby, your heart's more toward the middle of your chest." Olivia flashed a naughty grin in Madison's direction. "If you have a minute, would you mind coming into my office?"

Not waiting to hear an answer, Olivia turned on her heels, leaving Madison bewildered.

Madison shook her head, wondering how she had worked for this woman for so long. Closing the door behind her, she relaxed in her normal seat in Olivia's office. "Ok, I'm here. What can I help you with?"

Olivia sat behind her desk with the biggest grin on her face. The cat that ate the canary kind of grin. Madison became a little unnerved.

"How long have we worked together?"

Madison lifted an eyebrow answering cautiously. "We've been together for almost six years now. Are we going to have a trip down memory lane? Or are you letting me go?"

"You always go there, don't you? Sometimes, Madison, you can be so negative. No, I'm not firing you. You are my best employee."

"I'm your only employee," Madison smirked.

"Were getting off track here," Olivia said trying to steer the conversation back. "What I am trying to say is after all these years, you seem to always underestimate my talents."

Olivia slid a business card across the top of her desk.

Madison leaned forward placing a finger on it, turned it so she could read it.

Jerrica Kerrison
Account Executive/Business Analyst
Morrill, Hartford, and Donahue Co. Inc.

"Olivia, I already have this information. Her business cards you can get anywhere. The contact numbers on this card just ring back to the office. This really doesn't help my cause."

With her finger still on the card, Madison started to slide it back in her boss's direction. "You have very little faith in my abilities. Turn the card, honey," Olivia said.

Madison picked the card up, flipping it quickly. On the back of the card were listed two phone numbers with a home address. "How did you get these?"

Olivia looked very pleased with herself while answering, "I made really good friends with the young man in the file department. He loves my…southern charm."

"Oh, please don't tell me anymore," Madison put her hand up to stop her from continuing.

Olivia let out a hearty laugh at her comment.

Madison stared down at the business card now in her hand, suddenly feeling petrified. She had the information that she had been searching for suddenly sitting in her hand.

"Well, now you have everything you need to find her. Go get her, tiger," Olivia said, slapping her hands on her desk in celebration.

Madison looked up from the card, "Olivia, I'm afraid. I've spent days looking for this information and now that I have it, I don't know what the next step should be. I didn't think beyond finding …."

"That's just something you're going to have to figure out, honey."

✝

Friday arrived too quickly for Madison. She had barely gotten any of her work done all week and she couldn't take it home for the weekend because she was visiting her parents. She sighed deeply at the thought of visiting them.

She loved her parents, there was no question about that. What she didn't love were the lectures she would hear during her visit. She would hear about how she needs a better job and how she doesn't need to be working for Olivia. At least she wouldn't have to hear the moving closer lecture. She expected to be grilled on her dating habits and if she'd had met that special person. Madison's mind flashed to Jerrica's face and her stomach clenched. She needed to forget about her since she obviously had forgotten about Madison. Jerrica knew where to find her and she hadn't even tried calling her. She flipped the business card between her fingers. Madison lifted her head just in time to see Jaime walking toward her. She slid the card under her keyboard.

"Hi," Jaime said when she reached Madison. "I was going out for lunch today. Interested in joining me?"

Looking up into an innocent expression she answered. "Sorry, I can't. I am so far behind that I need to work through lunch."

"Yeah, it looks like you're burying yourself," Jaime said as she pointed to the multiple stacks of papers on the desk. "Well, maybe next week" She smiled and just like that, Jaime was walking away.

Madison glanced over her cubicle wall, looking around the room. It looked like she might be the only one working through lunch; the department appeared almost empty. Picking up the receiver, she called Olivia. "I'm going to get supplies. Do you need anything?"

"Actually, I need more markers and a few file folders. Thanks," Olivia drawled into the handset.

Entering the supply room, Madison started her adventure in finding supplies. Looking around the small racks, she started pulling items she needed. As she retrieved the last item, she turned to leave, stopping abruptly and staring at the figure in the doorway. Madison was in shock, dropping everything she was holding. She knelt down to pick the items up, noticing the door closing, trapping the two of them inside.

"We need to talk," Lauren stated sternly.

Madison rose, leaving the items scattered at her feet. "I'm not sure we have anything to say to one another," she replied coldly.

Madison noticed that Lauren was a little taller than she was, with attractive features and very strong looking biceps.

Madison's reply did nothing to change Lauren's mood. Lauren started walking in haste toward Madison, who backed up as quickly as she could.

When her heel rubbed against a rack, there was nowhere else to go. Lauren had her cornered. Madison tipped her head to look directly into Lauren's eyes as she spoke. "I said we have nothing to say to one another. Now, please move out of my way."

Annoyed, Lauren glared at the smaller woman. "I said we need to talk, and if this is the only way I can talk to you in private, then this is how it will be."

Madison saw the challenge in her eyes, deciding very quickly she wasn't up for this fight. "Fine, then say what you have to say."

Lauren stepped back out of Madison's personal space, "I want to get this out in the open. I don't like you."

"You needed to back me into a corner, in the storage room to tell me that? Tell me something I don't already know." Madison's sarcasm hit a bad nerve for Lauren.

Lauren tried to stay calm. She needed to do this for Jerrica, "Here's something you don't know. I know about you and Jerrica."

Madison found herself almost falling backwards into the racks in surprise. Reaching for a shelf, she regained some of her composure before replying. "I'm not going to discuss my personal life with you."

"Ok, fair enough. This isn't about you. It's about Jerrica, and therefore it includes you, much to my displeasure."

"Listen, I don't know what she has told you, but she has made it quite clear, by her absence, that her life doesn't include me." Her heart tightened. Madison fought back the tears that threatened to release, looking toward the floor.

Lauren caught the pain in Madison's eyes just before she lowered her head. "If you felt or feel anything for her, go to her. You're going to have to make the first move. She's not that strong. Jerrica is a wonderful woman and if you don't fight for her, well, you're a bigger fool then I thought you were."

Lauren backed farther away from Madison, who was still glancing at the floor. "Such fools," she retorted, leaving the supply room.

Madison heard the door latch, realizing she was again alone. Crumbling to the floor, she started to weep, shaken by their conversation. Several minutes passed before she could calm herself enough to get off the floor. Brushing off her pants, straightening her blouse, Madison brushed the last tear from her cheek and exited the supply room with her head held high. Madison's thoughts were no longer focused on work. She sat at her desk the rest of the day with a New England fog clouding her head.

"Hey, you going home sometime today?" a voice said through the haze.

Blinking a couple times, Madison was able to see Olivia standing next to her desk holding her jacket. "Ah, yes. I was just about to shut down my computer. Have a great weekend," Madison was able to mutter.

Olivia placed her hand on Madison's shoulder. "Have a good time at your parents' house. Try to get some rest. Maybe call someone?"

Letting go of Madison's shoulder, she headed toward the elevators.

Maybe the trip down to her parents would be the break she needed.

†

With a large cup of coffee in hand, Madison remotely unlocked the car door, then climbed behind the wheel. The sun was up and it was a beautiful Saturday morning. She'd had trouble sleeping, replaying her conversation with Lauren.

In fact, she'd barely slept at that apartment since that night with Jerrica. She needed to find something more permanent, maybe out of the city. She started the engine of her rental car, grabbing her sunglasses from the visor. With the car now in gear, her favorite CD blaring from the speakers, she left the garage. The streets of Boston were mostly deserted this time of the morning so it should take no time to hit the highway out of town. It would take her approximately a half hour to get home. She wasn't in any rush to get there early, just in a rush to get out of the city, so she kept very close to the speed limit.

Images of Jerrica and Lauren fogged up her mind and she sighed in frustration. This was going to be a long trip if she couldn't keep her mind focused on driving. The closer she progressed to her parent's house, the faster the interstate signs began to pass.

Madison took a sip of her coffee, then adjusted her hands on the steering wheel as she took the right exit for 1-95 North, toward Newburyport, toward Jerrica, instead of left toward Collins Cove. Twenty minutes later, she clicked on her GPS as she turned onto the ramp that would lead her into downtown Newburyport. Removing the business card from her jacket pocket, Madison glanced at the address on the back. Speaking into the navigation system, within seconds she had directions to Jerrica's home.

A queasy feeling came to Madison the closer she came to Jerrica's. Slowing the car down, Madison gradually drove up to the front of the house. *Come on, Madison, you have to find out either way,* she told herself.

Pulling into the short driveway, she turned the engine off, her hands shaking. With a deep breath filling her lungs, she exited the vehicle, cautiously walking toward the house. Her hands were still shaking as she pushed the doorbell. Rocking back and forth on her heels, she waited for the door to open. When a substantial amount of time had passed, she rang the bell a second time. When the second bell went unanswered, she realized Jerrica wasn't home. Disappointed, she returned to her vehicle.

Still having time on her hands, she decided a nice drive along downtown would help calm her anxiety. The sun was bright in the sky. It was a New England, balmy, fifty-four degree day and shoppers heavily occupied the streets. The hustle and bustle of pedestrians caused the motor traffic to decrease gradually to a crawl. Madison didn't care, she was in no hurry to be anywhere right at that moment.

Every other car seemed to stop for shoppers waiting to cross the road. When Madison approached a busy crosswalk, she too had to halt for foot traffic. Pressing the accelerator to continue on, a shadow of a familiar figure entering a restaurant caught her eye. Madison quickly switched her blinker on to enter what looked like an alley to the parking lot behind the restaurant. Turning the vehicle off, Madison noticed her hands were trembling again. Heading for the entrance, that queasy feeling returned.

The host approached her the moment she stepped in the door. "Table for one?"

"No, thank you. I'm just looking for my friend," Madison responded to the host as she cased the room.

With a grin, the host stepped back, motioning her toward the patrons. Madison walked into the dining area to get a better look around, hoping to find that familiar face. After glancing around the room with no success, Madison turned to leave. Her heart stopped as the face she now sees in her dreams, in her apartment, and just about everywhere else, strolled across the restaurant floor. She observed Jerrica walk to a table, joining a female companion. Madison stood completely still, observing the interactions of the two women. Madison felt the color in her face start to drain as she watched the women touch in a warm embrace. Jerrica's companion caressed her hair. The pair held hands as they started talking, engrossed in one another.

Madison thought she was going to be sick. She was too late. Jerrica had already found someone else.

"Miss, did you find your friends?" queried the host.

"They're not here. Thanks," she answered as she dashed for the door,

Gasping for air the instant she stepped outside, Madison felt bile rising in her throat. Bending over, as she rounded the side of the building, she tried to stop the nauseating feeling. Her heart was thumping loudly in her ears and her chest suddenly felt tight. Madison put a hand to her chest as she struggled to get her breathing under control.

Slow deep breaths. This is not the time to have a panic attack. She didn't need a scene in the middle of downtown. Holding onto the side of the building, her breathing steadied as she returned to a standing position. Moving as quickly as she could, Madison rushed to her car.

You have no time to get upset, you need to get away from here.

Finally out of the city, she eased the car onto the interstate. Feeling a small tear trickle down her cheek, Madison regretfully headed for her parents.

†

By the time she turned into her parent's driveway, her eyes were no longer red. Her face was devoid of the tear stains that had covered her complexion a short time ago. Shifting her car into park, Madison didn't move. Resting her head on her hands, she realized she was not ready for the show she knew was about to unfold.

Act one—Her parents would start their mutual interrogation the moment she walked in the door.

Act two—Then once she was alone and settled they would individually find her, to ask the intimate questions. Her mother would ask about her love life, wanting details that she wouldn't ask in front of her father. Then her father would wander in and ask about her money situation, advancing job opportunities, etc.

Act three—Tomorrow morning the pair would try to convince her that she needed to move home to settle down. They never mentioned that they want her to be with a man and have many grandchildren but it's always implied. Even though they know she enjoys the company of women.

Act four—Madison leaving early, not talking to her parents for months afterwards. End of show.

She knew the theatrical production well. She was not ready for this at all, she thought, sitting back in her seat. She didn't want to open herself up to more criticism about her choices. She was definitely not ready to share the ache that constricted her chest and reveal the broken heart hidden beneath. A movement on Madison's left made her turn her head toward the house. Looking at the kitchen window, she could see her mother's face peering out. With sarcasm in her voice Madison spoke. "It's show time."

She had made it to the trunk to retrieve her overnight bag when she heard her father speak. "Hey, butter bean! What took you so long? We expected you earlier."

Butter bean was her father's favorite childhood nickname for her. The trunk clicked closed as Madison looked up at the porch where her parents stood. "I left a little later than I had anticipated, took my time getting here, enjoying the scenery," she explained, avoiding their watchful eyes.

Her foot came to rest on the top of the stairs as her father approached. Slapping her on the shoulder, he grinned. "Just like your old man, spending lots of time in the car."

Madison smiled as he grabbed her bag, disappearing into the house.

Like your old man, Madison pondered. Was she really like him?

George and Audrey Jeffery welcomed two healthy children born only a few years apart into their joyful lives. Due to complications with Madison's birth, Audrey could not conceive any more children. They were a happy family of four, at least that's the picture they portrayed to all their friends. Unbeknownst to her, Madison would become the son her father would never have. Throughout their childhood, her sister Sarah went to ballet classes while she went to karate. When she was old enough, George signed her up for a softball league. Whether she wanted to play or not, she did it for him because it made him proud. She went to college for marketing because of him as well. George was a top-notch sales representative in his day and it was an honorable profession to be part of, he would tell her. Madison followed the path she felt her parents wanted her to take for most of her young life until her last year in college.

At that point, Madison felt it was time to be honest with her family and stop hiding her true self from them. During a short weekend visit, she admitted to her family that she liked being in relationships with women better than men. The family unit was outraged about this new development.

"It's just a phase," her mother had said to her. "Once you're out of college, you'll change your mind. Everyone experiments in college, or so I've heard."

That's how Audrey dealt with stressful events in her life, she would convince herself it was a temporary problem, and it would soon go away. Her father on the other hand backed away from her emotionally. She didn't know if it was intentional or not, but realized she had lost the close bond they had once shared. All topics were up for discussion with her father, except her personal life, he would leave that for her mother to inquire about.

When the screen door closed behind him, Madison could feel the distance between them increase. Unexpectedly, her mother stepped in her line of view, wrapping her arms around her.

"Hi, Mom," she said pulling away from the stifling hug.

"Sweetie, you look thin. Have you been eating?"

"I weigh the same as I did the last time I saw you, Mom."

Her mother led them into the house. "I thought you were thin then, so my question still stands."

Madison tried hiding a smile. "Yes, I've been eating just fine. Thanks for asking. So how is everyone?"

Madison followed her into the kitchen. The smell of corned beef and cabbage wafted through the air.

"Everyone is well. I hope you brought your appetite, I cooked a complete boiled dinner for supper," she said and smiled, confidently.

"I am hungry, but don't you think that's a lot of food for the three of us?" Madison asked as she walked to the stove.

Lifting the lid to the boiling pot, she could smell the aromatic fragrances that reminded her of her youth. Not hearing a response, Madison set the cover back on the pot, turning to face her mom. She was standing across the room leaning on the counter; Madison noticed the baffled look on her face.

"We've invited your sister and her family. Didn't I tell you? We know Sarah would want to see you, too."

"Oh yeah, I'm sure Sarah wants to see you," her father said in a non-descriptive tone as he entered the room,

"I'm going upstairs to freshen up and rest for a little while. Let me know when everyone gets here," Madison muttered as she headed out of the room.

"Madison, dinner is at five o'clock. Your sister will be here around three." She heard her mother call the words after her. "Please come down and socialize."

"Yes, Mom," she yelled back as she reached the bedroom.

Stepping into the room, she quietly closed the door behind her. *Peace at last.* Leaning her back against the door, she looked around the bedroom. It still looked the same as when she was in high school. Strolling to her desk, she pushed the papers around that were tossed on top. None of these papers held any important information, so she tossed them in the trashcan.

Without hesitation, she hopped on the bed. Everything in this room belonged to her. Things she had grown up with. The memories were everywhere. She was home, everything should feel right, but it didn't. Madison felt disconnected from her surroundings. The young girl who used to spend so much time living in the private world of this room was gone. What remained was a woman, looking for acceptance from her family and her own place in the world. The ache in her chest was a constant reminder of precious time lost. Fatigue was winning as Madison stretched putting her hands behind her head, closing her eyes. A twenty-minute power nap and she should be good to go.

†

"Madison Marie Jeffery, wake up this instant!"

Bolting to a sitting position, Madison stared at her sister who was standing at the end of the bed. "What the hell, Sarah?"

She rubbed the sleep out of her eyes, as she swung her legs over the edge of the bed. Turning her head to glance at Sarah, who was now walking around the side, Madison noticed the closed bedroom door. She recognized, all too well, the irritated expression on Sarah's face.

I was only sleeping. Now what did I do to piss her off? she wondered.

"Who's Jerrica?" Sarah said as she came to a stop right in front of Madison, "I asked you a question, Madison. Who's Jerrica? Answer me, damn it!"

Madison knew if she tried to stand, she would push Sarah backwards, or Sarah would shove her back on the bed. Folding her arms across her chest Madison looked up into her big sister's face. "Jeez, Sarah, give me time to wake up. Besides, that's really none of you damn business. Now, let me up."

Sarah stepped a little closer, emphasizing she had the upper hand. "It is my damn business when I'm sent up here to get you and you're calling out this person's name and… and…."

"And what, Sarah, what exactly are you accusing me of?" Madison's voice was elevating.

Sarah was not backing down, no matter how uncomfortable she felt about this situation. She wasn't going to let her little sister win. "Fine, you want to know what I'm accusing you of, you were calling out her name and inappropriately touching yourself in your sleep."

She could see her sister's cheeks flush as she finished her sentence. Madison found the situation amusing. "I can't be held responsible for what I do in my sleep, Sarah. You should have knocked first. Now, step back Sarah or I'll make you step back," Madison said as she placed her palms on the bed.

Sarah flinched, stepping back as Madison stood.

Madison summed up her older sister. Sarah looked like she had put on a little weight around the hips, but other than that, she still had the same build. Her golden hair flowed long and today she was wearing designer glasses and not her usual contacts. The sisters stared at one another. Madison hadn't noticed before that Sarah was shorter than her by at least three inches. The major thing that hadn't changed in Sarah was the arrogance.

Maybe today will be the day I knock that chip off your shoulder dear sister.

Sarah had to look up as Madison stood in front of her. "What if Robbie had been sent up here to get you? Can you image what damage you would have caused him if he had seen that?"

"I would hope with your parenting skills drummed into him, Robbie would have knocked first," Madison countered.

Sarah's face turned deep red with anger. Without another word, Sarah turned to leave.

Madison's ego needed to get in the last word so she yelled as Sarah was closing the door, "Please tell Mom and Dad I'll be right down. I need to finish up."

The door slammed shut without a reply. Madison smiled to herself.

The Jeffery sisters had never gotten along, not even as children. In their parents' eyes, Sarah could do no wrong. Sarah was the picture perfect daughter, student, wife, and mother. Madison couldn't compete with Sarah's flawless life. She was the pretty princess to Madison's tomboy. Sarah went to ballet and then as she grew older started the local pageant circuit. In high school, she was part of the popular crowd and on the cheerleading squad. What she lacked in intelligence, she made up for in popularity. Sarah had made no plans for further academic paths after high school. Within a year of graduation, she had a part time job, which lasted four weeks, became pregnant, and got married. Even though their parents' didn't approve of the pregnancy before marriage, their perception of their princess never wavered. The first-born grandchild could do no wrong in everyone's eyes. Robbie was born two months after their wedding. He would be ten this year. Robbie was the apple of his aunt's eye and the bright spot in all their lives.

"Madison, are you coming down?" Her mother called her from the bottom of the stairway.

Madison walked to the door, opening it. "I'm coming."

Taking the stairs two at a time, the aroma of men's cologne wafted in the air. The smell shocked her nostrils the moment she entered the living room, making her nose wrinkle. Her brother-in-law, Martin, rose off the couch, moving to give her a hug.

"What you smell is not coming from me," he commented, releasing her. "Your nephew has decided he needs to wear cologne. Girls like men who wear cologne, he says."

"Most women do, but they don't want to smell them states away," Madison said, waving a hand in front of her nose.

Martin chuckled, returning to the couch to continue reading the paper.

Madison followed the assaulting odor into the kitchen.

Her mother was the first one to see her. "Did you enjoy your nap sweetheart?"

Madison glanced at her sister who was scowling down at the table as she folded napkins.

"Actually, it was very pleasurable. Thanks for asking, Mom."

Sarah flinched, getting up in haste. "I'm going to find out what Robbie and Grandpa are up to."

Heading for the backyard, Sarah slammed the door behind her.

Her mother looked from the door to Madison who was raising her shoulders in mock confusion.

I win, Madison beamed inwardly. Turning her attention back to her mom, she asked,. "Why is dad outside with Robbie?"

"Well, I image Martin has told you this overpowering aroma is from my grandson," she answered, nodding her head. "Your father thought it might be a good idea if they spent some time outside in hopes the scent would diminish."

"I think a hot shower and a good scrubbing would do a better job."

Strolling to the sink to look out the window at the yard, she saw that little Robbie was running around with the football and her dad was hot on his trail. Madison looked down into the sink, feeling a little sadness as she realized her dad finally had a boy in the family. "I guess I should go out there and save George," Martin said, standing next to her.

"Martin!" Madison punched him the arm. "Don't sneak up on me, you ass."

Martin rubbed his arm were she had hit him. "Mother Jeffery, are you going to let her treat me like that?"

"I probably would have hit you, too if you had sneaked up on me like that," her mother said not looking up from the bowl she was wiping dry.

"Tough crowd," Martin smiled at them. "I'd better go outside were I'm appreciated."

Madison watched Martin act like a wounded animal as he joined the others. She stood at the window for a few minutes longer, watching everyone share Robbie's attention.

"So, Madison," she cringed when she heard her mother speak in a questioning tone. "How are you doing?"

Madison exhaled and turned around to face the inquisition. "I'm doing fine, Mom. The new job is good, very busy." Madison moved closer to the table.

"So, you're still working for, um…what was her name?"

"Olivia, Mom."

"Yes, Olivia. I thought that job was only temporary."

"I've only worked for her six years now. The experience and connections I am making now, I'll be able to take anywhere in my career," Madison answered, a little confused. Her father usually asked these types of questions. "Mom, is this really what you want to talk to me about?"

Audrey knew her tactic was transparent to her daughter and decided to be honest. "No dear, it's not. How are you really doing?"

Madison sat at the table across from where her mother was standing. "Honestly Mom, I'm doing fine. I'm not dating anyone and haven't been for almost a year now. I don't have any children I don't know about and since there's been no dating, there is no significant other. Olivia has signed a contract with this company for at least two years. Therefore, if I continue to work for her, I'll be in New England for the next two years. Did I cover everything?"

Audrey was making imaginary figure eights on the tabletop with her index finger, thinking. "You know I love you."

Here it comes, Madison thought as she sat back in her chair.

"I just worry that you're living alone in that big city. I want you to find someone, settle down, and be happy. That's not too much to ask, is it?"

"Why can't you understand that I am happy with my life? I'm only in my mid-twenties. I'm not ready to settle in my work or my love life. I'm not Sarah and will never be."

Audrey heard the anger in her daughter's voice. "Don't take that tone with me."

Madison looked down at the table.

"I never asked you to be Sarah. I just worry about the paths you are taking in life."

Closing her eyes, Madison counted, trying to control the anger that was building inside. Reaching the number ten, she opened her eyes, speaking just above a whisper, "You're talking about my career, right, Mom? Because, we will be headed for an argument real quick if you're talking about my personal life…again and the fact that you don't approve of my lifestyle."

Audrey paused as if debating her next sentence.

"Hey! That smells good. Is supper ready?" George asked as he entered the house with the tribe following close behind.

Audrey greeted her husband with a hug, whispering in his ear.

George forced a smile as he looked from his wife to his daughter. He could tell by the expression on Madison's face that the rest of the family had interrupted something important between the two of them and neither one of them seemed happy.

"Robbie, go give your auntie a hug," Martin said as he stepped aside.

Madison's face softened the instant she saw Robbie running toward her. Standing quickly, she picked him up in her arms, swinging him around in a tight bear hug.

"Auntie Roo," Robbie yelled as she carefully settled him back on the ground.

"You've gotten so tall since the last time I saw you. How's my handsome young man doing?"

"I'm doing great. I've missed you, Auntie Roo. Did you bring me something?"

The innocence of a child, Madison thought.

"Robbie, that's not polite. You don't ask people for presents," Sarah corrected her son harshly.

Madison could see the sadness in Robbie's eyes, knowing he would have to apologize. She interrupted him before he could speak, "As a matter of fact, yes, I did bring something for you, little one, but I think we are just about to have supper. I'll give it to you later, okay? Now I need you to do me a favor. Please take these folded napkins to the table, placing one at each dish setting for me. Can you do that?"

A big smile spread across Robbie's face as he carefully took the napkins from her hand and raced into the dining room. Robbie looked back at his dad, who gave him thumbs up as he exited the room.

"You shouldn't encourage him," Sarah commented dryly.

"Robbie just loves his Auntie that's all. He knows I'll always bring him something when I return home. It's no big deal," she said, returning to her seat.

Everyone started mulling around the kitchen as Sarah went to the sink to wash her hands. Sarah turned to face Madison. With an evil smirk on her face, she mumbled just loud enough for Madison to hear. "Well, since you don't have any children, I guess you wouldn't know any better."

Madison was on her feet in seconds rushing toward Sarah with anger in her eyes.

Sarah's grin broadened as she stepped behind an unaware Martin for protection.

Martin, who had been talking to his father-in-law, turned just in time to grab Madison's right arm as it reached for his wife.

"Hey," Martin cried out. "What's going on here?"

"Let go of my wrist, Martin, and step out of the way. This is between Sarah and me."

Martin realized Madison wasn't looking at him, but through him at Sarah.

"I don't think so," Martin tightened his grip. "Why don't you and I go out on the porch for some fresh air."

Still holding her wrist, Martin put his other hand on her shoulder, backing Madison toward the door.

"All right," Madison yelled, ripping her wrist from his grasp. "I'll go outside."

Audrey turned to her eldest daughter. "Wipe that smug look off your face, young lady, and tell me what the hell just happened."

Grabbing a spare sweatshirt off the back of a kitchen chair, Martin followed Madison outside, leaving her parents confused as to what had just transpired.

Madison followed the wraparound porch to the front of the house. The view from the front of the house was spectacular. Across the street from her parents' house was a panoramic view of Collins Cove. The sun glistening off the water always relaxed her. She never appreciated the serenity that the porch offered until now. Madison tilted her head toward the sky listening closely to the small waves lapping the rocky shore.

"Would you like to talk about what just happened in there," Martin inquired as he leaned against the railing.

"Yeah, your wife is a bitch," Madison said confidently, without looking at him.

She heard Martin chuckle. Madison turned to face him, resting her left arm on the railing. "Sarah just knows how to get under my skin."

Martin reached over, placing a reassuring hand on her shoulder. "Madison, you let her, so it's partially your fault. Yes, Sarah can be hard to handle sometimes, but it's like fireworks whenever you two are together. Again, I don't know what happened in there, but can we at least get along long enough to make it through dinner?"

"Tell your barracuda wife to stay off my back for the rest of the night and everything will go smoothly."

With a large smile, Martin patted Madison's shoulder and headed for the door to go back into the house. "Are you coming, Madison?" he asked, reaching for the door handle.

"I'll be right in. I need a little time by myself. Tell Mom and Dad I'll be right there," Madison said over her shoulder.

She heard the door click shut behind her and exhaled a deep breath. Sarah was right, she didn't have children, but that didn't give her the right to throw it in her face every chance she could. Sarah had the life she had dreamed about since being a child, a great husband, and beautiful son. She had a two-story dream home in the suburbs and their parents wrapped around her finger. Her parents were so proud of their first-born. Out of nowhere, Jerrica's face flashed across her mind, causing a sharp pain in her chest. Madison clung to the railing tightly. She struggled to clear her mind. She had to stop torturing herself.

By the time Madison reappeared in the dining room, the meal was on the table. She sat in the seat left vacant for her. Robbie was on her right, her mother on her left and positioned across, on the other side, was Sarah. They were sitting across from one another, with their mother as referee.

Martin was the first one to break the silence. "Well now that everyone is here, let's devour this delicious meal prepared by my wonderful mother-in-law."

"Thank you, Martin. You are my favorite son-in-law," Audrey said with a smile.

Sarah rolled her eyes as she passed Martin the bowl of cabbage.

Dinner moved along at a comfortable pace. Conversation at the Jeffery supper table was light and fluffy. Madison added to the banter when requested, but most of the time she kept to herself. When dinner was wrapping up and the table was being cleared, Madison stood behind her chair, as Sarah approached.

Standing directly in front of her sister, Sarah whispered into Madison's ear.

"I promised Martin I would be good and not start any trouble, but I've been holding this inside for years now."

Glancing around Madison to make sure they weren't being watched, she continued, "I want you to get back on your high horse and go back to the city. Everything was fine while you were gone. Therefore, you need to disappear and stay disappeared. Stay out of my life, my family's life and stay away from Mom and Dad."

Sarah looked into Madison's face. The hurt in Madison's eyes must have made Sarah feel guilty for what she had said but she would never apologize to her sister.

Their mother returned just in time to see Sarah walk away from Madison, leaving the room.

Madison tried to tuck her emotions deep inside as her mother put her hand on her shoulder.

"Are you girls playing nice?"

Madison spun around to look at her. Before she could speak, she glanced over her mother's head to see Sarah standing in the doorway. Without breaking eye contact with Sarah she replied to her mother. "We are just fine, Mom."

Sarah backed out of the doorway, disappearing into the kitchen.

Audrey knew something was wrong with her youngest daughter, but didn't want to pry, so she patted her on the shoulder, bringing dirty dishes back to the kitchen.

Madison stood alone in the dining room with her troubling thoughts. Was she that bad of a person that even her sister didn't want her visiting? First Jerrica stops coming to work to avoid her, and now her family didn't want her here either. Madison felt so lost not knowing where she belonged anymore. For the second time today, Madison felt like she was going to vomit.

"Mom, I'm suddenly not feeling well. I'm going upstairs to lie down," she called out, walking toward the stairway.

Madison was halfway up the staircase when her mother came to the bottom. "Baby, do you need anything?

Are you going to be all right? I can come up there if you need me."

"I'm going to be fine, Mom. I just need some more rest. That's all," Madison said as she reached the second floor.

With a massive ache in her heart, she closed the bedroom door, finally allowing herself to

weep silently.

Chapter Eleven

When Jerrica had awakened that morning, she had no real plans to leave the house. She would go for a run, shower, and finish up some work from the office. That was her original plan for a beautiful Saturday. Once her music player was on her arm, Jerrica was out the door into the cool air. She found she had more time with working at home to enjoy things she had long forgotten. Jerrica used to run every morning when she first moved to Newburyport. She loved the peaceful streets, taking in the exquisite architecture of the old homes that lined up in rows behind the brick laid sidewalks. It always amazed her at how extensive in size these historic dwellings were for single households. Many of these buildings were now modernized for multi-family apartments. Jerrica still thought this city was beautiful, that's why she had moved here. Odd things one thinks about while running. With her favorite music in her ear and the rhythmic sound her shoes made, Jerrica was able to clear her mind.

Glancing down at her watch, she elected to shorten her run and head back home to get more work done. Seeing her townhouse in the distance, Jerrica slowed her pace for a cool down period. She figured by the time she reached the front door, her pulse should be close to normal. With her schedule mentally in place, she smiled at the orderliness. Once in the house, she headed for the shower to cool off.

"Hello? Hello," she yelled into the annoyingly ringing phone.

"There is no need to yell, Jerrica, I can hear you just fine," said the voice on the other end.

"Katherine! I'm sorry. I had to hunt down my cell phone. I think the kitten was playing with it. You're lucky you caught me at all, I was just about to get in the shower," Jerrica said as she sat on the edge of her bed.

"I'm going to be up in your area today and I thought maybe we could catch some lunch, if you're up to visiting."

"That would be wonderful, when and where?"

"How about eleven forty-five at our favorite restaurant?"

"Eleven forty-five sounds great, so I'll see you there," she said smiling as she disconnected the call.

"Well, I had better hustle a little if I'm going to make it on time," she told herself.

Once in the shower, Jerrica realized her well-constructed plan was now out the window and she would have to re-evaluate the rest of the day once she returned home. Tossing on her favorite pair of jeans and a light yellow sweater, she walked toward the living room to grab shoes.

"Ah hell, let's live a little," she said, grabbing her high-heeled, calf-high motorcycle boots and sliding them on.

These boots gave her an additional inch in height and just having them on made her feel sexier somehow. The boot made her almost as tall as Katherine. She knew it was just lunch with a friend, but it had been so long since she felt sexy, she needed it, even if it was just through a pair of boots.

†

Jerrica pulled around the back of the restaurant to park, seeing that Katherine's car was already there. The car was empty so she assumed Katherine was inside. Jerrica stood under the entrance sign for the Starboard Gallery Restaurant. Keys and cell in left hand, wallet with ID in back pocket, she had everything. When she first entered, she viewed the room for her friend. Not seeing her anywhere, she decided to walk through the dining area. After circling the tables a couple times, Jerrica recognized a voice calling her name. She spotted Katherine a few tables behind where she was standing, trying to get her attention. Jerrica acknowledged her friend, walking in her direction.

With a big smile and open arms, Katherine enfolded Jerrica in a huge embrace. Before Katherine let her go, she kissed her on the cheek. They both smiled at one another, then sat down to talk. The server took their orders for drinks and an appetizer, and then disappeared quickly. When the table had settled down to just the two of them, Katherine asked her. "So, my friend, how have you been?"

"I have been doing great. Job is good. House is fine," Jerrica, said trying to sound upbeat.

Katherine tilted her head to the side, questioning the quick response with her eyes.

"How are your parents?" she asked. "Do you even know?"

"If you came all this way to give me a guilt trip, you can turn around and go home," Jerrica commented harshly.

"I'm not here to give you a guilt trip. I happened to run into your mom the other day and she told me she hadn't heard from you in a while. Then I started thinking that I hadn't heard from you either. I started to worry," Katherine said, as the server appeared with their food and drinks. She disappeared again just as quickly.

"Katherine, we've known one another for a long time now and you should know that if there was anything wrong, I would call you."

The table went silent as Jerrica sipped on her drink and Katherine took some of the appetizer.

"I have my doubts you would," Katherine answered finally.

Jerrica heard the disappointment in her voice. "When my marriage was breaking up, who did I tell first?"

"You told me. I know that. You've vanished from your family and your friends in New Hampshire. I know you better than you know yourself, Jerrica. You're worrying me." Katherine reached out to hold Jerrica's folded hands.

Jerrica wanted to slide her hands away, but knew Katherine was right. She was hiding something. Jerrica closed her eyes, considering if she should tell Katherine the truth.

Katherine rubbed her thumb on the back of Jerrica's hand. "Tell me…."

Jerrica began unfolding her tale, starting with Devin, the fact that she was working from home now and her confusion about Madison. She admitted to herself and to Katherine that she felt misplaced in her own life.

Katherine listened closely to her friend's troubles. Being the understanding friend, she spoke calmly. "I won't offer you advice. What I can offer you is my honest opinion, if you want to hear it."

Jerrica wasn't sure she was ready for one of Katherine's honest opinion speeches. They had been friends since they were in grade school and even though they were the same age, Katherine always seemed mature beyond her years. After graduation, they had split ways. Katherine attended the University of California at Santa Cruz and then went off to Stanford University of Medicine to be a doctor. She was now working on her last year of residency at a top New Hampshire Hospital. Engaged for two years now, her fiancé wanted to hold off getting married until she finished her residency. Katherine had always known she wanted to help people, so she chose medicine for her career.

Jerrica smiled at the memory of them as children. In some small way, Jerrica envied her for designing a plan for her future and staying with something she loved doing.

"What are you thinking? You spaced out of the conversation," Katherine asked as she saw a hint of a smile on Jerrica's face.

"I was just remembering our childhood together," Jerrica said with a doubtful smile. "Okay, doc, give it to me straight. I can take the pain."

"All right…I have supported you in every decision you've made. I stood by you during your divorce. I was the one who helped you come out to your parents. We have been through many things together, Jerrica, but I honestly do not know how I can help you this time. I think this Devin person is just trying to jerk you around. And about your problems with work, I think it's time to decide if this is going to be your career. You're still young enough to switch careers without too much trouble," she added, pausing to sip her drink. "Now…this thing with Madison. You told me that you weren't sure how you feel for her. My friend, if you think you love this woman, you need to find out. I'm not saying jump in the sack again right away, but take your time to get to know one another. Sex fades, sweetheart, you need to find out if there is something else between the two of you."

Jerrica knew she was right. Katherine was always right.

"You need to face your demons, Jerrica. You need to face Madison. That's the only way you're going to be able to move forward."

"So," Jerrica tried to change the subject. "How's the job and hubby?"

Katherine frowned at her friend. "Nice way of changing the subject, Jerrica. Patrick and I are not married yet, remember? There are no immediate plans to change that situation. Oh, and the hospital experience…loving it!"

Jerrica's smile grew bigger at her friend's answer. "I know you're not married yet, I just like to tease you about this long engagement."

Katherine made a silly face at Jerrica's comment, causing Jerrica to burst out laughing. *We're quite a pair,* Jerrica thought.

Katherine glanced at her watch. "Sorry to say this, but I have to go soon. I have an appointment at two with a representative from Anna Jacques Hospital. That's actually why I was going to be in your area today."

"I thought you were still doing your residency?"

"I have less than a year to finish. I'm keeping my options open," Katherine said as she fiddled for something in her purse.

"Does Patrick know that's why you're here today?"

"As a matter of fact, he doesn't. He doesn't control my career, Jerrica. He'll respect my decision if I choose to move to a different hospital than where he practices. Lunch is on me."

Jerrica watched as she waved down the server giving her eighty dollars without even looking at the bill, telling her to keep the change. Walking arm in arm back to the parking lot, the two women bantered back and forth about silly things, trying to end their visit on a positive note.

"Don't forget to call your parents," Katherine ordered as she pulled out of the parking lot.

Back at home, Jerrica set up her computer on the table with her files spread out in front of her. She had changed into her sleepy shorts and tank to be comfortable while working. She closed all the blinds so she could get some work done and not daydream. Stretching her arm, she grabbed the first folder. The rest of her exciting day was spent going through each new client's information. She paused only twice. Once to feed the cats, the second for her needs. When the pile started to dwindle down to just a couple of folders, she glanced at her cell phone for the time. It was midnight. What had happened to her Saturday? She had totally lost track of time.

Saving her work, she closed the computer. Standing up stiffly, she reached for the ceiling, stretching her aching body. She switched lights off as she exited the downstairs, then headed straight for bed. She seemed very tired all of a sudden. She flopped on the bed, quickly falling into a much-needed slumber.

Chapter Twelve

The loud pounding noise startled Jerrica from sleep. She sat motionless in the dark, wondering if she had heard something or just dreamt it. A few seconds went by in silence. Figuring it was just part of her dream, she started to lie back down. Inches before her head hit the pillow, the doorbell echoed through the house. Glancing at her nightstand, the clock read 2:45 a.m.

Who, the hell could that be? she wondered.

Tossing the covers off and grabbing her glasses, she exited the room with her baseball bat in hand, heading for the front door. Reaching the foyer, she clicked on the outside light and looked out the peephole. Gasping in surprise, she stepped back.

"Jerrica, could you please let me in?"

Jerrica stood frozen, not knowing what to do. She felt the blood drain from her body.

"Please, Jerrica, let me in. We need to talk."

"How did you find out where I live?"

"I'll explain everything to you if you just let me in. It's kind of cold out here."

Jerrica set the bat down, numbly reached for the deadbolt, and unlocked it. Unsure of what she was doing, she put her hand on the doorknob and pulled the door open.

Madison walked passed Jerrica, rubbing her biceps to diminish the cold.

Jerrica inhaled the sweet scent of her perfume. The foyer light was the only illumination in the downstairs, but Jerrica could still distinguish the worn shape-hugging blue jeans that accentuated every curve and a very complimenting form-fitted long-sleeve blue shirt.

"Let me get some lights on in here," Jerrica choked as she closed the door, rushing past Madison to click on the other lights.

With multiple fixtures lighting the rooms, Jerrica turned back to her visitor, "Please have a seat. Would you like something to drink?"

Madison glanced around Jerrica's home, amazed at the surroundings.

When she didn't answer, Jerrica stepped closer, repeating softly. "Madison, please come in and have a seat. Would you like something to drink?"

Madison managed a smile and a nod as Jerrica motioned her toward the front room. Jerrica entered the kitchen.

Madison was overwhelmed as Jerrica's private world engulfed her. She traveled by the open concept kitchen, glancing at what looked like a family portrait wall. She wanted to stop to examine the beautiful faces, but wasn't sure she had the right to enter her personal space that way.

Following the flow of lights, she entered what she thought could be the living room. The walls were a light neutral color, but in this light Madison wasn't sure of the exact color. There was a row of floor-to-ceiling curtains along the length of the wall in front of her. Everywhere she looked, she saw expressions of Jerrica, from the mismatched throw pillows on the tan couch to the exquisite painting of the mountains that hung above the fireplace. There was a mahogany coffee table in front of the couch with two wood accented recliners set parallel to the couch. Most of the furniture seemed modern and fresh. This was Jerrica's world and she could see how everything seemed to fit.

Where do I fit? Madison wondered as she made her way to the couch, sitting just as Jerrica handed her a glass of liquid. Madison examined the contents as Jerrica sat across from her.

"It's just water, ice with a slice of lemon. I didn't know what else to serve."

Jerrica watched Madison bring the glass to her lips. *Those lips…what those lips can do to her.*

Madison watched the blush develop on Jerrica's face and smiled. Madison took in the full vision that was Jerrica Kerrison, above the rim of her glass. From her semi-tussled hair, to the arousing look of her in glasses, to the tank top and boxer short set she filled out extremely well.

"So, Madison, why are you here at this hour?" she said, trying to get the conversation started.

Madison set her glass down in front of her. Her gaze met Jerrica's as she spoke just above a whisper, "I needed to talk to you. I know it doesn't really mean anything now that you're with someone else and that there is no place for me in your life, but I need to know what happened to you…to us. You just disappeared after…that night."

"Back up a little. What do you mean, someone else?"

Madison eyes couldn't conceal her sadness as she continued. "I was in town earlier today and happened to see you entering a restaurant. I watched as you met with another woman. The way you looked at her, I could tell the two of you have chemistry."

Madison tried holding back her sigh, but to her dismay her aching heart pushed it out anyway.

Remembering the events of the day, Jerrica shook her head, clarifying. "Yes, she and I do have chemistry."

Madison's heart sank as she took in Jerrica's words.

"Her name is Katherine. She is my oldest and dearest friend. But she is just my friend."

Jerrica watched Madison's spirits lift a little with this new revelation, but it was short-lived.

She again pressed on the original subject Jerrica was avoiding. "Then, if it's not someone else, then what? Talk to me, Jerrica. I can't stand it anymore—not knowing what happened…"

Jerrica lowered her head to stare at the glass resting on her knee. "What do you want to talk about? So much happened that night," she asked trying to buy herself some time.

Becoming extremely nervous, Madison slid to the edge of the couch. "What happened with you, Jerrica? Why did you let me take you home, take you to my bed, and then disappear without saying a word? Did you even consider how I would feel when I woke up the next morning alone?" Madison was fighting to keep her emotions in check.

Jerrica swished the ice cubes around, searching for a response that would satisfy Madison.

Madison wanted so much to jump up and hold her, to go back to that night when it was just the two of them. Watching Jerrica fight with her emotions was too much for Madison to bear. Standing, Madison turned to leave.

Seeing the sudden movement reflecting in her glass, Jerrica stood and grabbed Madison's arm. "Please don't go."

The contact sent a shock of excitement flooding through their bodies. Staring at the hand on her arm, Madison stood motionless. With eyes focused on the warm hand touching her, Madison spoke gently. "You feel that, don't you?"

Madison watched as the warm hand slid up her forearm onto her bicep before pulling away. The excitement that had begun when they touched lingered when contact was broken.

"Please stay," Jerrica whispered.

Seated back on the couch, Madison watched Jerrica returned to her chair, placing her glass on the corner of the table. Jerrica's chest nervously expanded with an intake of air then slowly, cautiously released it. "I was hoping that this conversation wouldn't happen," Jerrica commented honestly.

"What do you mean by hoping this wouldn't happen?"

"Being confronted when I don't have clear answers for you." she said, looking at her hands in her lap. "I thought if I gave us some distance, you would forget about that night, forget about me. You're a beautiful woman, Madison, and you can easily find someone else. I mean it was just sex, right."

Is that what Jerrica thought it was, just sex? That can't be true. Madison could feel the panic rising. Regaining enough composure, she left the couch, walking to stand in front of Jerrica. Kneeling to face her, she enfolded her hands around Jerrica's trembling ones.

Jerrica absorbed the warmth and electricity from Madison's touch, but couldn't look directly at her.

"Tell me you don't feel something every time we touch. Tell me your heart doesn't skip a beat whenever you look at me. Tell me that our night together was only sex to you." Madison let out a ragged breath, "If you can look me in the eyes and honestly tell me you feel nothing and that our night meant nothing, then I'll go, putting us in the past, and—"

Emotion overtook Madison, her throat constricted and moisture clouded her vision.

†

The sudden drop in conversation prompted Jerrica to lift her head. She could see the pain just behind the settling

190

tears, but as she looked beyond the raw pain, she saw a woman that was offering her more than just one night of sex. Jerrica reached out, brushing a stray tear from Madison's cheek.

"Yes. I felt…something," she replied in a low tone. "Yes, I get breathless every time we are in the same room. Yes, just yes...." She leaned in swiftly, pressing her lips to Madison's.

The contact increased as Jerrica pushed her chair back kneeling on the floor, their bodies pressing together. With a small moan, Jerrica's lips parted to receive Madison's sensual tongue. She felt dizzy as Madison's tongue played and taunted her senses. She held Madison's face in the palms of her hands while Madison caressed the bare skin of her back under her tank.

"Stop," Jerrica cried as she wrenched her face away. "We can't do this. I can't do this to you again."

Jerrica hands moved down to Madison's side trying to push her away. Madison's hands slid up to Jerrica's shoulders preventing her from fleeing the situation again. She turned her head away from Madison just as the flow of emotions cascaded down her face.

Madison felt her resistance ease, allowing her to draw Jerrica into an uncontested embrace.

Jerrica buried her face into Madison's neck in hopes it would dull the sound of her own sobs.

Madison tilted her head until her cheek was lightly brushing Jerrica's, softly whispering in her ear. "It's all right. We'll get through this."

✝

What are you afraid of Jerrica? Madison wondered. She waited patiently letting time pass by, holding the woman who was softly weeping on her shoulder. She could hear Jerrica's sobs transitioning into soft sniffles. The corners of Madison's mouth lifted as she felt Jerrica's arms strengthen around her waist pulling her in closer. "Jerrica, please talk to me."

Madison felt Jerrica tilt her head, their eyes meeting immediately. Madison gazed at the gorgeous face with puffy cheeks, a cute little red nose and exhaustion written in her beautiful eyes. Madison verbalized what she felt they both needed at that moment, "Before we say something we may regret out of exhaustion, I think we should get some rest. I would like to stay. I'll sleep down here on the couch, so there is no issue with sleeping arrangements."

Madison reluctantly released the embrace, rocking backward onto her feet to stand up. Her knees protested with a dull ache as she straightened her legs out to stand. Trying not to wince in pain, she extended her hand to help Jerrica off the floor. With Jerrica on her feet, Madison slowly brushed her sore knees.

Jerrica chuckled to herself as she watched the display unfold. "Either I'm a really bad house keeper or someone had trouble getting up off the floor."

"Are you accusing me of something?" Madison returned a sexy grin.

Giggling, Jerrica offered Madison her hand.

Madison's eyes glimpsed at the invitation of the open hand and then back to Jerrica's face.

"I can't have you sleeping on my couch. I don't even sleep on my couch, I'm too tall," Jerrica said confidently.

With a wary smile, Madison entwined their fingers and allowed herself to be led up the stairs.

Releasing her hand as they reached the second floor landing Jerrica stepped close enough to whisper in her ear, "The room behind you is the guest room where you will be sleeping."

When she stepped back, she could tell by Madison's posture and expression, this was not what she had expected. "The room is cluttered, but the sheets and blankets are clean. The bathroom is right here," she added, pointing to the door on her right. "And at the end of the hall is my bedroom."

Madison did not attempt to argue, she just nodded.

When Jerrica realized Madison wasn't going to protest, she walked toward her bedroom. Jerrica could feel a set of eyes on her as she entered the room. Turning she saw that indeed Madison was staring and did not attempt to avert her eyes when Jerrica caught her staring.

"Goodnight," Jerrica said as she slowly pushed her door closed.

Her first instinct was to rush to the mirror and inspect her reflection, but she resisted the urge. Right now, she was too tired to consider what she looked like at that moment. Leaning back on the closed door, she brushed her fingertips on her lips. She could still feel Madison's soft lips. The heat from deep inside returned. For a brief second, Jerrica considered asking Madison to join her, but pushed it away. As much as her body wanted Madison's touch, her mind had decided this was the right thing to do at this moment. She flopped on her bed, willing her mind to clear. Closing her eyes, she prayed for sleep.

†

Madison sat on the edge of the bed in the guest bedroom, wondering how she had ended up here. Looking around, she realized that Jerrica must not have many quests. The room contained boxes along the wall in front of her. There was a small office desk underneath the window, covered by more boxes. Leaning on the footboard was a mountain bike, not your typical décor for a guestroom.

She had watched Jerrica enter her bedroom and wasn't bashful when Jerrica caught her staring. Madison had hoped Jerrica would change her mind, but knew at 'goodnight' that she would be sleeping alone. Having forgotten her overnight bag at her parents' house, she decided to sleep in her shirt and panties. Maybe she could ask Jerrica to borrow something to wear so she could get home tomorrow. Or was that today, now? Lying back on the full sized bed, she pulled a blanket up to her waist and clicked the light off. Staring at the ceiling, she replayed the events of the evening in her head. "What am I doing?" she mumbled aloud, closing her eyes.

Chapter Thirteen

The sound of running water surprised Jerrica from a restless sleep. Her eyes focused in on her alarm clock, which read just after one in the afternoon and she swiftly remembered she had a houseguest. In an instant, the water had shut off and the townhouse fell silent. When the bathroom door opened, Jerrica's heartbeat quickened, listening to the footsteps. Tilting her head, she glanced at the now partially opened door, seeing Madison step into view.

"Good afternoon, sleepy head," Madison said as she leaned on the door casing. "Would it be possible for me to borrow some clothes to wear home? I forgot to bring any with me."

Jerrica caught her breath as she stared at Madison, wrapped only in a towel. "Uh-huh…you can find t-shirts…in the top drawer of that dresser and sweats in the…bottom," she offered, absently pointing in the direction of the dresser.

With a smile, Madison rushed across the room, gathering the items she needed then retreated into the hallway. She mouthed thank you to Jerrica as she left the room.

Jerrica watched every move and was mesmerized by the exquisite flow of motion. She was also unexpectedly aroused. Closing her eyes, taking in a deep breath, she called out. "Madison."

A few seconds went by before Madison re-appeared in the doorway. She stepped into the bedroom and their eyes locked onto one another. Madison could see the desire in Jerrica's eyes and shivered with excitement.

With hesitation Madison spoke softly. "Jerrica, you need to be very clear on what you want me to do here. I won't have any more regrets lingering between us."

"I need you to hold me. I need to feel you…" Jerrica replied shyly.

She grabbed the blankets, flipping them down as Madison tossed her towel on a nearby chair, climbing under the covers.

Madison's body slid onto the sheet as she covered her naked form with the blankets. Madison sighed as Jerrica slipped out of her cloths, removing the last barrier between them.

Jerrica turned on her side, her back to Madison, hair brushed off her shoulder. She heard a low groan from Madison as she slid behind her, molding their bodies together.

Sliding her arm over Jerrica's side and onto the tight abdomen, Madison pulled Jerrica closer.

Jerrica moved back into Madison's embrace. She closed her eyes, enjoying the feelings rushing through her body. Jerrica felt safe, but aroused at the same time.

Madison sighed next to her earlobe. "You're driving me crazy. I want to make love to you."

Jerrica's hips twitched with excitement.

Pausing only long enough to take in a deep breath, she whispered. "I can't hold it back any longer, I love you, Jerrica. I have since the moment we met."

Madison felt Jerrica tense, but she didn't struggle to get away. She couldn't see Jerrica's expression as she continued. "This has never happened to me before. Every time you're near, I want to hold you, protect you from anything that might do you harm. I would give you the moon if you asked me,"

Madison was vulnerable. "These past weeks have just about killed me, not being able to talk to you. Not being able to tell you how I felt."

Heart exposed, Madison waited for Jerrica.

Jerrica was quiet, reeling from what she just heard. *So it was true, Madison loved her,* she repeated in her mind. Her heart swelled with joy and fear. Fear that if she gave her heart, Madison would crush it. Devin had damaged her so much, she couldn't go through that pain again. If she couldn't verbalize how she felt, maybe she could show her.

The stillness in the air grew between them until Madison could take no more. "Jerrica, say something."

With tear-filled eyes, Jerrica rolled to face Madison. Jerrica closed the small gap between them, kissing Madison sensually, but firmly on the lips.

The kiss deepened, her lips parted to receive Jerrica's soft probing tongue. Madison's mind was telling her she needed to know how Jerrica was feeling, but her body was clouding her judgment.

Not releasing the kiss, Jerrica eased Madison onto her back, covering her body with her own. Licking the edge of Madison's lips, she pulled away, looking into eyes filled with love…for her. For the first time in her life, she truly knew that someone loved her. With a touch as soft as a feather, she trailed light kisses down Madison's neck, making her way between her breasts.

Madison inhaled quickly when Jerrica took a nipple in her mouth. "Mm…mm…" escaped Madison's parted lips as Jerrica circled the bud with her tongue.

Gently biting the erect nipple, Jerrica changed positions to entice the other breast with her mouth. She moved lower, carefully kissing the soft exposed skin of

Madison's abdomen. She wanted to make the pleasure last for both of them this time.

Madison jerked her hips as Jerrica slid between her legs, kissing her inner thigh. Every nerve was in overdrive, making every touch ache with desire. "Oh, my God," Madison groaned as Jerrica's mouth touched her.

Stroking the sensitive skin with her tongue, Jerrica slid her tongue between Madison's tender folds, the tip of her tongue delicately flicking the swollen bud. Jerrica slowed her pace not wanting to move too quickly. The soft moans emanating from the trembling woman under her, encouraged her to continue the sweet torture.

Madison lifted her hips, opening herself to Jerrica as the euphoria took her higher and higher with each caress. Her hands clutched sheets as the spasms ripped through her. "Jerrica…," she breathed as the swift orgasm roared its way across her.

The sound of Madison calling her name caused a tear of joy to run down Jerrica's cheek, mixing with Madison's beautiful fragrance. Jerrica lessened the pressure as the ripples of bliss that assaulted every inch of Madison's body began to subside. Leisurely, she moved back, kissing the soft skin of Madison's thigh. As she slid herself fully over her lover, Jerrica smiled down at the beautiful woman. Placing her hands on either side of Madison, she pushed to a sitting position, straddling Madison's hips. "Look at me."

Through the fogginess of passion, Madison gradually opened her eyes. Jerrica paused briefly, watching the light haze of ecstasy clear. Jerrica's green eyes sparkled as she held Madison's gaze. Whispering, Jerrica released all her fears and doubts, finally being able to verbalize how she felt. "I love you."

Madison's eyes filled with tears, spilling over. Lifting her hand to Jerrica's face, she lightly rubbed her cheek with her thumb as she spoke. "Don't say anything you don't mean."

Jerrica covered the soft hand on her face with her own. Turning her head, she kissed the palm with tenderness. "I don't say things I don't mean." She nipped Madison's fingertip.

There was much more they needed to say to one another, but desire was all too consuming and Jerrica's body was silently screaming for release.

Seeing the smoldering passion in those green eyes, Madison reached up with her other hand, brushing Jerrica's hard nipple. Massaging the breast gently, Jerrica arched backwards, releasing Madison's other hand. With expert hands, Madison continued pleasuring each sensitive nipple until they became needy.

Jerrica fell forward, positioned on hands and knees above Madison. The rage of fire ran through Jerrica, slicking her core.

Madison felt the warm moisture on her lower abdomen as Jerrica groaned.

"I need you," she whispered breathlessly in Madison's ear.

Madison pulled Jerrica's lips to hers, kissing her deeply, thoroughly. She moved her hand between Jerrica's thighs, filling her completely. The movement of Madison's hand was slow, taking her new lover on the long journey to rapture.

Caught in the steady climb for release, Jerrica whimpered as she separated her lips from Madison. On her knees, with her hands on either side of Madison's head, her body began a slow rhythmic motion, keeping pace with the movement of Madison's hand. The urgency of her release raged within her as she increasing the tempo of her hips. She felt the passion rapidly building with every downward thrust.

Madison felt Jerrica's body tighten around her fingers.

"Yes, right there," she moaned.

Madison shifted a little, keeping the constant rhythm with Jerrica's body.

Jerrica threw her head back, her hair cascading around her shoulders.

"Oh God…yes …yes…"

The primal urging of Madison's fingers that were filling her entirely, Jerrica's body shuddered when the orgasm tore through her body. Trying to hold her position, her arms collapsed and she slipped forward overcome with complete bliss.

Madison held her close. Their bodies molded together, her hand positioned between Jerrica's thighs.

Jerrica's body trembled with each spasm that rushed through her, one by one taking her higher into the abyss of sexual pleasure. When she thought she couldn't take anymore, her raspy voice pleaded with Madison. "Please…stop."

Madison stilled her hand, slowly slid it out from between them, resting it on Jerrica's back. Lightly stroking Jerrica, Madison held her close.

When she was able to gain some control, Jerrica spoke quietly. "I wish I had a better word to describe how I feel, but all I have is…extraordinary."

"You are unbelievable. I've never known anyone like you. You were made to be loved," Madison answered.

Jerrica slid onto the mattress, resting her head on Madison's shoulder. The warmth of her arms enfolded Jerrica in a safe and comfortable embrace.

Running her hand through the auburn hair, Madison whispered. "I love you more with each passing moment, Jerrica Kerrison."

Smiling, Madison tilted her head to place a delicate kiss on the end of Jerrica's nose.

Jerrica wrinkled her nose, making a funny face. Just then, Jerrica's stomach made itself known and she blushed at the sound. "I guess my stomach is telling me it's time for nourishment," she said and giggled.

"Something is telling us to get out of bed," Madison joked.

Placing a light kiss on her lips, Jerrica rolled over, exiting the bed.

With great admiration of the beautiful body, Madison's vision followed her to the bathroom. Stopping just inside the doorway, she turned, grinning. "You can join me, but only if you're good," she allowed before disappearing into the room.

Hesitating for only a second, Madison rose out of the bed and dashed to the bathroom. Once in the doorway, she watched Jerrica turn the shower on and step in. "Define good."

With mischief in her tone, Jerrica commented sensually. "Are you coming?"

Simple washing became a spirited game of touching and tasting. Each participant determined to be victorious. Sounds of soft moans and laughter resonated throughout the townhouse. The average shower that normally takes fifteen minutes stretched to almost an hour. Jerrica thought she could get used to these long showers until she realized she was famished. Turning her back to Madison, she reached to the handles of the shower, shutting the water off. The disappointed look on Madison's face made Jerrica chuckle.

Once dressed, they made their way downstairs. Jerrica browsed around the kitchen looking for her pets.

"Are you looking for the kitties?"

Jerrica nodded her head in surprise.

"I already fed them. I didn't want them to wake you," Madison said leaning against the counter.

"Thank you. Why don't you go relax in the living room? I'll bring in coffee and goodies," Jerrica said as she claimed two mugs out of the cabinet.

Jerrica felt the sudden heat on her back.

"Are you sure you don't need my help," Madison said, placing a small kiss on the back of her neck.

She trembled at the sensual touch, choking out. "I'm fine…go…sit…or we'll never eat."

With a gratified smile, Madison left the kitchen. Sitting on the couch, a thought entered Madison's mind. *Maybe I do belong here after all.*

Just as she turned her head to her side, she witnessed the smallest kitty hop up next to her. Without hesitation, the kitten crawled into her lap and began to purr. The kitten started to fall asleep as Madison absently patted her.

A tray of bakery goods and coffee in hand, Jerrica entered the room. "It's not much, but it will at least stop us from starving," she said as she set the items on the table.

She was surprised to see the kitten in Madison's lap. "I didn't know you had company."

Madison smiled. "I guess she likes me."

"I guess so. She doesn't normally visit when I have guests. Her name is Baby Kitty."

"Well, hello, Baby Kitty," she cooed, scratching behind an ear, "You are a precious little one, aren't you."

Jerrica watched the interaction. Her heart felt happy, making her smile.

Seeing the broad smile, Madison questioned her. "What are you thinking?"

"I was thinking how precious you are," she said, kissing her lightly on the mouth. Jerrica handed her a cup of coffee and a warm croissant. Turning, Jerrica grabbed her mug, and food for herself, making herself comfortable next to Madison. Picking up the small remote from the table, Jerrica clicked it once opening the wall of curtains.

Madison's eyes grew wide as the beauty of the bay revealed itself to her. Her eyes took in the subtle movements of the water against the rocks along the shore. The sun glistened off the water, making it look like it went on for miles. Flocks of geese were playing in the distance. The panoramic view was breathtaking. "This is an amazing view."

Jerrica smiled, watching Madison's almost childlike expression of awe. They sat in silence while devouring brunch.

"I think we should talk. I feel I need to explain myself to you. I'm ready to answer your questions from last night," Jerrica commented finally.

Madison wanted to look at her, but fear prevented her from completing that act. Both hands tightly wrapped around her cup to the cat's disappointment, Madison waited anxiously for Jerrica to continue.

"I don't want this to be an uncomfortable situation between us," said Jerrica as she stretched out her legs onto the coffee table. "I want us to be honest and open with one another."

Madison's eyes focused on the floor as she answered in a whisper. "After what's happened between us today, I thought we could leave all that behind and move forward."

Jerrica tilted her head to look at Madison, but her hair covered the side of her face.

"That's exactly why we need to talk. If there is to be any future for us, I don't want any doubts or misgivings about that night to stand silently between us," Jerrica said as she pushed the hair back from Madison's face.

Holding onto the phrase, *any future for us*, Madison tilted her head to look into Jerrica's tender eyes.

"Since the time I saw you that first day in the ladies' room, I knew something was different about you. I couldn't seem to concentrate when you were near. I found myself desperately trying not to think about you and the way you took my breath away from just seeing you across the room. Then after the night we spent together, I knew things would be different," she paused to choose her words carefully. "I was frightened of you and the unfamiliar feelings you were creating deep inside of me. I didn't know what all these new emotions meant because I've never felt this way before, not with anyone. When I left that morning, I knew I had made us different. I knew I was different somehow. It took a good friend to make me realize what I was feeling. I've been hurt in the past and what you were offering, honesty and love, terrified me," she finished, settling her hands on her lap.

Madison leaned forward to look at Jerrica's features as tears filled the green eyes.

"My past isn't clear of mistakes, Madison. I'm no angel and will never claim to be. I've been through a few failed relationships in my life. I was even married once," she offered, taking in a deep breath, "to a man."

Jerrica watched the confusion cross Madison's expression. "My first same-sex relationship was with a closeted lesbian about a year or so ago."

Jerrica looked out the window, lost in pain-filled memories. An unexpected warmth covered her hands, making her looked down into her lap. A smile displayed on her face as she entwined Madison's hand with hers.

"I want to be honest with you. I thought at one time I was in love."

"Thought?" Madison replied softly.

"I know now that I mistook my sudden freedom and lust-filled intentions for love."

"Are you sure it's love this time?" Madison asked, with some hesitation in her voice.

Jerrica pondered the question briefly. Lifting her dark green eyes to meet the inquiring brown ones, she answered, "I have never felt for her what I feel for you. I left that night out of fear. I was a coward and should have stayed. I have wasted so much time living in fear."

Madison leaned in, brushing her lips against Jerrica's. "I love you," she managed to whisper as she softly trailed kisses on her face. She placed light kisses on her cheek, down to her jawline, burying her face in the scent of her neck.

Jerrica felt a chill run down her spine as Madison kissed and nipped her neck. Slanting her mouth to her ear, Jerrica spoke seductively. "Call in tomorrow, stay with me another day."

Jerrica felt a gentle bite on the base of her neck.

Madison licked her way to her ear whispering. "I was hoping you would ask,"

She pulled back to look into Jerrica's eyes.

The cat jumped off her lap as Madison followed Jerrica's body as she lay back on the couch.

Jerrica slid her hand into the thick black hair as Madison eased on top of her. "I would have begged you to stay if I needed to," she purred, in a low throaty voice.

Chapter Fourteen

A dull ache slowly woke Jerrica from her slumber. The sensation was coming from her left arm that was cradling Madison's head. Having spent the afternoon enjoying the pleasures of a new lover's touch, they had fallen asleep tangled into one another on the sofa. She smiled as she watched Madison sleep, fascinated by this beautiful woman she held in her arms.

"What are you smiling at," Madison said as she slowly opened her eyes.

"I'm sorry. Did I wake you?"

"I felt your breathing change, so I knew you were awake. So tell me about the smile?"

"I was thinking to myself, how fortunate I am to have such an incredible woman in my arms."

Madison moved in close enough so that she was almost touching Jerrica's lips. "I think I'm the one who is fortunate," she breathed as she pulled away.

Anticipating a kiss, Jerrica felt disappointed when it didn't come to fruition. Jerrica sighed as she watched Madison push back from her.

"I'm afraid if we don't move soon, I won't be able to move my lower extremities," she explained staring into Jerrica's pouting face.

A smile quickly replaced the pout. "I know what you mean. I can no longer feel my fingertips on my left hand."

They both laughed heartily at the comical state they found themselves in. With helping hands, Jerrica was able to get herself into a sitting position. Once sitting, she stretched her upper body. She rubbed her arm first to get the sleepy numbness to go away.

Madison slowly stretched as her feet hit the floor. Looking up, she giggled as she noticed Jerrica was watching her.

Tossing Madison her clothes, Jerrica finished getting her wrinkled clothing on. "I need to go to the store," Jerrica announced as Madison moved to a standing position, sliding her own sweats on, "I haven't been shopping yet this week, and I don't have anything suitable for us to eat. I only need to pick up a couple of days worth of groceries."

Placing her hand in Jerrica's, Madison spoke, "We can go together. Let me buy you supper. I'll cook for you."

"Fine, you can cook supper only if I can cook breakfast," Jerrica said with a twinkle in her eye.

Madison felt a rush of heat blaze inside her at the thought of spending the whole night in the same bed. Clearing her throat she answered her. "Deal!"

✝

The unfamiliar car parked in the driveway suddenly changed her plans. Circling back, she found an empty parking spot on the street where she could see the townhouse, but not be seen by the inhabitants. She had a perfect view of the front of the house. It was a waiting game now.

An hour or more had passed when unexpectedly two figures emerged from the house. Even though the sun was setting, one form was easily recognized, the second was new to her. Their hands were entwined, shoulders almost touching and their playful body language was easy to read as they walked to the waiting vehicle. They were lovers. Proving this, the couple exchanged a passionate kiss. Their bodies pressed tightly together, hands reaching under material to touch soft curves.

The strong hands of the observer held the steering wheel tight, in frustration, watching the intimate scene unfold. Reluctant to let go of one another, the two parted and entered the vehicle on either side. They backed out of the driveway, heading in the direction of town, unaware someone was watching their interactions.

Once the taillights were out of sight, the heartache hit hard, causing the watcher to raise both hands, clutching her chest when the pain rushed through her. Time continued to move forward as the gasping for air, slowly transitioned into even breaths and muscles relaxing. Staring into the light of evening, the reality of the situation came into completion, causing tears to escape from the beautiful blue eyes.

"I've lost her," Devin whispered into the air for no one to hear.

†

The supper was cooked to perfection; each enjoying the long missed home-cooked meal. The conversation was light during the meal, simply wanting to enjoy one another's company. A hand reached out to grab Jerrica's wrist as she stood to bring her dish to the kitchen.

Jerrica looked down at the warm hand touching her, to the worried expression on her lover's face. "What's wrong?" Jerrica asked, tilting her head.

"I'm afraid…I'm afraid that this, what is happening between us isn't real, that it's just a fantasy. That I'm going to wake up and find out I dreamt the whole thing." Madison lowered her eyes in sadness.

Placing the plate on the table, Jerrica reached out cupping Madison's chin in her hand. Gently lifting her face so their eyes could meet, she moved in closer to whisper. "Oh, baby, there is no reason to be afraid. What is happening between us is very real."

Brushing stray hairs from Madison's face, Jerrica continued. "There is no doubt that I want you. My body aches to have you touch me. But it's more than that, way more…" Jerrica leaned in, lightly brushing her lips across Madison's lips, teasing her. Jerrica moaned, pressing her lips firmer, welcoming Madison's sleek tongue. Jerrica could feel the passion rushing to her core as Madison tried to get up.

Jerrica moved away, breaking their physical contact and starting toward the kitchen.

Madison fell back into her chair, gasping. She had seen Jerrica's mouth curl up into a devilish grin before she turned to leave the room. "Are you teasing me, Ms. Kerrison?"

Jerrica smiled at herself as she placed the plate in the dishwasher. She spun around in time to see Madison enter the kitchen with her plate. "I don't know what you're talking about Ms. Jeffery." Her eyes twinkled as Madison reached around her to place her dishes on the counter.

Bodies now touching, a surge of warmth rushed across her as she felt Madison's lips nipping her ear. "I can play this game, too," she said, beginning an assault of kisses on her welcoming neck.

The trail Madison's lips were leaving on Jerrica's skin, made her shudder. Jerrica placed her palms on each side of Madison's face as her kisses were traveling down between her breasts.

"Uh, you need to stop or I won't be responsible for my actions," she said trying to catch her breath, as she lifted Madison's face.

"That's a problem?"

"I was hoping we could spend some time cuddling and maybe talking."

Madison's grin widened, but Jerrica continued. "I mean mostly talking. We really don't know one another that well. What's your favorite color, book, and movie…music? What were you like growing up? Whatever you feel you want to share."

Jerrica leaned forward, placing a soft kiss on Madison's forehead as she removed her hands.

"You pick a fresh bottle of wine. I'll grab the glasses from the table and I'll meet you in the living room," replied Madison.

Jerrica nodded in agreement and they both went about completing their tasks. Within moments, they were both sitting on the couch. The darkness of evening had set in, so Jerrica closed the wall of curtains. Handing her the wine, she lifted Madison's other arm behind her head. She cuddled her head on a soft shoulder.

Madison lightly kissed the top of Jerrica's head. "Tell me about Jerrica…."

Jerrica inhaled slowly and began. She shared her stories of growing up in New Hampshire, her marriage and the time spent after the separation at Lauren's cabin. Jerrica felt heartsick as she omitted the abuse she endured by his hands. She revealed very little of her relationship with the closeted lesbian. At that moment, she wasn't ready to explain the complex connection between Devin and herself.

Jerrica casually sipped wine, snuggling closer. When she finished, she placed her glass on the table, snuggling back into what was becoming her favorite spot, wrapping her arm around her lover's waist. The room fell quiet as several minutes passed by. Jerrica sat patiently before tilting her head to look into Madison's face. Gazing into complicated eyes, Jerrica shyly smiled, waiting for Madison to speak.

With a sharp intake of air, Madison began an edited version of her life. Skipping past most of her childhood, the college years, she quickly went through her short job history and working for Olivia. She had left out so many personal details that she felt a pang of guilt in her stomach. Haunted by her own private demons, Madison surmised if she couldn't face them herself, she couldn't share them either.

Jerrica heard a tone in Madison's voice she had never heard before and felt the muscles involuntarily tense in her shoulder as she spoke. Jerrica could tell something was amiss, but didn't want to ruin the moment.

Madison took a gulp of wine, relieved that she had gotten through her tale. They sat for a long time just holding one another. Feeling the arm around her waist tighten, Madison smiled with contentment.

Turning, Jerrica maneuvered so she was straddling Madison's lap.

"You seem to like this being on top position," Madison said, grinning.

Jerrica's eyes were sparkling as she started to tickle Madison. Jerrica roared with laughter as Madison tried to wiggle out from under her captive hands.

"Oh, you think this is funny, do you," Madison snickered as she reached up quickly to grab at Jerrica.

Knowing she was about to lose this battle, Jerrica bolted to a standing position, hopped backward over the coffee table, putting escaping distance between them.

Surprise came and left quickly as Madison realized by the space between them that Jerrica was trying to flee.

Not waiting for Madison to get the best of her, Jerrica sprinted toward the stairway giggling, and disappeared.

Rounding the couch quickly, Madison chased after her quarry toward the master bedroom. Where else could Jerrica run to?

"You'll never catch me," she bellowed, running into her room laughing.

Sprinting into the room, Madison spotted her bounty jockeying on the other side of the bed, chuckling at her.

The moment Jerrica dashed to her left toward the bathroom Madison vaulted over the bed. Grasping the bottom of Jerrica's shirt, Madison yanked the material toward her.

The unexpected shift in motion caused Jerrica to lose her balance as the momentum of her body swung her around in a circle.

Capturing her in a tight embrace, Madison swiftly tossed both of them on the bed. She successfully secured Jerrica's hands above her head and pinned the rest of her body with her own. They both laughed heartily as they lay pressed against one another. Lowering her head into the warm curve of Jerrica's neck, she could feel her pulse rapidly beating. Trying to calm her own heartbeat, Madison breathed in deeply. The combination of Jerrica's scent and her light recognizable perfume assaulted her senses, and she growled softly.

Trying to wiggle from her confines, Jerrica froze when she heard the sweet noise.

Madison felt Jerrica stiffen and quickly lifted her head in bewilderment. As their eyes met, Madison could see her own desire reflected in Jerrica's eyes. They lay motionless, falling deeper into one another. Her tight grip on a pair of wrists loosened as she fell farther into those green pools.

Lightly brushing Madison's cheek with her fingertips, Jerrica slid her hand into the thick black hair. Clutching the hair in her fist, she pulled Madison toward her. Their lips met in a fevered hunger, their appetite for one another growing rapidly. Hands were everywhere, pulling clothing up and off, touching scorching skin. Rapture came quickly and was brutally intense, the two taking the journey together as one.

When they floated back to earth, Madison half lay on Jerrica, her head resting on her shoulder. She could hear the rapid heartbeat under her ear and smiled with satisfaction, not only physically, but emotionally as well.

Jerrica could feel the brisk rise and fall of Madison's chest slowly decrease as time slipped by. She softly scratched up and down Madison's back, sighing peacefully. She brushed the moist, tousled hair off Madison's face as she tilted to the side to look at her.

"That was amazing," she said, looking into her half closed brown eyes.

Madison's smile grew wider, "Maybe next time we'll take our time?"

Jerrica raised an eyebrow at the assumption. She kissed her on the forehead. Pulling back, she whispered jokingly. "You are presuming there will be a next time."

Madison used her forearms to position herself above Jerrica. With a cat like grin, Madison answered. "I presume nothing. I love you and I'm not going anywhere, so there will be plenty of time for more of …this…." Lowering her head she took Jerrica's lips in a deep kiss.

Enjoying the newness of love, they spent the rest of the night in discovery, awakening not only the body's senses, but also their souls. Love wrapped itself around them like a familiar blanket, clinging to one another and holding onto the profound love they felt.

With dawn rapidly approaching, their bodies exhausted with satisfaction, they finally drifted into a deep slumber, wrapped in one another's embrace and love.

Chapter Fifteen

The light rays of day crept sporadically throughout the room, gracefully illuminating the once darkened area. An unfamiliar sound in the hazy distance of sleep conveyed to the owner of the home, that somewhere a kitty was getting into trouble. Taking inventory of all her functioning body parts, she stretched, becoming aware that there was a restriction around her waist. Lightly grasping the wrist of the loving arm that encircled her, Jerrica carefully raised it, quietly scooting out of bed. The hunt was now on to find the disturbing noise.

Tiptoeing to the opposite side of the bed, the volume increased. She knelt on the floor, peering under the bed. She found her prey and it was sitting on a discarded pair of pants on the floor. The culprit stared back at her with surprised eyes. With a warm smile, Jerrica reached out pulling the pants and a surprised Baby Kitty out into the open. Once the kitten was no longer hiding, she bounced herself across the floor, finding a warm sunspot to lie in.

"Now, this is an interesting sight to wake up to," Madison said, spying a very naked Jerrica on the floor.

Jerrica leaned forward, placing a quick kiss on her lips, pants still grasped in one hand. "Oh?"

She stood, smirking down at her sleepy eyed companion.

With her hand on the waistband of the pants, Jerrica turned to toss them into the laundry hamper when a muffled vibration halted the motion. The cat looked up from its tanning spot on the floor in curiosity. "So, that's what you were after," she said to the kitten as she retrieved her cell phone from the pocket.

Her thumb brushed the screen just as the pending phone call transferred to voicemail. She had missed twenty-seven calls, sixteen texts, and had twenty-three messages pending. She tipped the screen so Madison could see the screen.

"Who's been trying to call?" Madison asked as Jerrica sat on the edge of the bed.

Moving the screen with her finger, Jerrica replied, "They're all from Lauren."

Madison sat up as Jerrica called Lauren on the phone, motioning Madison to be silent. Jerrica waited anxiously for Lauren to pick up. In moments, she heard the familiar voice droll out the repetitive phrase.

"Jerrica Kerrison's office. This is Lauren speaking." "Lauren, its Jerrica. I see you called me hundreds of times?"

"Where the hell have you been? Yes, I've been trying to get a hold of you since I came in this morning."

"I misplaced my phone," she said dryly, "What's going on?"

"There's something serious happening here, but nobody knows exactly what is going on. I've gotten four calls already this morning from Mrs. Burnham, wanting to know if I had heard from you yet today."

"You heard from Mrs. Burnham?"

"Yes! The last time I talked with her, she left a heated message for you to call her right away. This whole place is abuzz. This makes me nervous."

"Well, it terrifies me. Let me collect myself and I'll give her a call."

"Call me back as soon as you know."

"No problem."

Jerrica rested the phone on her leg as her chin dropped toward her chest. Deep in her thoughts, Jerrica barely felt the supportive hand rest on her shoulder.

"I only heard part of that conversation and it didn't sound good. Are you ok?"

Breathing in deeply and letting it go, Jerrica lifted her head, turning to look at Madison. "It seems that Ms. Donahue's personal assistant would like to talk to me as soon as possible." Her voice was just above a whisper, "I've been with this company for more than six years now, and have never had any personal interaction with her. I wonder why now?"

In her best supportive voice, Madison tried to be positive. "Well, the only way you're going to find out is to call. There's no time like the present. I'm right here to help you through…whatever this is."

Jerrica felt comfort from Madison's support, but had to prep herself before she called, "I need to throw some clothes on first, then I'll call the office."

Madison removed her hand as Jerrica slid off the edge of the bed, headed toward the bathroom. She adjusted the blankets around her as she watched Jerrica disappear through the door. Grabbing the nightshirt off the stand beside the bed, she slipped it on. With a quick look around, she realized her shorts were MIA, so she would have to search for them later. Jerrica reappeared from the bathroom, wearing an oversized t-shirt and a pair of running shorts. She had pulled her hair into a high ponytail and when she walked toward her, Madison was almost sure she could smell toothpaste.

All this for a phone call, she must be nervous, Madison thought.

Walking around the furniture to return to her position on the edge of the bed, phone in her left hand, Jerrica displayed a weak smile as she tapped the phone, dialing the office. As she listened to the automated directory, Jerrica tapped the correct extension.

Madison watched as Jerrica drummed her fingertips on her leg, feeling powerless to help. A transformation in Jerrica was noticeable as she spoke into the phone.

Jerrica's voice was an octave lower. She even sat a little straighter. Put on hold, Jerrica let out the breath she had been holding tightly. This was nerve-wracking for both of them. A shiver ran up her spine when she heard her voice in the phone.

"Ms. Kerrison, thank you for getting back to me so quickly."

Jerrica could hear pleasantry in her acknowledgement, but heard the sternness and sarcasm in her tone. "It's my pleasure, Mrs. Burnham. How may I help you today?"

"Speaking on behalf of Ms. Donahue, your presence is required tomorrow at nine a.m. for a meeting in her office."

Mrs. Burnham paused, sounds of shifting paper could be heard in the background as she spoke. "I would advise you to be here at least ten minutes before the meeting to be briefed on topics, and on any paperwork Ms. Donahue might want you to go over."

Jerrica didn't even have time to respond when the very business-oriented assistance resumed her duties.

"Ms. Kerrison, do you understand all the information I have given you thus far?"

With sudden shock, Jerrica answered. "Yes, Mrs. Burnham, I understand everything. I look forward to seeing you tomorrow."

"Very good then, Ms. Kerrison, we will expect you tomorrow morning. Have a good day."

The line cut off before she was able to say goodbye. Tossing the phone toward the headboard, Jerrica leaned back on the bed, covering her eyes with her forearm.

Feeling a little confused, Madison slid down the bed to lie next to Jerrica. Leaning on one elbow Madison softy brushed her knuckles against Jerrica's cheek whispering to her. "Honey, are you all right? What's going on?"

Jerrica took a few seconds to collect her thoughts before she removed her arm from her eyes, angling her head to look at Madison. She saw the concern in her eyes and reached out to take her hand. "I will be going into the office tomorrow," she squeezed the hand, "I have a meeting with Ms. Donahue at nine."

Madison's quick intake of air was not comforting to Jerrica.

Quickly reaching for her hand, Madison brought Jerrica's palm to her lips, kissing it softly. "I'm sorry, honey. The news just surprised me."

"How do you think I feel?"

"What can I do to help?"

"Nothing," she said sitting up. "This is not how I wanted us to spend the day. Let's just enjoy our day together and I'll worry about tomorrow…tomorrow."

They sat together not knowing what to say. Madison fumbled with the hem on her shirt, trying to figure out how to make everything all right again.

Jerrica stood. "I'm not going to let that one phone call ruin our day. Why don't you go to the kitchen and make us some coffee. I need to call Lauren back to tell her what is going on."

She grabbed Madison's hand, yanking her to her feet. Pulling her fully into her arms, Jerrica quickly kissed her, then, turning her toward the door, she slapped her ass to get her moving. "Now go," Jerrica said with a smile as Madison headed for the hallway.

A sense of joy came to Madison as she spied her pair of shorts on the floor. Slipping them on, she smiled at Jerrica and left the bedroom as instructed.

Jerrica made a quick call to Lauren, both women trying to figure out what was going on, but with no success. Within minutes, she was standing at the bottom of her stairs watching and listening to her lover hum around the kitchen making coffee. With a loving smile, she joined the private party.

Chapter Sixteen

The car shifted into first gear as they approached the parking space. The ride to work had been very quiet as both occupants were deep in thought for the same reasons. Jerrica reflected on what became of the rest of yesterday. They had spent the rest of the day talking and laughing, just enjoying whatever the other one had to offer. They ended the day savoring the blissful pleasure of one another's bodies. Nevertheless, always, in the back of her mind, her thoughts returned to today's impending meeting.

Madison had just spent the best weekend of her life. She had finally admitted aloud to Jerrica that she loved her. The big surprise was that she found out someone loved her in return. Everything was perfect until they entered the real world. Jerrica had tried very hard to not let the worry creep into their day, but Madison could see, every once in a while, the distracted look in her eyes. When the car came to a complete stop, Madison looked around puzzled. She hadn't realized they were in the parking garage already. She glanced at her as the car was shifted into park and the car ignition turned off. They sat wordless for several minutes, contemplating their thoughts.

Jerrica cleared her throat, giving an unspoken instruction that it was time to leave that private world. She reached out to Madison, touching her arm before she exited the vehicle.

Looking into worried eyes, Jerrica spoke in a whisper. "I don't know what is going to happen today," she said, almost choking on her words. "And nobody knows about us yet, so—"

Madison placed a finger on Jerrica's lips stopping her from continuing, she knew what she was trying to say. They were going to have to act as if they didn't know one another intimately. They would both be professional.

Jerrica lightly kissed the finger touching her lips, seeing a smile develop on Madison's face. Emotions running on overload, they shared not only a last kiss, but their fears as well.

†

The numbers in the elevator ascended rather quickly today. Madison looked around the empty elevator. She didn't want to be there. Straightening her long sleeve navy blue shirt, Madison rocked back and forth on the heels of her sneakers, anxiously waiting to get to her desk. Trying to look as professional as possible, in her weekend clothes, she put on a big smile just as the doors opened. Few heads turned to look in her direction as she exited the elevator and hurried to Olivia's office. Lightly rapping her knuckles on her door, Madison was rewarded with Olivia's bellowing voice. "Yeah, come in."

Approximately ten minutes later, when the elevator doors opened again, another familiar figure entered the department. With shoulders back, head held high, Jerrica confidently walked toward her office. She did not glance around. She kept her eyes focused on the partially opened office door. Passing by her staff she commented, "Good morning," but offered nothing else.

When she entered her office, she used the end of her briefcase to push the door closed behind her. The office looked the same, but cleaner. There were no remnants of broken glass or stains from a wet carpet. Jerrica smiled to herself as she dropped her case next to her desk. She leaned on the edge of her desk, staring at her wall clock. The hands on the clock seemed to slow down as she stared. Jerrica was anxious to find out what was going on.

Not wanting to stare at the annoying clock any longer, she strolled to the windows. She could see her reflection. The charcoal pantsuit she had chosen today made her look powerful and in control. Unfortunately, her nerves were anything but. Adjusting her outfit, she glanced again at the clock. Inhaling deeply and exhaling loudly, she was as ready as she was ever going to be today.

†

"Well I'll be damned," said Olivia as Madison opened up her office door.

"Good morning Olivia," she responded, shutting the door quickly.

As casual as possible, Madison made her way to the front of her boss's desk, depositing herself in the empty chair.

Olivia sat quietly for a second, concentrating on Madison.

She could feel Olivia's eyes burrowing into her. "Stop staring at me!"

"Oh, my God, you slept with her again," Olivia blurted out the moment she figured out what was different with Madison. "It's written on your face!"

"Olivia, lower your voice please. These walls are paper thin."

"I'll take that as a yes. So was it as good as the first time?"

"You're incorrigible, you know that, right?"

"Well, it has been a while. So dish."

"Later, I promise. Something is going on around here. Have you heard anything?"

Olivia looked uncomfortable, as she answered. "I don't know exactly what is going on, I only heard it involves your new squeeze."

"Well, I knew that. We came in together. Her meeting is upstairs at nine," she said, looking at her watch. "She should be leaving her office any time now."

Olivia and Madison tried not to be conspicuous leaving the seclusion of the office and walking to Madison's desk. While Olivia was explaining the multiple files on her desk, Madison glimpsed movement in front of her. Looking up, she saw Jerrica exit her office. Her face was stern, her look confident as she stopped at Lauren's desk. Whatever information they exchanged, it was brief, giving Jerrica a chance to glance over Lauren's shoulder at Madison.

Their eyes met for only a second, but it was enough to make Jerrica smile as she walked toward the elevator. Four sets of eyes were glued to her every movement.

Once the elevator doors had closed, only one set of eyes continued to look in that direction. With her eyes locked on the closed doors, Madison suddenly felt like she couldn't breathe and she stumbled backward.

Olivia gently grabbed her elbow, pulling her down into the nearest chair.

Confusion set in on Madison's face and she looked up.

Catching her stare, Olivia said softly. "Take it easy, my friend. You need to relax and breathe for me. She can hold her own."

After several minutes, Madison had control of herself and told Olivia she was fine.

Olivia was skeptical at first, but conceded, returning to her office.

Alone at her desk, Madison felt the worry building again as she rotated her head, looking at the last place she had seen the woman she loved.

†

Jerrica was alone in the small wood and polished steel elevator. As she watched the numbers increase, the fidgeting with her hands began. The soft ding sound echoed in the small space as it announced the destination. Collecting herself just before the door opened, Jerrica plastered on her best fake smile, holding her head high as the doors slid open.

Stepping out onto the executive's floor, she walked boldly to the executive secretary's large half-moon shaped desk. Before she could officially address the woman behind the desk, the receptionist confirmed her arrival. "Good morning, Ms. Kerrison. Ms. Burnham has been informed of your arrival and will be right out."

"Thank you," she said, rotating on her heels toward the waiting area. After a few moments, an adjacent door opened and Ms. Burnham entered the spacious foyer.

Their hands met in a firm handshake. "Ms. Kerrison, thank you for coming in so early. Would you please follow me?"

There was no conversation as she followed the well-dressed older woman down a small hallway to a larger office.

Ms. Burnham proceeded to her desk, motioning Jerrica to the chairs positioned in front of her. "Please have a seat. Ms. Donahue will be with you in a moment," she said with a pleasant smile.

Jerrica was getting irritated with the power game she felt they were already playing with her. They made her hurry to get there and now they were making her wait, proving that once again, if you have money, you have power. After waiting twenty minutes in a rather uncomfortable chair, she became increasingly aggravated.

She shifted in her seat, about to speak up, when the intercom sounded and a flat-toned voice sounded. "Please bring Ms. Kerrison in."

Ms. Burnham rose the same time Jerrica did. She picked up a very large manila envelope off her desk. "Please follow me."

Jerrica tried not to look surprised as she entered an enormous office. Glancing around the room, she saw a sitting area with two leather bound couches facing a gas fireplace and a bar on her right. There was a fifty-two inch flat screen TV with a full media center built into the wall on her left. Rows of windows connecting the left wall to the right were behind where Ms. Donahue sat. The centerpiece of the whole room was a massive mahogany desk with a gray-blue marble top. The presence behind the desk didn't even move when they walked into the room nor make an acknowledgement as they approached her desk.

Motioning to one of the two seats directly in front of the desk, Ms. Burnham placed the envelope on the desk, turned and exited the awkwardly quiet office.

The chair Jerrica rested herself in was in the center, right in front of Ms. Donahue. Sitting up as straight as possible, Jerrica graciously crossed her legs, again meant to wait. Glancing at the woman behind the desk, Jerrica remembered why she had considered working for this company right out of college. Alexandra Donahue was one of the most influential women in the world of finance. Mr. and Mrs. Donahue started a small firm two years after they met. With her husband's inheritance and her mind for numbers, their firm quickly made the list of Forbes Top Ten Businesses to Watch. When she and her husband decided to merge with Morrill and Hartford, their small firm was already worth one hundred and fifty million. The rumor around the financial world was that the merger was necessary because Alexandra's husband had fallen ill. He died two years after the merger, long before Jerrica had started working for them. After his passing, Ms. Donahue had become the controlling stockholder in the company and was the driving force behind the company.

After a few minutes, Ms. Donahue looked up. "Good morning, Ms. Kerrison. I'll be with you in just a moment," she said, as she reached over, retrieving the manila envelope.

The contents of the envelope she deposited in one hand and tossed the empty packet lazily on the corner of the massive desk.

Jerrica observed with curiosity as Ms. Donahue reviewed each document thoroughly.

Once she scrutinized the last document, she laid it down, adjusting her glasses. Looking directly at her employee, she remarked, "Ms. Kerrison, may I call you Jerrica?" Not waiting for an answer, she continued. "You are probably wondering why I called you here today."

"I assure you that all my accounts are up to date and…" Jerrica stopped as Ms. Donahue held up her hand.

"Your work performance is fine. Even though I would like to have you on site more, I have had no complaints thus far with our current working arrangement. The reason I brought you here today is that we have run into a little problem with one of our top clients."

Jerrica tensed, but Alexandra didn't seem to notice.

"Are you personally familiar with Daniel & Daniel's Inc. company financials?"

What is going on here, Jerrica thought. "Yes, I just sent the quarterlies. What seems to be the issue?"

"You are aware that Morrill, Hartford, and Donahue have been courting Daniel & Daniel, Inc. to take on all of their accounting needs, domestic and abroad?"

"Yes, I have heard."

"Well, it was almost a done deal. I received an emergency call this weekend, directly from the president of D & D. He informed me that his company is considering leaving MHD and are now entertaining offers from our competitors."

Jerrica was stunned. "The Daniel company is locked into a contract with us until end of this year. They can't legally leave us."

"Oh, yes they can. They can buy out their contract." Alexandra removed her glasses, placing them on her desk.

Quickly crunching numbers in her head Jerrica replied, "That would be just more than half a million dollars. Is he aware of those figures?"

"Yes, it would be and he is aware of the cost. Our job performance has been immaculate for his company. According to his file, we've gone beyond for them in some cases. Our feedback reports have always been top notch. This whole situation is baffling," she said rubbing the bridge of her nose and replacing her glasses.

Trying not to show emotion, the explanation to Alexandra's quandary flashed into her mind. *Devin!* Jerrica raised her hand to her forehead, rubbing it lightly with her fingers, giving herself thinking time.

"Jerrica," Alexandra said it with such powerful certainty that Jerrica snapped her head up. "We haven't lost them yet. We have an invitation to meet with them. Be warned, we are not the only firm that received this invitation. I have heard of at least four other firms that have been invited as well."

"An invitation to what?"

"To a working weekend at their Nantucket estate," she explained. "MHD is scheduled for an early morning meeting on Saturday. Ten, I believe."

Ms. Donahue shuffled papers around her desk, looking for the invitation.

Jerrica was speechless. Just under the surface of this calm cool exterior, she was furious. She knew that something, no, someone, was trying to sabotage her career. Calming her inner rage, she tried to speak logically.

"Ten a.m., that's fine. I can have a proposal ready by Friday. My assistant and I will go down Saturday morning and re-sell MHD."

"That won't do. To show Mr. Daniel that we are committed to our business future's together, you will be going down on Friday. All the other representatives will be there on Friday, so will Morrill, Hartford, and Donahue. I have already arranged for you, and your personal assistant to spend the night at the Nantucket estate. I talked with the younger Ms. Daniel and she said she would make all the arrangements."

Of course she did. Jerrica replied a little harshly. "Those arrangements are not going to work for me. I think it's unprofessional for us to have a professional meeting of this importance in a personal setting. They are trying to set us up for failure."

Sliding her Armani reading glasses down her nose to look over them, Alexandra spoke in a deep tone, with authority. "Ms. Kerrison, remember you still work for Morrill, Hartford and Donahue and this is part of your job. This is not a request. Trust me, if I could send someone else, I would have, but you are familiar with their account and they personally requested you to attend this meeting."

Jerrica knew she had just lost the power struggle.

The two women stared at one another, as the room grew eerily quiet. With her index finger, Alexandra pushed her glasses back up her nose, then turned her attention to her computer. "Stop at Evelyn's, I mean, Ms. Burnham's desk before you leave this floor. She has the new contracts for the Daniel & Daniel, Inc. to sign, should they decide to re-sign with us. If they decide to terminate their connection with us, they will have to come to our office to do so and this time it will be more costly for them." Alexandra started clicking her keyboard, without another word being exchanged.

Exiting the office, Jerrica had all she could do to hide her irritation. Smiling politely, she took the envelope from Ms. Burnham's hand. Within seconds, Jerrica was standing at the elevator doors, pressing the button repeatedly. Once in the elevator, she tried to calm herself down, but the more her mind thought about what had just happened, the higher her temperature rose. She was at a full march the moment the doors opened. Approaching her office, she motioned quickly for Lauren to follow her, leaving the office door open.

Jaime and Lauren looked at one another, then back to the open door.

Lauren stood, grabbing her note tablet, rushed after her boss, closing the office door behind her.

Across the room, Madison watched everything unfold. She knew something was wrong and felt powerless to help. She would have to wait for an opening to see Jerrica.

Lauren entered the room expecting to see something broken on the floor. Instead, she found Jerrica leaning on the front of her desk, head down, and both hands grasping the edge of the desktop. She approached the desk cautiously. "Jerrica, what happened?"

Lauren could tell, as she moved closer, that Jerrica was trembling, but she did not answer her. Standing at arm's length from Jerrica she stopped and waited patiently. Time passed slowly. Lauren wasn't sure how long they had been standing in Jerrica's office before Jerrica sighed loudly.

With eyes that held uneasiness in them, she focused on Lauren. "We have been requested to attend a business meeting this weekend."

Jerrica kept eye contact, speaking in a monotone. "Morrill, Hartford, and Donahue are about to lose one of their top clients. The client specifically requested me to attend this meeting to represent MHD. You will need to accompany me to Nantucket." Jerrica moved her hand, grabbing the envelope, and handed it to Lauren.

These meetings were not out of the ordinary. Lauren couldn't understand what the big issue was. Grabbing the large envelope, Lauren proceeded to open it.

Jerrica lowered her head, listening to Lauren read aloud. Jerrica closed her eyes as the room went silent.

"You've got to be fucking kidding me," Lauren barked as she glanced up from the documents.

When Jerrica didn't budge, Lauren continued her ranting. "You realize this is her doing, right? First, she screws with your personal life, now she wants to mess up your professional life, too. This woman is freaking crazy." With each word, her tone became more elevated. "Jerrica say something!"

In an alarmingly calm voice, Jerrica retorted. "What is it that you want me to say? She's put me in a difficult situation. I've thought about all the angles. It won't make any difference if I tell the company we were involved at one time, they would send me just the same. If I tell her father the truth, MHD would lose the account. I'll lose my job and ruin my reputation." Sighing, she lifted her head to stare at the wall. "She has the control now."

"Bullshit!"

"I don't have a choice. I have to see it through."

"Does Madison know your connection with that evil bitch?"

Jerrica turned her head in surprise. "She knows that my first female experience was a closeted lesbian, but that's all. I never mentioned who she was or how I met her."

"Well don't you think you should fill her in on that information, since you're staying overnight at her home?"

"I can't, especially now. Our relationship is too new and if she knew about my personal connection to the Daniel corporation, to Devin, I might lose her. As soon as this blows past, and it will, I'll tell her everything."

"You underestimate her. I think this is a mistake."

"Well, it's my decision to make," Jerrica locked eyes with Lauren. "And promise me you'll say nothing."

Lauren stood her ground, biting the edge of her lip in frustration. "Okay, I promise."

Lauren exited the office with a knot in her stomach. She knew this situation was just a train wreck waiting to happen. Sitting at her desk, she typed a very short interoffice e-mail.

Madison's anxiety cranked up a notch when she saw the look on Lauren's face. She knew something was wrong. She wanted to rush to Jerrica. Staring blankly at her computer screen, Madison wanted to cry. Through her mist of pending tears, Madison noticed her e-mail icon. In desperate hope that it was Jerrica, she clicked to open it.

Ms. Jeffery,
Jaime and I will be taking an extended break at 10:15 a.m. I would appreciate it if you would cover our department while we are gone. Thank you for your assistance.
Sincerely,
Lauren Blanchet
Assistant to Ms. Kerrison

The corners of Madison's mouth turned up. Clicking out of the e-mail, she waited patiently. Approximately five minutes passed and Madison watched Jerrica's employees leave their workstations. Snatching a folder off her desk, she made her way to Jerrica's office door, lightly knocking. Hearing a soft greeting from the other side of the door, she entered the privacy of Jerrica's office. Feeling a rush of emotion as their eyes met, Madison dropped the folder in her hand and rushed to her, enveloping her in a secure embrace.

Jerrica let herself be taken in by the warmth and protection Madison's embrace promised. Molding her body into Madison's, she returned the hug. Precious moments went by before Jerrica lowered her arms to her side.

Madison felt the sudden chill and released the embrace. Stepping back her heart broke as she peered into emotionless eyes. "Honey—" Madison choked.

"Madison, I'm fine."

Madison noticed the flat tone in the use of her first name.

Jerrica retreated to her desk chair, putting distance between them. It was only a few feet, but it felt like the Grand Canyon to her.

Madison seated herself, feeling confused. Something had happened while Jerrica was upstairs.

While moving papers around on her desk Jerrica repeated the conversation, she had with Alexandra Donahue. When she had finished she looked into caring eyes, trying not to reveal what she was trying so desperately to hide.

Madison tried to be encouraging. "Well, this happens all the time in this business. I'm sure you will persuade them to stay with the company. I have confidence in you! I don't understand why you're so worried."

"Who said I was worried?"

"I can see it in your face and hear it in your voice."

"I guess I am a little worried. This is an extremely large client for this company. It will affect my position here if I can convince them to stay. I'm also not much for traveling and I hate rushing to put together a presentation."

"Well, you have a very competent staff that will help you. You will have Lauren to assist you and keep you company on the trip. Besides, it's only one evening."

Jerrica looked down at her desk again. "I'm glad someone believes in me and my abilities," she said in a low voice. "I don't know…what the rest of this week is going to be like… so, I think you…should stay in the city, at least until…this weekend is over."

She regretted saying it the second it left her mouth. Jerrica's eyes focused on her desktop. She didn't see the flash of shock and hurt that passed across Madison's face.

Sliding to the edge of her seat, Madison glanced down at the floor as she replied. "If you think that will help you? I don't want to do anything to distract you."

Jerrica could hear the disappointment in her voice, but didn't or couldn't answer back. Jerrica looked up just as Madison was standing to leave.

When their eyes met, Madison whispered unevenly. "I love you."

"I love you, too."

Her eyes lowered to the floor as she made her way to the door. As Madison reached for the door, she heard Jerrica's voice whisper. "Maybe I could stay in town a little longer today, and we could have supper together?"

"If you can find time to fit me into your busy schedule that would be great. Call me later if you can," Madison replied over her shoulder, closing the door behind her.

Chapter Seventeen

With music blaring in her ears and a heavy lead foot on the gas pedal, Jerrica hurried toward Lauren's house. She had turned on what Lauren liked to call screaming music, to help drown out all the noise going on in her head, but it didn't seem to be working today. It had been almost two and a half days since she had seen Madison. She had purposely-avoided contact with her. The last time she had physically seen her was when she left her office on Tuesday. Their dinner date that evening never materialized and Jerrica hadn't returned to the office the rest of the week.

They had talked briefly on the phone the next day, but the conversation seemed labored. Jerrica was frustrated with herself for not telling Madison the whole truth to begin with, possibly avoiding all this trouble. Lauren was right. As soon as all this was over, she would invite Madison for a nice dinner, maybe even a massage. She smiled. She would have to admit to Lauren that she was right about telling Madison the truth. She would never hear the end of this one. With a big sigh, she tapped her GPS, taking the exit ramp toward Lauren's house.

†

"Are we in a race?" Lauren yelled above the music.

Jerrica didn't hear Lauren speak as she swerved in and out of the traffic lanes.

Tapping the radio off, Lauren yelled again. "I said, are we in a race?"

"You don't have to yell, I'm sitting right here," Jerrica said, quickly glancing in her direction.

"Well, you didn't hear me the first time. Besides you still haven't answered my question."

"No, we are not in a race. Why?"

"Have you looked at your speedometer lately?" Lauren asked pointing to the instrument panel.

"Are you telling me how to drive?"

"Do I need to?"

"No." Jerrica lifted her foot from the accelerator a little.

Clicking the radio back on, adjusting the volume to a respectable level, Lauren reclined in her seat, letting the warm sun grace her features for the long journey ahead. Fifteen minutes into the trip, Lauren was comfortably snoring.

I'm not the only one who falls asleep on trips, Jerrica thought as her smile broadened. She reached her hand forward, turning up the music. On the almost hour ride to the Cape, Jerrica tried hard not to think about the upcoming weekend. The ambiguity of the true reason for this trip continued to resurface in her psyche. To everyone else, this was all about a competitive business move. Jerrica knew this was more than business, it was personal.

✝

Lauren was jarred out of her slumber as the car was slowly loaded onto the Nantucket Ferry. Stretching her arms up to the roof and her legs as far out on the floorboard as possible, Lauren tried blinking the sleep out of her eyes. Glancing at the multiple cars around them, Lauren realized where they were.

"Hey, my sleepy travel companion," Jerrica said.

"I am real sorry about that. I didn't expect to fall asleep."

"That's okay. Do you want to go top side?"

Looking at her surroundings again, Lauren replied. "Why not, it's a beautiful day. Go ahead up. I want to get a sweatshirt out of my bag first."

"Are you sure?"

"Go, Jerrica, I don't need a babysitter," she said, lightly tapping her arm.

A child-like smile crossed Jerrica's face as she exited the vehicle.

Lauren watched as Jerrica disappeared between the seas of parked cars. Lauren sighed heavily as she flipped open her cell phone to call her husband. Lauren listened to the ring from the phone. Jerrica wasn't the only one keeping secrets.

The top deck of the bow on the boat was Jerrica's favorite place to be. Her fingers were lightly wrapped around the banister, her eyes closed, head tilted toward the sun.

When Lauren finally located Jerrica, she stood only a few feet away, observing her friend in silence. There was a small breeze traveling across the deck and it brushed Jerrica's hair away from her face. A light mist of water touched her cheeks as the large vessel cut through the waves. Her stylish sunglasses were hiding the dark circles caused by the absence of sleep. The once barely noticeable worry line on her forehead had become more visible in the past few months.

Lauren could also see the difference in her shape now that she had removed her blazer. As her eyes traveled the length of Jerrica's form, Lauren acknowledged to herself with sadness that her closest friend was becoming dangerously thin. Her sky blue blouse seemed to just drape off her shoulders, then gather loosely at her waist where the material was tucked in. Her slacks, ones that used to show off her curves, now just hung on her hips, almost voiding her shape. A new belt was the only item keeping her pants in place. Lauren stepped closer, announcing her presence.

"It's beautiful out here, isn't it?"

Jerrica opened her eyes, looking at the familiar face. "It is now that you're here."

"Flattery will get you everywhere," Lauren said then paused. "Jerrica, what's going on with you?"

"Wow, that came out of nowhere."

Lauren giggled. "Listen, we don't have time to ease into a conversation. We have only twenty minutes before we dock and I can tell you need to talk."

Jerrica knew she wasn't going to get out of this one. She was going to have to talk. "You and I both know what this meeting is all about. It's not about business, though she has put a lot of effort disguising it as such. This is about Devin's need for control or should I say control of me."

Jerrica leaned her back against the railing. "I honestly don't know what is going through her head right now. We as a couple have been finished for almost a year now. Does she think that she will win me back if she threatens my career? I don't know what to expect when we get there and that frightens me."

Holding her hands in the air, Lauren said, "Don't ask me what she is thinking, you're the one who dated her. So what is your plan of attack?"

"I really don't have one. The one thing I know for sure is that the meeting tomorrow is our top priority. We need to dazzle them with our presentation, so we keep their account." Jerrica hesitated. "The rest… I'll have to play by ear."

"Well, playing by ear is better than nothing at all."

Jerrica's expression saddened as she looked off into the distance. "I barely talked to Madison this week. I think I made a mistake not telling her the whole truth about Devin."

"I told you, you should have been up front with her. I watched her mope around the office the past few days. I don't understand how two people who love one another have such communication trouble. This is the beginning of your relationship. This is the time when you tell one another everything about your past, plus your dreams and your hopes for the future."

"This is all new to me, Lauren. I've never really done this before. I know I've screwed up, big time. I'm going to call her once we are settled. I'll ask her out for dinner to talk. Hopefully I can salvage what we've begun."

"If you truly love one another, everything will work out."

"I hope you're right, Lauren. I hope you're right."

Chapter Eighteen

The drive from the ferry terminal to the Daniel residence would normally only take them about fifteen minutes. However, getting off the ferry was going to take a lot longer. Even though the staff on the ferry was expert in unloading vehicles, the tourists were not as adept. Impatient visitors jockeyed for position to get off the ferry first and tempers began to flare. The hand gestures were flying and the colorful language that people yelled back and forth only made departing the vessel harder. Two pain relievers and thirty-five minutes later, Jerrica's front tires finally rolled onto Nantucket Island.

With a child's wonder, Lauren took in the sights as they drove toward the estate. She had visited the island once when she was a youngster, but never this far across. She marveled at the historic buildings and the small towns— which time seemed to have forgotten— as they passed through. The drive went by quickly. When they turned into the Daniel's driveway, Lauren gasped. Her hand covered her mouth and her eyes grew wider as the property grew larger the closer they approached. The newly renovated two-story New England colonial was painted a medium weather gray with white trim and had what looked like floor to ceiling windows in just about every room. Looking just past the house, all she could see was the blue of the ocean in the near distance.

"So this is what's it looks like to be wealthy," Lauren muttered.

Jerrica smiled at Lauren's reaction as she steered toward the oversized garage located left of the main house.

Jerrica found a spot to park just past the building. Turning the ignition off, Jerrica examined the volume of vehicles already parked. She pushed the button to pop the trunk as she got out. Almost making it to the back of the car, she saw someone rushing toward them.

"Ms. Kerrison, how have you been?"

"Good morning, Peter," she replied as he reached in her trunk to grab her bags. "I would like to introduce you to my associate and friend, Lauren."

"It is afternoon now, Ms. Kerrison," he responded with a wink, then turning toward Lauren, he greeted her. "Nice to meet you, Ms. Lauren. You women are the last to turn up. The older Ms. Daniel is in the parlor awaiting your arrival."

Jerrica smiled weakly at him, trying not to show her nervousness. She had never met Devin's parents. She had always done business through Devin or their attorneys.

"Well, follow me," he said with a glint in his eye. "Even though I know you know the way, Ms. Kerrison."

Lowering her head in embarrassment, she whispered. "Yes, Peter."

He led them from the garage to the main house.

The door opened the moment they stepped up onto the porch. A portly old woman stepped out to greet them. Her hair had gotten a little grayer since the last time she had seen her, but her kind beautiful eyes were the same.

With open arms, the woman greeted her. "Well, Ms. Jerrica, it's been a long, long time. I was so happy to hear you would be attending this shindig."

"Molly, you look great," commented Jerrica as they hugged.

"I never thought I would see you here again, Ms. Jerrica."

Stepping back Jerrica replied, "I never thought I would be back." Leaning in so only Molly could hear. "Is she here?"

Molly nodded and glanced up.

A statuesque silhouette appeared behind Molly. As the person stepped forward, her face was illuminated from the reflection of the sun. The woman was dressed casually in a pair of white slacks and a pink cotton blouse.

Jerrica could tell, even though the woman was on an upper doorway step, that she was at least two inches taller than her or Lauren.

Deep blue eyes gazed from Jerrica to Lauren as a welcoming smile developed. Extending her arm, she spoke coolly. "You must be the representatives from Morrill, Hartford and Donahue."

Taking the offered hand in hers, Jerrica replied, "Yes, we are. I'm Jerrica Kerrison and this is my associate, Lauren Blanchet."

"I'm Victoria Daniel."

Jerrica felt the hand tighten around hers. Scrutinizing eyes stared down at Jerrica. "Ms. Kerrison, it's so nice to finally meet you. My daughter speaks very highly of you," she paused to clear her throat. "And your company. Ms. Blanchet, welcome to our home."

Slowly Victoria released her grip and Jerrica tried to reply professionally, "Well, Mrs. Daniel we hope that we can continue doing business for you."

"I think that this is what this weekend will determine."

Turning she addressed Peter. "Please take these ladies to the guest cottage."

Victoria smiled turning her attention back to Jerrica. "Since you two are the last ones to arrive, we've had to set you up in the cottage with a representative from a competing company, instead of the main house. Peter can introduce you to them when you reach the cottage. We do have an agenda for today and tomorrow. This afternoon, everyone is free to roam and enjoy all the many amenities we have here at the estate. Between six and seven, on the back veranda, we will be serving hors d'oeuvres. At seven p.m., dinner is in the formal dining area. Drinks and conversation will follow dinner in the family room. Please remember ladies, this is a formal, but social affair and we would like the business talk kept to a minimum at least for this evening."

She paused briefly. "Your meeting tomorrow is scheduled for ten a.m. All meetings will be in Mr. Daniel's office on the west side of the house. We've allotted one hour for each company. We do request that all representatives stay on the property until all meetings are over, just in case we have any additional questions. All presentations will be no later than three tomorrow afternoon. This should give everyone plenty of time to catch the late afternoon ferry to the mainland."

Jerrica wanted to argue, but thought better of it and nodded her head in understanding.

Victoria looked at Peter again. "Peter, please take these young ladies down to the cottage to get settled."

She looked once more directly at Jerrica., "If you are unsure of the locations of any of these events, please ask Peter or one of our other staff members to show you the way. I'm glad you could make it and I hope you have an enjoyable time."

With that, she abruptly turned, disappearing into the house.

Peter and Molly were quietly talking amongst themselves as the two women just looked at one another in puzzlement.

Lauren shrugged her shoulders and turned toward their guide.

Noticing that everyone was ready, Molly stepped back, playfully tapping her husband's arm. "You take good care of my girl, now. Remember, Ms. Jerrica, if you need anything later, you just call."

"Thank you, Molly," Jerrica leaned forward, kissing the woman's cheek as the group started the walk to the cottage.

Peter guided them around the house on the semi-wrap around porch and onto the granite stone pathway that would wind its way to the cottage.

There wasn't a piece of dead grass anywhere in sight on the perfectly manicured lawn. Strategically placed walls of shrubs almost concealed the Olympic size in-ground pool as they passed. Once they were by the row of shrubs on the farther side of the pool, the cottage came into view. The guest cottage was a smaller version of the main house. The house was situated close enough to the main house for interaction if the guest wanted, but far enough to give privacy.

Peter placed the luggage on the front porch, pulling a handkerchief from his front pocket and wiping his sweat-covered brow. "Ms. Jerrica, would you mind getting yourselves settled? You know where everything is located. I still have to go get the furniture placed for this evening and I'm starting to get plum tired."

Jerrica smiled. "Go on, Peter, we will be fine. Don't let that old bitty work you too hard."

"It's not the old bitty I'm worried about, it's my Molly. These parties are her specialty and she'll have my backside if I don't do things just the way she wants them."

With a sassy grin, he bowed to Jerrica and then to Lauren. "It was nice to meet you, Ms. Lauren. I'll probably see you both later."

Turning, he started back up the path.

"He's a character," Lauren said with a giggle.

"Yes, he is," she observed, watching him walk away. "Shall we go in?"

Jerrica's hand reached for the handle of her bag as the cottage door opened.

"Do my eyes deceive me or is that the great Jerrica Kerrison I see in front of me?"

Lauren looked from her boss to the striking voluptuous blonde-haired woman in a tiny black string bikini who was standing in the doorway. The expression she witnessed on Jerrica's face told her they knew one another.

Releasing the handle, Jerrica bounced up the steps. "Hello, Courtney! How have you been?" Jerrica embraced the woman.

Lightly kissing one another on the cheek as they stepped back, Courtney let her gaze wash across Jerrica. She was not trying to hide the pleasure of what she saw. "I had heard we might be sharing the cottage with other reps, but I didn't think it would be with the top financial guru and her henchman from Morrill, Hartford, and Donahue."

Either she was trying to flatter them or was searching for a fight. Lauren couldn't decide which one.

Jerrica smiled, her face flushing lightly as she turned to retrieve her bag again. "Courtney darling, you haven't changed. Isn't it a little too cool in the sea to be swimming?"

"Oh, silly, Jerrica, the pool is heated. It's nice to know you are concerned for my well-being."

"Concern is a strong word," Jerrica faked a smile. "It's always a pleasure running into you, Courtney."

Lauren lifted her bag from the porch landing, walking toward the doorway.

"Oh, it could be pleasurable, darling," Courtney whispered as she placed another small kiss on Jerrica's cheek. Stepping aside, Courtney remarked. "May the best woman win."

"Oh, I plan to, darling," Jerrica replied as she entered the guesthouse.

Lauren said nothing as she passed by the smug woman. She heard the front door close abruptly as they walked through the large open concept kitchen-living room area, traveling down a long hallway toward what she figured were the bedrooms. The closed doors on the first two bedrooms made them realize someone had already claimed them. They reached the first open door and both women looked in to see if the room was empty. Lauren jumped in the room yelling, "This one's mine!"

Jerrica laughed at her enthusiasm, but continued to the last bedroom at the end of the hall. Standing in the doorway, looking around the room, memories of a time gone by flooded her mind. Taking one-step forward, she placed her luggage on the stand next to the door. The room hadn't changed. The queen size comforter on the bed matched the curtains in the large window that overlooked Nantucket harbor. Tiny boats, with captain's wheels and little life rings covered almost every inch of this room's décor. The nautical theme of the room even crept its way into the en-suite bathroom. She made her way to the bed, sitting on the edge. Lost in the memories, she lightly brushed her hand across the soft material, unaware Lauren was watching her.

"Well, I don't have to ask if you've been in this room before," Lauren commented as she walked in, tapping closed the door behind her.

Jerrica closed her eyes, falling lazily back on the bed.

"Would you like to explain to me what just transpired between you and Courtney darling at the front door?"

Jerrica grinned as Lauren sat on the other side of the bed looking down at her. "Courtney and I have a very brief history."

"No kidding. Do you care to elaborate?"

"Not really."

Lauren crossed her arms across her chest. "Well, too bad. We have plenty of time before we are due for cocktail hour. Spill it, Jerrica."

She sighed. "I've known Courtney for a while. When you travel in the same financial circles long enough, you start to meet your competition regularly. Do you remember when I had to go to Phoenix a while back to prepare that manufacturing company for the government audit?"

Lauren thought a second, then nodded her head.

"Well, I ran into Courtney in the hotel lobby. She was there on business as well."

Lauren fell back on the bed next to Jerrica.

Both sets of eyes were staring at the ceiling as she continued. "To cut to the chase, we had dinner later that evening and one thing led to another...."

"Wait," Lauren rolled on her side, propping herself on her elbow. "I thought devil woman was the only one you have been with...besides Madison...."

"Devil woman; creative name, Lauren," Jerrica said with a smile, "Yes, Devin was my first intimate experience with a woman. Courtney and I just had a one-night kind of thing. It wasn't an important event in my life —not enough to make it part of my bio. Besides, Courtney isn't gay, she's bi-curious and I am sure her husband wouldn't want to know she's been involved with a woman or anyone else for that matter. He's the jealous type."

"That goddess," Lauren said, pointing to the door, "has a husband?"

"Yup, and I've met him, too."

"Wow!" Lauren paused to think. "You got to tap that! She's gorgeous and God knows you do need the experience."

Jerrica grabbed a small pillow, smacking Lauren with it.

Lauren playfully blocked it as they both laughed.

Sitting up, Jerrica became serious, "We have five hours before we are required to socialize. I would like to spend at least three hours prepping for tomorrow. Then I can take you around the property to see the cliffs and the beach. If we time it right, we can be back here in plenty of time to change and be at the main house just after six. "

"I'll go retrieve the paperwork out of my case and maybe you can rustle up some food. I'm hungry."

"You got it. I'll call the main house and have someone send something down."

Alone in the room Jerrica tried to call Madison on her cell. The phone didn't even ring, switching directly to voice mail. The tone in her voice said more than the brief message she left. Clicking the phone off, Jerrica tossed it on the bed, sighing in despair. Once Lauren returned to her room, they started working. Jerrica had turned on a radio for background noise and she paced the floor as she recited her speech, pointing to imaginary graphs that would be part of her PowerPoint presentation.

Lauren sat on the bed with her back against the headboard, notebook in her lap, studying her boss. She watched Jerrica go through the motions, and jotted down ideas and comments that they would discuss later.

They made a good team. They worked straight through the afternoon. They paused only once when the pitcher of lemonade, and a fruit and cheese plate arrived. They could occasionally hear joyful laughter on the breeze throughout the day. The noise of the carefree visitors only fueled the determination growing deep inside the women of Morrill, Hartford, and Donahue to be the best at their jobs. When Jerrica finished her speech, she sat down on the bed to discuss Lauren's notes and suggestions. After a few more rewrites and a chart insertion, they were both satisfied with their work for the day.

Peering at her watch, Jerrica realized that they were actually a little ahead of her schedule and would have more time outside.

Taking no chances, Lauren separated the presentation into two folders.

Jerrica took one folder, placing it between the mattress and box spring.

Lauren would take the other folder into her room and hide it somewhere for safekeeping. No one was going to steal what they had worked so hard to produce.

†

"I'm glad you decided to schedule in a trip to the beach," Lauren said, pushing sand between her toes as they walked the edge of the water.

"Is that a compliment or are you being sarcastic."

"Take that any way you want to."

Jerrica slapped Lauren on her arm and they both laughed. They strolled along the beach enjoying the sun, sand, and sounds of the water. And one another's silent company.

†

The dark blue eyes narrowed as they followed Jerrica and Lauren's walk down the beach. A low giggle escaped her throat as she remembered her unpleasant dealings with Lauren, a protective woman with a quick sarcastic attitude.

She would have to find a way around her to get to her prey. A broad smile grew on the lovely young face as she continued to enjoy the view of the beach. She observed every move the pair made until finally they disappeared into the guesthouse. Devin decided it was time to get dressed for her guests.

Jerrica Kerrison you will be mine, she vowed.

Chapter Nineteen

Moving her hand across the fogged mirror, Jerrica smiled at her reflection. The hot shower had been invigorating, having removed all the sea and sand smell that had entered her pores. Wrapped in a towel, she softly towel dried her hair, gently combing it out. Leaving the bathroom to clear out from the mist, she went to her bag to retrieve her underclothes. She wouldn't wear a bra to accommodate the cut on the back of her dress. Pulling on her bikini and garter belt, she carefully pulled her thigh high nylons over her shapely legs. Once the underclothing was attached, she returned to the bathroom to finish hair and make-up. Finishing all the prep-work, she was finally able to wiggle the long flowing dress down over her shoulders. The wide shoulder straps on her dark blue empire dress accented the sparkling silver trimmed neckline. The front dipped just enough to show a little cleavage, but not enough to give anything away. She displayed a blue sapphire pendant on a silver chain around her neck and matching earrings.

Lauren smiled when Jerrica opened her door.

"Hey, just in time. Can you zip me up?" Jerrica asked as she turned around.

She stepped into the room, closing the door behind her. Lauren straightened the crisscross straps on her back then fastened the zipper. Lauren noticed the back of Jerrica's dress revealed a lot of skin.

Jerrica spun around to get a good look at what Lauren had picked out. Lauren was wearing a strapless floor length dress, the color of lavender. The pleated material under the bust line highlighted the empire waist design. The pleats followed the flowing fabric to the floor, giving the illusion that Lauren was taller than she actually was. Beautiful diamond studs adorned her ears. Her hair was long enough to cascade past her shoulders, so she wore no necklace.

"You look great," Jerrica commented.

"Don't sound so surprised," Lauren said putting her hands on her hips. "I like your hair style. You can see more of your features that way."

Jerrica turned away before Lauren could see her blush. "Now where did I put those shoes?"

†

Later, on the terrace, Jerrica took a quick look around, staking out the terrain. When she spotted her hosts sitting at the far table under a deck umbrella, Jerrica tapped her associate on the shoulder. Calculating her steps, she made her way to the table with Lauren close behind.

Victoria Daniel established eye contact with Jerrica first. "Ms. Kerrison, I see you finally decided to join us." Standing, Victoria extending her hand in greeting,

"I don't think you have met my husband, Franklin," she said, turning to the older man who was slowly rising, "Franklin, these are the representatives from Morrill, Hartford and Donahue, Ms. Jerrica Kerrison and Ms. Lauren Blanchet."

They shook hands, awkwardly. His eyes met hers as his grip tightened uncomfortably around her hand. His amber eyes studied her openly, never releasing her hand.

"You're right, darling, I haven't had the pleasure of ever meeting Ms. Kerrison. I'm glad you and your associate could make it."

Never breaking eye contact, she replied. "I don't think I've had the delight of meeting you either, Mr. Daniel. If I had met someone as dapper as you, I'm sure I would have remembered."

Franklin laughed heartily, releasing his grip on her hand and sitting back down. Turning to his wife who was now sitting beside him, he commented, "She's a sharp one, Victoria. Maybe their company does have a chance."

"Thank you for coming tonight and I'm sure we'll talk again real soon," Victoria stated.

"It would be my pleasure," Jerrica answered as she backed into the small crowd, disappearing from the elder Daniels' view.

Jerrica and Lauren moved their way through the crowd to the edge of the terrace. Leaning up against the railing, Jerrica took a sip of her drink to help calm her nerves.

Lauren waited as her boss slowly regained her composure. "I think that went well," she said sarcastically.

Jerrica couldn't help but laugh, letting the tension melt away. Where they were standing, Jerrica had a good view of the crowd and the doors. As she swept the room with her eyes, some faces looked familiar and she was able to place which company they worked for, but other faces she didn't recognize.

The waiters were very efficient with their given tasks. Their glasses never reached empty before the staff graciously refilled them. Food trays were always floating around for those who enjoyed expensive caviar on dry crackers or a fresh variety of imported exotic sushi. The Daniel family didn't do things half way.

Jerrica and Lauren were talking amongst themselves when the sudden decrease in the group's volume caught their attention.

The crowd parted like the Red Sea as Devin Daniel graced the terrace with her presence. She was captivating in a black halter style, form fitted A-line dress with cut out-sides. Her blonde hair was pinned up in the back, making the long curls flow down past her shoulder. The halter-top was trimmed in gold and diamonds. All eyes watched as she glided from guest to guest saying a few words of welcome to everyone she passed.

Her eyes quickly scanned the crowd. Finding her prize at the edge of the veranda, she stifled a grin of satisfaction as she glided toward her parents. The volume of voices returned to normal the moment she reached her parents' table.

"Talk about a grand entrance, the queen is here," Lauren said before sipping her drink.

It was only a brief second that their eyes had met, but Jerrica recognized the look in those pools of blue, Devin was on the prowl. Glancing up at the colors of the dimming blue sky with scattered puffy white clouds, transitioning into the darker early evening covers of pinks and yellows, Jerrica whispered to the heavens. "Oh, Lord, help me."

Jerrica made every effort not to watch Devin leave her parents, working her charm as she greeted more guests.

Like a snake, Devin slithered from group to group making introductions and joking with those she knew closely.

It was obvious to Jerrica that she was going to make her wait. Turning her head to look out across the grounds, she sighed in frustration. Time dragged on as Jerrica absent-mindedly started rotating the almost full flute of Champagne in hand.

"Is our Champagne not to your liking, sweetheart?"

Jerrica glanced down at her glass, then up into the determined face.

Devin extended her hand. "Why, Ms. Blanchet, or may I call you Lauren?"

"Ms. Blanchet is fine."

Jerrica glared at Lauren as Lauren took Devin's hand.

"Very well, Ms. Blanchet, I am so glad you could attend."

Retrieving her hand, Lauren retorted. "Did I have an alternative?"

Devin openly laughed as she offered her hand to Jerrica. "Ms. Blanchet, you never change." She grasped the other hand being offered. "Ms. Kerrison, I'm so glad you could attend as well."

Holding up her half of appearances, Jerrica replied. "Please call me Jerrica and thank you, Ms. Daniel, for the gracious invitation. You have a very lovely home here."

There was a strong tension between them as they stared at one another. Devin held onto Jerrica's hand as she leaned in closely to Jerrica's ear.

"We will talk later, my love," Devin whispered, releasing her hand. "Enjoy your time, ladies.," She turned to leave.

"Bitch," Lauren whispered.

Devin whirled on Lauren. Standing within inches of Lauren's face, Devin stared defiantly into her eyes, "Jerrica, please tell your pit-bull to heel or I'll have her physically removed."

Lauren didn't move nor break eye contact. She wasn't going to be the first one to back down.

Jerrica reached and placed her hand on Devin's soft shoulder.

Feeling the warm touch, a touch she hadn't felt in a long time, she slanted her head to look at Jerrica.

In a low tone, Jerrica voiced seductively. "Devin, please, this display is not necessary. I promise we'll talk later."

Jerrica received the results she was hoping for when, graciously, Devin stepped back.

With a quick smile, she returned to her other guests like a proper host.

Stepping forward Jerrica squinted at Lauren. Her voice only loud enough for Lauren to hear. "Are you trying to break this deal for us?"

"I won't cower to her and you shouldn't either. If they want to keep doing business with MHD then let the business speak for itself. Don't sell your soul along with it."

"I'm not selling my soul." Jerrica sounded surprised. "And I take offense to that."

"I have always been honest with you, Jerrica. You need to really stop and look at the whole picture going on here." Lauren sipped her Champagne again. "I'm real sorry if that hurts your feelings, but it's true."

Reaching out, she brushed Jerrica's forearm with her fingertips, smiling shyly.

As if on cue, a butler stepped out from the house and announced they were serving dinner in the formal dining room. The parade of people began to file into the house.

Jerrica was happy to see the gathering heading away from them, all but one person. An attractive man about six-feet tall, wearing a sleek black tuxedo was cautiously walking their way. The man looked like he might be in his early fifties, but Jerrica wasn't sure.

"Lauren Reynold, is that you?" the baritone voice asked.

Lauren, head tilted to the side in confusion, replied. "It's Blanchet now, but Reynold is my maiden name. Do I know you?"

The corner of his mouth curled up as he raised a hand to his chest. "Lauren, it's me, Andrew...Andrew Chasson."

Lauren stepped forward, raising a hand to the side of his face. They embraced lovingly.

Shock was the only expression you could read on Jerrica's face. She had no idea who this person was or how he knew Lauren.

When Lauren stepped away, she was blushing. "Mr. Chasson, this is my boss and friend, Jerrica Kerrison. Jerrica, this is a very old and dear friend of mine, Andrew Chasson."

"Call me Andrew," he replied as they shook hands.

"I don't mean to put a damper on the moment, but I think we are expected in the formal dining room."

His hand took Lauren's in his, raising it to his lips and softly kissing the back. "May I see you later, after dinner? Maybe catch up?"

Lauren lowered her eyes. "That would be lovely, Andrew."

His eyes reflected joy as he relinquished her hand and looked at Jerrica. "It was nice meeting you as well, Jerrica."

Without haste, he disappeared into the house with the other guests.

Jerrica turned her head to look at Lauren who was still looking in the direction Andrew had gone. She could tell by the faraway look in her eyes that there was a lot more to this story then just running into an old friend.

"Would you like to explain that to me?" Jerrica pointed toward the house.

"Nope," answered Lauren as she glanced at Jerrica, then back at the house. "I'm hungry, let's go eat."

Chapter Twenty

The final guests filtered into the dining room, seating themselves in the scattered empty chairs. Jerrica sat across from Lauren. With everyone seated at the long rectangle oak table, Jerrica could now sum up the competition. Jerrica calculated that there were sixteen people sitting at the table. The Daniel family counted for three, between familiar faces and other mannerisms, she figured ten, including she and Lauren, were there for the competition, but there were two men and one woman that she just couldn't place. One of those people was Lauren's friend, Andrew. She wondered what their role was for this weekend. Were they friend or foe? From her vantage point, she could see everyone she needed to watch.

There was quiet chitchat during dinner as the wait staff fluently served a superb four-course meal. When dessert was finally served, consisting of fresh strawberry puree drizzled on a decadent piece of New York cheesecake, Jerrica graciously declined. This didn't go unnoticed by the hostess.

"Why, Ms. Kerrison, did you not care for your dessert?"

"It looks absolutely delicious, Ms. Daniel, I'm just not much for such lavish sweets. But thank you for your concern about my eating habits." Though civil, her tone bordered on sarcasm.

The room went deadly silent as every head swiveled toward Victoria Daniel to see what her response would be.

Always graceful and dignified, Victoria lifted her glass, acknowledging Jerrica's statement with a smile and a nod.

Jerrica repeated the motion, putting an end to the dinnertime show. Jerrica peered above the rim of her glass at Lauren as she sipped her drink. The smirk on her face told Jerrica she approved of the recent interaction with the elder Daniel.

The room remained strangely silent during dessert. The sound of silverware touching china plates echoed though the room until everyone had completed their dish. Mr. Daniel placed his napkin beside his plate. Standing, he made an announcement. "Ladies and gentlemen, if you would care to, please join me in the family room for pleasantries."

Like good little lab rats following the master with the cheese, everyone stood and did what was instructed, everyone except the representatives from Morrill, Hartford and Donahue. They sat quietly until they were the only two, besides staff clearing the table, left in the dining room.

"We could have showed up tomorrow and missed all of this," Jerrica said as she waved her arms in exasperation., "I don't understand why they wanted us to come tonight. They've spent all of five seconds with us all evening. This is all bullshit."

"You forget who's behind this," replied Lauren as she got to her feet., "Shall we go?"

"Let the record show, I don't want to do this."

"It has been noted, boss lady. Now put on that fake smile and let's go mingle."

Since they were the last ones to enter the family room, every head turned when they appeared. Before Jerrica had a chance to look around, Andrew and an unknown woman entered her personal space. Jerrica watched, as a strange feeling seemed to pass through Lauren and Andrew as their eyes met.

"Ms. Kerrison, is it okay if I steal Lauren from you for a little while?" Andrew said not even looking in Jerrica's direction.

"Andrew, I don't want to leave Jerrica here by herself." Lauren's voice was just above a whisper.

"I think I can entertain her for a while," said the mystery woman. She held out her hand. "I'm Paula."

"Jerrica."

"Well, I guess everything is settled. Shall we go find a quiet place to talk?" Andrew held out his arm.

With a smile to her boss, Lauren turned, wrapped her hand around Andrew's elbow, and floated away.

Jerrica couldn't believe that Lauren had just left her there. Jerrica almost felt like a third wheel on a date, being pawned off on the wingman. In this case, it was the wing woman. Jerrica felt very uncomfortable. As fate would have it, a staff member was walking around with more trays of Champagne. She motioned for him to come over. Removing two glasses from the tray, she handed one to her guest. Before the waiter could leave, Jerrica asked if she could order a stronger drink. After taking her request, he politely excused himself, making his way toward the bar area.

"I know who you are," Paula commented.

"Excuse me," Jerrica said, choking on the Champagne.

"I have been wracking my brain all evening trying to figure out who you were. You're Jerrica Kerrison from Morrill, Hartford, and Donahue. I recognized you from your article in Forbes magazine." Paula sounded excited as she continued. "I must have read that article about twenty times."

"I'm glad you enjoyed it," Jerrica said flatly.

Paula didn't seem to notice as she rambled on with excitement.

Jerrica tried to pay attention to the clueless woman who was chatting away. Often she would add a 'righ't or 'that's interesting' to the conversation, to make it sound like she was listening. She consumed the stronger drink in two gulps; seconds after the waiter had put it in her hand. Jerrica's eyes were just about to glaze from boredom or maybe it was the alcohol when Paula stopped talking.

"I'm sorry, could you repeat that?" asked Jerrica, suddenly aware Paula was waiting for an answer.

Paula smile widened. "I asked you to clarify what you meant in your article when you said and I quote, 'Life is such a short drive. Why not stop at every exit to see where it takes you.' Did you mean professionally or personally."

"Yes, Ms. Kerrison, do explain your meaning," interjected Devin.

Jerrica spun around to find Devin standing just behind her.

Paula stood next to Jerrica waiting for her to answer.

Devin was baiting her again.

Totally ignoring Devin, Jerrica turned to Paula, "I'm sorry, but I've suddenly developed a headache. Maybe it's the alcohol. Would you please excuse me?"

"Ms. Daniel, could you please give your parents my apologies for having to retire early?" she said, turning to Devin.

Devin nodded her head as Jerrica cased the room for Lauren.

"Ms. Kerrison, why don't you go rest and I'll make sure your associate knows of your location," Devin's phony concern was written on her face.

"Thank you, Ms. Daniel, I would appreciate your assistance. Goodnight, ladies." Jerrica graciously smiled at both of them, then withdrew from the room.

Chapter Twenty-One

The two-inch heels and restricting gown made running out of the main house impossible. It took longer for her to get to the cottage than anticipated. She had planned to have enough time to change into a more suitable outfit before Devin's arrival. She estimated it would take at least twenty minutes for Devin to slip from the party without someone connecting that both of them were absent. She left the bedroom door partially open. She was pulling down the last window blind when she heard the front door open. Jerrica stood perfectly still with her back to the windows, staring at the doorway, anxiously waiting. Devin entered the room with so much arrogance that Jerrica could feel it from across the room. Her anger began to fester low in her belly.

Devin strolled toward Jerrica, but stopped at the edge of the bed.

Jerrica watched as Devin slid her hands down her lower back, over her curvy buttocks, tucking the dress as she seated herself on the bed. Her gaze didn't wander as Devin crossed her legs. When their eyes finally met, Jerrica uttered, "Why, Devin?"

Devin pondered the question a moment then wetted her lips. "Because I love you."

"What you are doing to me, you don't do to people you love. You hide your cruel actions and selfishness under this blanket you call love. "

Devin looked at her hands in her lap, her confidence wavering. "You wouldn't talk to me. You totally shut me out of your life. I had to get your attention."

Tossing her hands in the air in frustration, she turned to one side. "There are better ways to get my attention than ruining my career."

"Ruining you?" Devin's voice went up a few octaves. "What about me?"

Standing, she stepped closer. "You never gave me a chance, us a chance. You walked out on us! You told me you loved me."

Jerrica could see the hurt in her eyes, hear the anger in her voice. "I tried to give us a chance. You're the one who destroyed us. I told you from the beginning, I wouldn't hide who I was ever again and that's what you wanted me to do. You haven't been honest with your parents or yourself," Jerrica said and sighed., "I can't deny that we had something special together, but I realize now it wasn't love. Maybe it was admiration or lust, but we weren't in love."

"No! Don't say that, Jerrica! I know you love me! I know you do!"

Without any warning, she lunged at Jerrica, knocking her off balance as she pushed her against the windows. Devin pinned Jerrica's arms above her head, then captured her lips with her own.

Jerrica struggled to get away, but the weight of Devin's body prevented her from escaping. A shapely thigh shoved between her legs and further kept her off balance.

Devin pulled her lips away, burying her face in the crook of Jerrica's neck. "I know you love me. I know you do."

Jerrica could hear her repeating that phrase several times near her ear. "Devin, let me go," Jerrica pleaded, trying to push her away.

Devin shifted her weight again to hold Jerrica captive, but freed at least one hand.

Panic rushed through every vein in Jerrica's body as she not only felt, but also heard the material of her gown being ripped open, exposing her flesh.

"No, stop!" Jerrica screamed as flashbacks of a previous life flooded her mind. Quickly placing her shoe on the low windowsill, Jerrica pushed as hard as she could; sending them both tumbling toward the bed.

Devin released Jerrica as she tried to catch herself before falling to the floor.

Jerrica fell to her knees, but was able to scramble to her feet, pulling the ripped side of her dress closed.

Devin kneeled on the floor breathing heavily. She used the edge of the bed to help her stand. When Devin finally turned around, Jerrica was in full swing, slapping her hard across the face. "How dare you! I am not something you can just take! You do not own me, Devin Daniel!"

The look on Devin's face as she held her hand to the side of her face was worth the pain now radiating through Jerrica's hand.

Devin's eyes narrowed. "How could you hit me?"

"You're lucky that's all I did! You were forcing yourself on me! What did you expect me to do? I am not one of your whores!"

"I don't know what I expected. I guess I hoped if I made you see we belong together, that you would come back to me. Everything just got out of hand." A bright red handprint was beginning to develop on her cheek.

Jerrica walked to the door. With one hand on the doorknob, she motioned to Devin. "I want you to go. Now!"

Jerrica reached in her bag, retrieving the phone as Devin walked toward her. She held it out for Devin to take, "Take this! I don't want any of your gifts."

A flash of anger raged through Devin as she ripped the phone out of Jerrica's hand and pitched it at the wall.

Jerrica watched as the brand new phone struck the wall, shattering into millions of pieces and scattering across the room. Jerrica looked at Devin in surprise.

"I don't want the fucking phone, I want you."

"Well, you can't have me," she said as she opened the door.

"Mark my words, Jerrica, once you get tired of your pretty little girl toy, you'll be back. You've never been able to resist me."

Confidence filled her voice. "I just did, Ms. Daniel. Now, please leave."

Jerrica watched as Devin's blonde hair swayed on her back as she left. Was Devin referring to Madison? Jerrica locked the bedroom door before she sat down on the bed. Her hands were shaking as the adrenaline rush was beginning to wear off. Without warning, tears started trickling down her face. She could feel the sobs building in her throat. A soft knock on the door startled Jerrica. She didn't answer; instead sat motionless until she heard the loving voice on the other side.

"Jerrica, are you okay? It's Lauren."

Jerrica rushed across the room to open the door.

Lauren wrapped the sobbing Jerrica in her arms. Trying to comfort Jerrica, the only way she knew how, by holding her tight. Lauren felt helpless, not knowing what exactly had transpired that evening. Acting more like a Mom then an employee, Lauren help Jerrica change into sleepwear and into bed. Lauren noticed the large rips in the gown as she draped it over a nearby chair. She held Jerrica's hand as she recounted what had occurred that evening between Devin and her, pointing absently to the pieces of cell phone on the floor.

Lauren heard the panicked tone in her voice.

Jerrica could see the anger in Lauren's eyes, but was too weary to argue with her. The last thing she remembered before she passed out from exhaustion was Lauren kissing her on the forehead, and then turning off the light.

†

The unexpected sound of music shocked Jerrica from her slumber. Reaching up, she flipped the switch to shut the alarm off. She pulled back the blankets about to get out of bed, but halted when she heard a light snore beside her. Cautiously rolling over, Jerrica saw a beautiful woman sleeping soundly on the other side of the bed. Jerrica smiled as she watched Lauren sleep. She slipped out of bed, heading for the bathroom to change. When she re-entered the room, she was in her jogging t-shirt and shorts. Jerrica softly touched Lauren's arm to wake her.

Lauren turned onto her back, slowly opening her eyes.

"Good morning. Thank you for staying with me. I'm going to the beach for a run. Maybe you should hop in the shower to wake up and then order us some breakfast."

"How are you doing this morning?"

"I'm doing okay, better than last night. Can I borrow your phone?"

Lauren nodded as she yawned some of the sleep away.

Jerrica picked up Lauren's cell phone from the nightstand. Walking to the windows, she dialed Madison.

Lauren sat on the side of the bed, observing.

Within seconds, Jerrica clicked the phone off. "Voicemail again," she said handing the phone to Lauren. "I'll be back."

The sun was rising slowly in the sky. She did her warm up stretches on the wooden walkway that led to the deserted beach. There was a small breeze coming off the water, which made her happy she had put her hair in a small ponytail. The music was blasting through her ear buds as she started down the beach, with a muddled mind and a sad heart.

Chapter Twenty-Two

"You look lost, can I help you with something, beautiful?" Devin said with a devilish smirk.

"I was looking for someone," the surprised woman replied, trying to shade her eyes from the rising sun, not able to see the person addressing her.

Devin sized up the familiar woman standing at the bottom of the porch stairs. Her black hair was styled perfectly to accentuate her sun kissed skin and she had amazing bedroom brown eyes. She was a little shorter than herself, but had a very nice build. She pleasantly filled out a light blue polo shirt, khaki pants, and black Doc Martin shoes. "Who are you looking for?"

"I'm looking for Jerrica Kerrison."

As if a light switched turned on in her head, Devin remembered. This was the woman she had seen Jerrica kissing the other day. Devin narrowed her eyes. Thinking quickly on her feet, Devin stepped into the light, completely revealing herself. Her golden hair flowed freely in the light breeze and her blue eyes stared at her new victim.

This woman was gorgeous and she knew it. Madison stifled a small gasp as she recognized the one of a kind, double-breasted navy blazer; Jerrica was the owner of that garment. The blazer was the only thing this woman was wearing. The blazer was just long enough to cover her intimate parts at the top of her thighs.

Devin's smile grew wider when she saw the recognition of the garment in the stranger's eyes. She stepped forward just enough to lean on one of the porch columns. "I'm afraid you just missed her," she said, running a fingertip up and down the lapel. "We were up late last night with… business…and she needed to get a run in this morning to wake up. She's on the beach right now."

†

Madison was puzzled. She hadn't heard from Jerrica since Thursday and even then, the conversation seemed filled with tension. Now here she was, in unfamiliar surroundings, looking at a half-naked woman, who was wearing one of Jerrica's favorite blazers, with no Jerrica to talk to or explain what was happening.

Devin continued on happily. "I don't know why she insists on running every morning. I can find many other ways for her to get her exercise. You know what I mean?" Devin winked, running a finger on the bottom seam of the jacket. "Would you like to wait for her?"

Madison felt her heart splinter into millions of pieces. *Jerrica how could you do this to us?* She wailed inside. "No, thank you. It's…not…that important."

Madison turned her back to Devin as tears started to fill her eyes. She didn't want this wicked creature, who relished her pain, to see her cry. Starting up the path, she could no longer contain the pain constricting her chest and began to cry openly.

†

"Madison?"

Devin spun her head around to see Jerrica running up the walkway from the beach.

Jerrica reached the porch, gasping for air and trying to speak. "Who was that?"

Bending at the waist, breathing heavy, she heard Devin answer. "I don't know, she didn't give her name."

One hand on her hip and one holding onto the banister, Jerrica's irritation for small talk with Devin was beginning to show. "What did she say?"

Devin retreated toward the entryway, stalling before answering over her shoulder. "She was looking for you."

"You bitch," Jerrica ran toward the main house.

†

Jerrica fell to her knees as the cloud of dust from the leaving car engulfed her. She was panting so hard, she thought she might pass out right there in the driveway. She had to get back to the cottage to get her keys. She had to catch her. Her muscles were burning, making every movement more excruciating then the last. Jerrica painstakingly returned to the cottage to find Devin and Courtney in the kitchen. Jerrica observed them playfully touching and kissing one another. Oh, my God, she slept with Courtney!

Lauren exited the bedroom, ready for their presentation as Jerrica stood in the doorway.

Jerrica rushed toward the kitchen and its occupants.

Lauren stepped in between Jerrica and the cuddling couple just as she lunged at them.

"You are a fucking bitch, Devin! I should choke you with my bare hands. You're trying to destroy my life!"

"I don't know what you're talking about," Devin replied as she scooted behind a bewildered Courtney for safety.

"That's bullshit and you know it," Jerrica shouted over Lauren's shoulder. Lauren was trying very hard to push her friend backward.

"Oh, please. If I wanted to destroy you, it would already be done." Glancing up at the clock, Devin smiled, "You might want to start getting ready, your meeting is in less than an hour…darling."

Mustering up her last bit of energy, Jerrica growled as she pushed Lauren to the side, charging Devin. Courtney didn't stand a chance as Jerrica shoved her away, wrapping both hands around Devin's neck. The momentum pushed Devin back into the counter.

By the time Lauren and Courtney were able to wrench Jerrica away from Devin, she was beyond reason.

Jerrica was yelling and kicking, as Lauren dragged her toward the bedroom.

Glancing back at the kitchen, Lauren knew Devin was fine as nurse Courtney was tending to the wounds. Lauren slammed the bedroom door behind them, dropping Jerrica to the floor. She had had enough. "Get your ass in that shower right now. You are behaving like a child! You can behave better than this! I want to kill her, too, but someone has to be the adult around here."

Jerrica stood, opening her mouth to talk, but Lauren stopped her.

"I don't want to hear it! Get in that shower and cool off!"

Jerrica lowered her head in defeat. Without further conversation, she entered the bathroom.

Twenty-five minutes passed before the bathroom door opened. Entering the room fully dressed for the meeting, Jerrica slowly walked to the bed where Lauren was sitting. Gracefully sitting down, she turned to face Lauren. "I'm sorry I put you through that. I didn't hurt you, did I?"

"No, you didn't hurt me. What happened?"

"Madison was here."

"Madison was here, when?"

"I thought I saw her when I was returning from the beach. She seemed to be conversing with Devin. As I got closer, she ran toward the main house. Not having my contacts in or my glasses on I wasn't sure it was Madison to begin with. When Devin finally told me she was looking for me, I ran after her, but she was gone. I wanted to chase her, but because of that damn scheduled meeting, I couldn't. My anger just took control the moment I got back here."

"Do you know what they talked about?"

"No, but it couldn't have been good. She left in a hurry without waiting to talk to me."

"I hate to add to your troubles, but did you see where your blazer currently is?"

Jerrica briefly looked puzzled, lowering her head in disbelief when the answer popped into her head. "Devin's wearing it, isn't she?"

"Yes and if you put two and two together, I think you can figure out what Madison might have thought or even been told by that crazy bitch."

"Shit! Can I borrow your phone?"

Snatching it from Lauren's hand Jerrica tried dialing Madison. Again, it went straight to voicemail, but this time she left a message saying they needed to talk. A dejected Jerrica dropped the cell phone into Lauren's hands.

Ever the supportive friend, Lauren commented. "You need to keep trying. She'll have to pick up sooner or later." Her tone changed, becoming sterner,

"Devin is still in the cottage, Jerrica. We are leaving in five minutes. I won't have any trouble getting you out of here, will I?"

"No, I promise."

"Good. Now go put some lipstick on and we'll leave."

Lauren cautiously opened the bedroom door, glancing down the deserted hallway. They made their way toward the front door, carrying their luggage, when a voice behind them stopped them in their tracks.

"I will make sure you leave here with nothing, Jerrica. You will have no career and you will be alone."

They both turned around to see Devin standing in the hallway, enraged.

"You will be begging me to take you back. You'll plead with me for your life back," Devin snarled.

Jerrica forced a calm smile on her face, but her anger was bubbling just under the surface. "Maybe you should hold your breath while you wait for me to come back," Jerrica snickered. "Oh, and by the way, I want my blazer."

Without a word, her eyes locked on Jerrica's, Devin unbuttoned the blazer, letting it fall off her shoulders, down to her waist, sliding it off her arms. Standing nude in front of both women, she extended her arm, with the blazer dangling from her fingertips.

Jerrica sauntered over, scooped the jacket over her arm and rotated on her heels. As Jerrica reached for the door, she turned to look at Devin.

"I hope you enjoyed my sloppy seconds," she said, nodding to the doorway where Courtney stood. Jerrica laughed as she let the screen door slam shut after her.

Lauren was the only one to speak as they walked toward the house. "If you take away the crazy bitch part, she's not too bad on the eyes."

Jerrica genuinely laughed.

Chapter Twenty-Three

Mr. Daniel had built his office to intimidate all who entered. Dark wood bookcases, stretching from floor to ceiling, covered most of the walls. Some sort of reading material covered each shelf. Jerrica doubted he had taken time to read even one. Walking to the oversized desk, she skimmed the smooth top with the palm of her hand.

"Explain that grin," Lauren demanded.

In a low tone Jerrica replied. "Let's just say, I've had a few experiences in this room already, on this desk especially." Winking evilly, she added, "It's very smooth on the skin."

Lauren giggled as Jerrica crossed the room, with a wide smile on her face, toward the table where they were to set up.

The oval conference table was located near the corner of the room, not giving Lauren and Jerrica much room to work in but they would make do. The presentation was ready when the first member of the Daniel corporation entered the room. One by one, they all filed in. Jerrica tried to hide her contempt as Devin was the last one to appear.

Before Mr. Daniel seated himself, he introduced Andrew, Paula and the other men she had seen last night. "I would like to introduce you to the lawyers from Mcane and Mills law firm out of Boston. They will be our legal counsel for these proceedings."

Everyone smiled and shook hands.

Formalities over, Jerrica cleared her throat, beginning her presentation. She used the full sixty minutes to her advantage. She had timed it out down to the last second. She passed out packets with figures and graphs.

Lauren offered them writing utensils with the company's logos, just in case they needed to take notes.

Jerrica amazed them with her quarterly trajectories and the projected company growth charts.

Even Devin, who was still irritated with Jerrica, seemed mildly impressed by what Morrill, Hartford, and Donahue would be offering in the new contracts.

The speech was finished, the questions and answer time over and Jerrica packed up the presentation. A peaceful feeling came upon her as she closed her laptop. No matter what happened now, she had given it her all. That thought and that thought alone, was gratifying for her. Jerrica pulled out the large envelope containing the official new contract. With case in hand, she walked around the table, presenting the envelope to Andrew.

"Thank you, Ms. Kerrison. We'll be in touch."

Jerrica turned to see Lauren smiling at Andrew.

Jerrica quickly moved though the rooms, the urgency to get away from those people seemed crucial to her sanity. Lauren was close behind, surprised that a woman wearing three -inch heels could move so quickly.

Jerrica graced the porch with only two steps before hurdling herself over the steps, landing perfectly on the path. It only took seconds for Jerrica to reach her car, her hand on the handle.

When Lauren reached the car, she panted, "Jerrica, stop, we can't leave yet. We need to stay for questions."

"Shit! Give me your phone."

Lauren handed it over. "Why don't you hold onto it for now. I'm not expecting any calls."

Jerrica dialed the number burned in her memory repeatedly, each time no answer. Discouraged, she slid onto the hood of her car.

At a loss again, Lauren sat next to her friend, sharing the comfort the silence was offering. Every fifteen minutes, Jerrica redialed Madison's number. To her dismay, the result was the same.

Seeing the young women's discomfort from the main house, Molly had Peter bring them out two lawn chairs and a pitcher of lemonade. With Peter's insistence, Jerrica reclined in one of the chairs, trying to relax.

She was anxious to get off this island and find Madison. Repeating her actions, she tried the cell phone and again no answer. The day dragged on as they watched each pair of representatives exit the house after their meetings. Molly had brought them a tray of finger sandwiches for lunch but Jerrica didn't eat. Her stomach was tied in knots.

All the reps seemed to be muddling around the yard, not knowing what to do next. They were all stuck, waiting.

By two forty-five, Jerrica was anxiously pacing by her car. She fidgeted with her hands waiting to escape from this hell. Peering at her watch, she realized they needed to leave soon or they would miss the late day car ferry to the mainland. "That's it," Jerrica said, exasperated. "Lauren let's—"

"May I have everyone's attention?" Andrew said from the porch, interrupting Jerrica.

Everyone moved a little closer to the house to hear him better. Having everyone in earshot, he spoke. "The Daniel family and the board members of Daniel & Daniel, Inc. would like to thank you for your cooperation this weekend. We will consider each offer. There were no further questions, so everyone is free to go."

Andrew stared into Lauren's eyes, smiling, and then he vanished back into the house.

Jerrica was already at the car when Lauren turned to find her. With a screech of the tires, the women of MHD were on their way home.

Chapter Twenty-Four

It was a long two hours before Jerrica's front tires drove onto the mainland. Driving her way toward the exit gate, she recognized a familiar face standing by the gate to the parking lot. Jerrica stopped her car in front of Lauren's husband.

"I called Brandon to pick me up." Lauren smiled at Jerrica. "Let him grab my bag out of the trunk."

Closing the door behind her, Lauren bent down to speak her words of wisdom. "Jerrica, don't screw this up, go after her."

"I love you, Lauren."

"I love you, too, now go!"

For the average driver, the drive would have taken at least an hour and a half to get back to the city. For Jerrica Kerrison it took a minute or two more than an hour. She entered Madison's building at a run, going into the first elevator that opened. Arriving at her door, the loud knocking began. Reaching into her pocket, she realized she still had Lauren's phone, and she repeatedly dialed the apartment number. From Jerrica's position in the hallway, she could hear a clear ringing from inside the apartment.

"Shit!" she said aloud. "Where the hell could she be?"

Tapping the cell phone on the hood of her car, Jerrica honestly didn't know what to do next. Madison was not answering her cell. She wasn't home and Jerrica had no way to contact her family.

What do I do now? she agonized.

Pulling the car door open, it came to her. *Olivia!* With trepidation, Jerrica dialed Olivia's number, holding her breath as the phone began to ring.

"Olivia Hutten, how may I help you," answered the strong southern accent.

"Ms. Hutten, this is Jerrica. We work together at Morrill, Hartford, and Donahue."

"Yes, Jerrica, I know who you are," Jerrica heard the tone change in Olivia's voice, "How can I help you?"

"I'm not sure if Madison has said anything to you about me but—"

"I know enough. How can I help you?"

"Have you heard from her?"

"I haven't heard from her since she left for Nantucket. Is there a problem?"

"There was a misunderstanding on the island and I really need to talk to her. I've tried her cell phone, her home. I'm running out of options," Jerrica's voice was shaking with distress.

"I see." The phone briefly went quiet. "Jerrica, I would advise you to go home and collect yourself. I have a few other numbers I can try to reach Madison for you. I will contact you later if I have news."

"That's all you can do?"

"Ms. Kerrison, right now, this is your only option. Can I reach you on the number you dialed from?" Olivia's voice became elevated.

Defeated, Jerrica replied, "Yes, this number is fine. Thank you, Ms. Hutten, for your help. I hope to hear from you soon."

Dropping the phone on the seat next to her, she started the journey home.

The house seemed emptier to Jerrica as she closed the door. The diminishing evening illumination only added to the feeling of despair that was taking control of her soul. Her steadfast furry companions came rushing to her feet.

At least someone still loves me, she thought.

Settling herself into her normal routine, she went about her business, feeding the cats, changing into something more comfortable, and fixing something to eat. Jerrica sat with her knees to her chest, staring off into the storm clouds that had rolled in, her untouched dinner still on the table. The sudden ring of the cell phone brought her out of the numbness that had inched its way into her thoughts.

"Madison?"

"Ms. Kerrison, this is Olivia Hutten." Hearing no reply, Olivia continued, "I'm sorry to say I was unable to find her. I'm sorry I couldn't assist you."

"Thank you, Ms. Hutten," was all she could assemble for a response, clicking off the phone.

The tears didn't come easy, but when she finally let the full picture of the situation develop in her mind, the storm clouds unleashed their fury. She allowed herself to sob.

You win, Devin, I have nothing.

Chapter Twenty-Five

A clash of thunder shattered her less than peaceful sleep. The last thing she remembered was talking to Olivia. Rubbing her eyes, she slowly sat up. Jerrica summarized that she must have cried herself to sleep. Rotating her neck from side to side, she tried to not only clear her mind, but also loosen her stiff neck. She jumped from her sitting position hearing a knock on her door. Sprinting around the furniture, Jerrica's hand flipped on the porch light the moment her out-stretched hand could reach it. Not worrying about her safety of who might be on the other side, Jerrica wrenched the door open. Rushing forward, she enclosed a rain soaked Madison in her arms, crying uncontrollably.

Madison buried her face in Jerrica's neck and their hot tears joined. In the darkened foyer, two frightened souls held tightly onto one another.

"I'm sorry," Madison whispered.

"I'm the one who needs to apologize," Jerrica replied between tears. "I don't want to let you go, but you should get out of those wet clothes before you catch a cold."

A small giggle escaped Madison. "If I didn't know better, I would think you were trying to get me undressed again."

Jerrica chuckled in Madison's ear, releasing some of her fear.

Jerrica's college sweatshirt and plaid pajama pants felt comfortable to Madison as she sat cross-legged on the couch closely facing Jerrica.

Jerrica lifted Madison's hands, entwining their fingers, linking not only their bodies but their hearts as well. Glancing from their connected hands to Madison's face, Jerrica spoke softly, "I have been so scared I had lost you. There are things I need to tell you—"

Madison cautiously interrupted. "Jerrica, I know."

Not fully registering her words, Jerrica continued. "I want to explain what happened on the island, but more than that, I—"

Jerrica stopped speaking when she felt a light fingertip on her lips.

"Jerrica, I know about your past with Devin Daniel. I also know everything that transpired with her these past few days."

The confused expression was visible on Jerrica's face.

"Seeing that woman in an article of clothing belonging to you...broke my heart. I didn't want to believe that you would cheat on me, but she was very convincing. I couldn't compete with a woman like that, and since we never really made promises to one another..." Madison fell silent for a moment, taking a deep breath. "After leaving the island, I just drove around in a fog. I had no place to go."

Madison wiped a stray tear from Jerrica's cheek, mirroring the pain in her eyes. "I stopped at Olivia's briefly. I needed to talk to someone. Once my mind finally cleared, I knew there was only one other person who would know the truth, even if I didn't like what she had to say...I called Lauren."

"You called Lauren? Why didn't you call me?"

"I was angry at you and hurt. That's why I didn't call you."

"I'm so sorry," replied Jerrica's weak voice.

"I knew even though Lauren and I don't get along, she has always had your best interests at heart. She was hesitant to tell me any information you should have already told me. She did finally give in and supplied me with facts that helped fill in the blank spots of your past and present connection to Devin, including all the events of this weekend."

"I thought if I could just get through this weekend, I could spare you having to be involved with my past life."

"Spare me or yourself, Jerrica? I think that's what hurts the most, the thought that maybe you didn't trust us, or me for that matter, to open up about everything."

Tightening her grip, head lowered, Jerrica tried to explain. "This is all new to me, Madison. In my previous relationships, no one had ever been interested in my journeys of life before they became a part of it. I'm not good at letting my guard down, but I want to try for you, for us. I am so sorry I hurt you."

"Jerrica, do you love me?"

Lifting her head as tears cascaded down her face, she answered. "Yes, more than I'll ever be able to show you."

Touching her hand to a moist cheek, their eyes making firm contact, Madison spoke "Well, we can start building our future off of that. Everything else will work itself out."

Love and a promise of a future together surrounded Jerrica and Madison as they leaned forward, meeting in the middle, to share a kiss. A kiss that quickly turned into lust filled wanting.

Madison pulled her lips away, gasping for air, as Jerrica traced soft kisses down her jaw line. The moan escaped Madison as Jerrica nibbled on her earlobe, letting the tip of her tongue follow the shape of her ear.

"Madison, my love, about our future..." Jerrica whispered.

Epilogue

Evelyn Burnham entered the executive office as she did every morning, with a smile and her arms filled with paperwork. Her presence in the room was immediately recognized.

Alexandra Donahue spun her chair around to face her assistant. "Good morning, Evelyn. How are you this morning?"

"Good morning, yourself," Evelyn replied. "We seem to be in a good mood this morning."

Alexandra lifted a packet of papers in her hand, waving them around. "She did it, Evelyn. Ms. Kerrison got the Daniel Corporation to re-sign with Morrill, Hartford, and Donahue for another five years. There are a few small provisions they want to add to the contract but they signed on the dotted line. They have even included a handsome bonus for Ms. Kerrison as well."

"That's wonderful, Ms. Donahue," she said, placing the pile of papers on the desk.

"Oh," she said, pulling a manila envelope from the bottom of the pile. "This was delivered by courier about ten minutes ago."

Her eyes still glued on the contract, she waved her hand. "Go ahead, and leave it. I'll get to it."

The click of the door brought Alexandra out of her euphoria enough to notice that Evelyn had departed her office. Setting the contract in front of her, she reached for the unmarked manila envelope. With the envelope opened, she slid the papers into her hand and began the task of reading them.

To: Alexandra Donahue of Morrill, Harford, and Donahue Company, Inc.

From: Blanchet, Pranvil and Colby, Law Firm Boston, MA on behalf of Jerrica Kerrison.

I, Jerrica A. Kerrison, do formally tender my resignation as Accounting Executive of Morrill, Hartford, and Donahue as of today's date. My legal representative will be contacting your firm directly regarding forwarding of 401k, pending pay or bonuses...

Alexandra Donahue's eyes widened and her mouth gaped open as she continued reading the letter. Standing up abruptly, sending her chair crashing into the windows behind, she threw the papers on her desk. As she slammed her fists down on her desk she yelled. "Damn it! Damn it all to hell, Evelyn, get your ass in here!"

The end or just the beginning?

About the Author

Riley Jefferson

So I have to sum up who I am in so many words or less… How do you describe the love of words since you were a child? Growing up in New England, the changing seasons helped color my imagination. My writing journey started in poetry but blossomed into fiction writing, lesbian fiction writing to be exact. I love weaving the stories that people will enjoy.

I still enjoy the character of New England till this day with my loving wife, two cats, and one dog.

Finding Her Way is my first publication.

Other Books from Affinity eBook Press

HER—Lisa Ron Fox has been looking for that one person who will make her feel complete-her perfect match. Together with her friends, Megan and Tree, Fox continues her quest while dodging exes and clingers, laughing a lot along the way.When she meets Madeline, she instantly knows that she finds HER.Madeline has her own problems-notably a domineering husband.Can Fox win her heart? Can they make a life together?This story will make you laugh, cry, and hold your breath as the story unfolds. With the right person love can conquer all.

Bayou Justice—Ali Spooner Hell hath no fury like a woman scorned. When Kara, Sasha's, new lover is taken hostage as a diversionary tactic to allow the drug dealing Bellfontaine brothers to escape justice, Sasha springs into action. Kara is released physically unharmed, however, her emotions, and budding career in the District Attorney's office are left in shambles when she is held blame for their release, Appalled, by the failure of the criminal justice system, Sasha exacts her own brand of justice for the acts committed against her lover. From the Bayou's of Louisiana to the jungles of South America, Sasha plots her revenge.

Out of Retirement—Erica Lawson Melanie Stokes was a doctor—a very good one, or so she hoped. She was calm and cool under pressure, and very little fazed her. Until…Caitlin Joseph ran a small retirement home for older women in need. The fact that everyone in the house was gay was a coincidence, although it did cut down the number of women agreeing to live there.Mel took up an offer to do some relief work for a local community center when their regular doctor was away on holidays. As soon as she arrived at the home she knew something was different about the place. Was it the little old lady chasing the paper boy down the street or the sign saying "Dykes Retirement Home"?But there was something about the place that also appealed to her. Sure, Caitlin was cute as a button, but it was more the fact that she took very good care of her charges, despite their rather bizarre behavior.The older women seized the opportunity to introduce a woman into Caitlin's lonely life, using any means possible to keep Mel coming back. Their plans were boosted by the introduction of another woman into the house, who set hearts a fluttering and blood pressure rising. Now if she was a lesbian it would have been perfect…

Letting Go—JM Dragon A failed relationship puts Stella Hawke's life on the brink of chaos.

When her grandmother falls gravely ill in Ashville, Stella ends her army career to take care of the woman during her last weeks. Little does she know that an old army comrade, socialite Reggie Stockton, whose family owns the local newspaper, also lives in Ashville. Will she allow herself to accept Reggie's help to turn her life around and let go of the past? This is a journey where both women re-evaluate what they want out of life. Will that path lead to happiness or to a parting of the ways?

Requiem—JM Dragon & Erin O'Reilly In the final book of the When Hell Meets Heaven Series, Olivia and Amelia reluctantly join forces with Parker and Remington to save their lives and those of the ones they love. The only problem—will three alpha females and an ex-nun be able to work toward a common goal and not kill each other before they complete their mission. The four women are up against the formidable strength of DOCO along with a corrupt politician, bent on mass destruction. Can they complete their mission knowing that a requiem will be the harbinger of their end should they fail.

Through the Darkness—Erin O'Reilly Becca Cameron is a loner—by choice. She lives in a hundred year old farmhouse built by her great grandfather. A tragic accident in her home a year earlier drove away her lover, and Becca tries to accept what she cannot change and hang on to the belief that love can conquer all. Chase Hunter, had a meteoric rise in the Eastman Corporation and was, at thirty-four, the youngest vice-president. To Chase, her work was all consuming leaving little time for friends or lovers. There was simply no place in her life for anything but her job. When Becca and Chase meet at their work place, the attraction is spontaneous. Life begins to look brighter for both women as work takes a second seat to romance. Unknown to either woman, someone is watching their every move…Will passion outweigh doubt? Can love conqueror fear?

Beginning of the End—Alane Hotchkin What happens when life doesn't go exactly as you planned and you must protect others from your own fate? Escaping a horrific childhood, Nikki longed to find happily ever after in adulthood. What she found was Hell. Or did it find her? Finding the courage to break the cycle of betrayal, she opens her heart one last time. Alex lived a childhood others dreamed of. Her father never once denied the young rebel a thing. All her life she dreamed of protecting others; to follow in her father's footsteps. Soon though she learned sex and fists made the most powerful of weapons. Alex controls the women in her life through fear and sex, will breaking the cycle be too much to overcome? Will loving Nikki be enough to change her, or is Alex beyond help? Alex would give Nikki the world, but at what price? When a person's tightly controlled reality snaps what then…? This is the Beginning of the End for one of them and the ultimate sacrifice for the other. But who is who in this game of life?

Galveston 1900: Swept Away—Linda Crist On September 7-8, 1900, the island of Galveston, Texas, was destroyed by a hurricane, or 'tropical cyclone', as it was called in those days. This story is a fictional account of Mattie and Rachel, two women who lived there, and their lives during the time of the 'great storm'. Forced to flee from her family at a young age, Rachel Travis finds a home and livelihood on the island of Galveston. Independent, friendly, and yet often lonely, only one other person knows the dark secret that haunts her. Madeline "Mattie" Crockett is trapped in a loveless marriage, convinced that her fate is sealed. She never dares to dream of true happiness, until Rachel Travis comes walking into her life.   As emotions come to light, the storm of Mattie's marriage converges with the very real hurricane. Can they survive, and build the life they both dream of? This second edition of one of Linda Crist's best-loved novels maintains the original story, while incorporating some reader-pleasing passages that were cut from the first edition.   As an added bonus, the short story "Something to Celebrate" is included at the end of the novel, detailing further adventures of Rachel and Mattie.

Rapture: Sins of the Sinners—A. C. Henley & Fran Heckrotte   A serial killer is targeting young lesbians throughout the state of Texas.Texas Ranger Cochetta Lovejoy is assigned to the case. Convinced she knows who is committing the murders, Ranger Lovejoy is willing to do whatever it takes to put the perpetrator behind bars--even if it means stretching the limits of the law by manipulating the judicial system. Detective Agnes Kelly-Elliott is one of Ft. Worth Police Department's finest investigators.   When Ranger Lovejoy appears on the crime scene of a recent murder, Agnes fears a dark secret that, if revealed, could destroy her family ties, and end her career. This is a dark, gritty, graphic tale of desire gone awry, and flawed characters looking for redemption in all the wrong places.

Till There Was You—S. Anne Gardner Julia is a woman used to power and is not afraid to use it or impose her will to get her way. She appears to have the world but a part of her is empty and cold as a frozen tundra. Julia rides in the mornings to clear her head and to make plans for what she is about to set in motion. Theodora, known as Teddy, is trying to put together a marriage filled with uncertainties. She felt once upon a time that she would have a great love but that has eluded her. One morning these two women meet and from the first instance, it is explosive. The attraction is undeniable, the fears very real and the end without question will change them both forever.

Denial—Jackie Kennedy   Time spent in Somalia has Doctor Celeste Cameron accustomed to living and working in a war zone. Coming back home to America, Celeste is glad to see the end of the peril she has been in—or so she thinks. Danger seems to follow Celeste and she finds it in the shape of Amy. What Celeste feels for Amy scares her more than anything she has faced in war zones. Amy has the same feelings, but is in denial and vows to marry Josh, Celeste's twin brother, no matter what. When fate brings them together again, will they give in to their mutual attraction or will they once again deny what they feel.

'55 Ford—Erin O'Reilly Andrea McBride, the author of four books, wants to find someone to restore an old '55 Ford truck that she inherited in a real estate purchase. She will only settle for the best and finds RJ Whittaker who many proclaim to be the best restorer among millions.

In Name Only—JM Dragon—Sequel to The Fix-it Girl Can an agreement forged out of necessity actually work?

An Affair of Love—S. Anne Gardner From a dark past, a forbidden love, a secret comes. Among the confusion and the chaos of an unwanted reality, two women find something they neither want nor can deny.

Desert Heat—Dannie Marsden For Luce Diamond, an undercover policewoman, her life is in shambles. Her longtime lover left her and an automobile accident that resulted in a child's death haunts her.

Taming the Wolff—Del Robertson ONLY ONE WOMAN...HAS THE POWER...TO TAME THE WOLFF...

Private Dancer—TJ Vertigo Reece Corbett grew up on the mean streets on New York City, abused, used and in trouble with the law. Faith Ashford grew up wealthy, with all the creature comforts that money provides. When they meet fireworks begin.

Miriam and Esther—Sherry Barker Miriam thought her life would play out in the bustling metropolis of Dallas, but after a life-changing accident, she moves to the small town of Cool Lake, Texas to get her head on straight and regain her senses.

McKee—A.C. Henley Private Investigator Quinlan McKee has returned to Los Angeles after a three-year absence, only to find herself embroiled in a world of child slavery and police corruption.

Bailey's Run—Ali Spooner Bailey Chambers mourns the loss of her lover, Nessa, in an unsolved carjacking. When Tommy, Bailey's brother becomes a victim of a gay bashing, Bailey assumes his case will be handled the same way as her lover's—lackadaisically. Desi Dexter assigned to Tommy's case, feels Bailey's disdain toward her and her partner. Through tenacious police work, Desi, is able to uncover the reason for Bailey's attitude, and convinces her that she is sincere in solving the case. Mutual attraction sparks, and before they can move forward with their fledging romance, Desi, and her partner Braxton, uncover the presence of a serial killer. What will happen to Bailey, when, Desi, becomes engrossed in another case, can their relationship survive?

E-Books, Print, Free e-books

Visit our website for more publications available online.

www.affinityebooks.com

Published by Affinity E-Book Press NZ LTD
Canterbury, New Zealand

Registered Company 2517228